The Flattery of Knaves

Book Two
of the
The Absence of Pity Trilogy

Also by Richard A. McDonald

Moral Chains –Book One

Love to Justice – Book Three

Forthcoming

The Presence of Hope Trilogy

The Counsels of the Wise and Good – Book One

Vanity and Presumption – Book Two

Sobriety of Understanding – Book Three

Copyright © 2016 Richard A. McDonald

All rights reserved.

This book is a work of fiction and, except in the case of
historical fact and character, any resemblance to actual
persons living or dead, is purely coincidental.

ISBN: 1536868736
ISBN-13: 9781536868739

"They took us to Crematoria Three and Four, there we saw Hell on this Earth. Large piles of dead people and people dragging these bodies to a long pit....
Some of our group threw themselves, jumped, into the pit, alive..."

Dov Paisikowic - born 1924 –Velky Rakovec – Czechoslovakia

Prisoner number A-3076 – Slave Labourer - Auschwitz-Birkenau Crematoria no.1 – 1944

Died 1988.

Chapter 1

March 1941 - Bletchley Park – England

Friday the 21st of March 1941, seventeen days after the Lofoten Islands raid.

By now, the British Pathe News film had been shown in Cinemas. The newspaper reports and the BBC detailed the success of the raid. They said there were no casualties, although an officer had shot himself in the leg, you couldn't make it up!

Archie knew the reasoning behind the deception, he'd suggested it. He'd also written three different 'Top Secret' reports, detailing the accidental finding of German Enigma equipment during a purely coincidental raid. Each report said they'd found different pieces of equipment, no report mentioned the murder of POWs or the deaths of two British soldiers killed by the Royal Navy. One day someone might ask him how many versions of the truth there were. His answer would always be; one more than you can see.

Nevertheless, he decided he'd write down the truth, every single word, he'd keep a diary, and one day, he'd use it. Even for a consummate liar, even unshackled by moral chains, even untold, the truth was still a priceless commodity.

The Bletchley Park section of their team knew that Conner, Archie, and Rebecca were absent during the raid. They'd seen them reappear afterwards, tired and drained, throwing themselves into work and trying to forget something.

When Archie and Rebecca returned on Sunday the 9th of March, Conner had already spoken to Mary Driver about Spud. He did that before he even handed over the Enigma equipment prize to the boffins. Twenty minutes wouldn't lose the war, and she took precedence for that short time.

Archie and Rebecca were closer, not visibly, or so they thought. There was nothing to see, they were friends, more intimate friends, family perhaps, but man and woman?

Never.

No one spoke directly about it, then two days after the Pathe news came out, all Bletchley Park knew the story. Building Thirteen's Operational team left, the raid happened, some hadn't returned, and no one could talk about it. There'd be no funerals, there were no bodies. Building Thirteen knew that Mary Driver was heartbroken and trying to hide it, poorly.

The Chosen Men had returned from leave on Monday the 17th of March. The men checked and serviced their equipment then continued to work hard on physical fitness and skills. The Manor became a mini training centre; Archie had commandeered a neighbouring field and set up an obstacle course and target range. War involved innumerable hours of sitting around just waiting for something to happen. Archie told them they should always be planning, practicing and preparing to kill someone, always. He didn't say explicitly that he always was.

He made the men work hard, and always for a purpose, they wouldn't waste any energy. Initially, he was telling them exactly what to do, later he would just let them set their own regime; once he was sure they were taking it seriously.

The intelligence team at Bletchley were working hard too, but there was a void and Conner knew he had to fill it.

*

Friday 21st March 1941 – Bletchley Park

This Friday, though, was a dry but frosty spring morning. The air smelt different, the promise of growth, perhaps of hope for better times to come. Conner had a promising idea, one that would work, endure and bear repetition.

He drove his car into Bletchley Park with Archie and Rebecca, parking directly outside their building and collected everyone, taking them outside. While he was doing that, Rebecca unloaded some small rose bushes with their roots in damp sacks of earth from the boot, Archie helped and had a spade. Smudger drove the remaining

Chosen Men behind them in their truck, parking behind the car. The men stepped out of the truck and stood beside the building.

Archie and Begley dug the first hole in the empty earth on the right-hand side of their building then passed Smudger the spade.

Archie took Begley by the shoulders and looked into those huge bug eyes.

"Begs, we need you even more now son, alright," he said with gritted teeth emphasising the words.

Begley looked back at him, said, "yes, sir," and became a man, Archie's man.

Archie then stood aside. He didn't want to do this, not in front of everybody.

His teams stood in a crescent shape around the four fresh holes mingling silently, exchanging half smiles and nods.

Rebecca handed one rose bush to Mary Driver. She uncovered the roots, placed it gently in the ground, stepped back and waited.

"Sergeant Jeremiah Patrick Murphy," said Mary Driver.

"Private Joseph James Dempsey," said Ben Dempsey.

"Private Stuart Buddy," said Davey Stubbs.

"Private Elwyn Tarrian," said Rebecca Rochford.

Each member of the team placed a small handful of cold, dry soil in each hole before Smudger with his huge hands pressed each area down firmly. The soil was excellent, Archie had brought it from the rear garden of the Manor the previous night.

As they spoke, Archie looked around to see others joining their small group, standing slightly apart from his two teams. From the rear of that second group, he heard the sound of a single violin playing a wordless version of 'Flowers of the Forest,' a traditional lament for fallen soldiers. It was Alan Turing playing, and Conner was standing next to him. The haunting melody and scraping sound of the violin triggered unwelcome feelings in his mind, so Archie took another few steps further away from the group.

Just when he thought he might not cry, Alan started to play 'Molly Malone', and Spud's death, in particular, began breaking him down. Spud had watched his back in Calais, and he hadn't watched his well enough, he'd killed him and the others. He had survived, and he tried to concentrate on that. If he hadn't killed Spud someone else would have, that should help. It didn't.

He turned around and took a couple of steps further forward, away from watching eyes and listening ears. Tears just flowed silently out of his eyes and down his impassive face, as never before. It was a long time since he'd cried and a few years' worth were coming out.

He was sure no one would notice him, then a small hand appeared next to him and took hold of his right hand, gently placing a new white cotton handkerchief in his palm.

"You look like shit you know," said Rebecca.

He wiped his eyes and face until the small white cloth was damp.

"And you... picked a bad time to make your first ever funny joke! Don't you dare make me laugh," he whispered to her, gritting his teeth and biting his cheek at the same time, still looking straight ahead.

The music stopped, and one pair of hands started clapping loudly. It could only be Smudger with his huge bucket hands, others joined in the spontaneous applause, for the music and the dead he thought.

His eyes were dry now so he risked a sideways glance at his friend, she wasn't crying, but had scratched her nose with a dirty hand leaving a mark of earth on it. He turned to face her, she looked up at him, and he used her hankie and his tears to gently clean the top of her nose.

"I hope there's no snot on that," she murmured with a mischievously straight face.

This time, he had to smile at her, with her and for her. Then he looked up and over her shoulder to see every face in that small crowd of people looking at him and smiling too.

'Oh Christ, what have I done now?'

The others drifted away slowly. Archie nodded at Conner and Alan, who'd stayed beside him. The ceremony was perfect, there was a permanent memorial now, as long as the roses lasted. He remained where he was, breathing clean, fresh air and feeling a definite warmth from the morning sun. He felt Rebecca squeezing his hands to attract his attention, he hadn't realised he was holding her hands and looked down at her.

"Mary's pregnant and you have to sort it out," she said.

Oh for God's sake, why is this down to me? How can I fix that! Was all he could think.

"What do you need me to do?" was all he could say.

*

After the rose planting, Archie called Conner into the private room with Rebecca, just the three of them.

"Conner," he said, "Rebecca and I think you deserve a break, a week at least. We'll handle everything while you're away."

He agreed so readily it took them by surprise, also when he said he might take two weeks, perhaps he was even more tired than they'd thought.

Conner said he'd go immediately and went back to the cottage to collect his luggage.

After he'd left, Rebecca said, "You'll have to watch him carefully when he gets back."

"No, we. We'll have to keep an eye on him, we're a team now."

*

Thursday 3rd April 1941 – Faroe Islands

Private Arnolt Neumann's wounds had almost healed, in the small well-guarded hut that he and his four comrades from the Krebs had shared for the last three weeks. The injuries he'd suffered would have killed him had the British not treated them properly. The medical care was excellent and food plentiful, but it was bland English rations. They'd been allowed to write letters home, yet had no contact with other German prisoners, and Arnolt knew what that meant. The British Commandos had the Enigma machines and papers from the Captain's cabin, the *'Krebs'* was hardly a significant military target.

From the open boat, that had taken him and the British officers from the *'Krebs'* to the Destroyer *'Somali'*, he'd seen smoke and fires from three of the Islands. He'd heard no signs of a fight so he knew there must be many prisoners, yet they'd not seen any of them.

He knew what that meant too; the British were going to keep them separate from other prisoners for the war's duration, or they were going to kill them. That was why he'd written a coded message in his letter home, and why they planned to attempt an escape. Although they couldn't understand the English words spoken, they knew instinctively why the British Commandos had been arguing on board the *'Krebs'*.

Not knowing where they were was the biggest problem and the hut's whitewashed windows gave nothing away. They were collectively ashamed of their abject surrender, with time to think and reflect, they intended to regain some self-respect. Arnolt was the eldest and smartest in his small group so he appointed himself their leader.

That same evening, six well-armed guards collected them from their hut, so he began to make his plans. They marched in complete darkness and subdued silence from the hut to a nearby dock and a small, old looking tugboat. He assumed the British were taking them from an Island, probably to the mainland. They'd discussed overpowering a guard, stealing a weapon or two then a small boat, perhaps this tug, which they could navigate to Norway given a chance.

The two guards they saw on the tug were old and had uniforms marked *Home Guard*. Once on board, the elder of the two Guards locked them in a small room containing just two old wooden benches. Arnolt talked the others through his makeshift plan. They would shout and bang on the door, feign an illness and take their chances. They could smash the bench and use parts as weapons, they'd have to wait until increased engine noise drowned out the sound of the breaking wood. This would be their best and possibly only real opportunity.

The tug, which was as old and noisy as Arnolt suspected, went steadily and straight for thirty minutes. They decided to risk shattering the bench, so Arnolt listened at the door, hearing nothing immediately outside. He moved to the bench, placed his foot firmly on it and began pulling the wood slowly upwards, it bent easily and was near to cracking when he gave it one final pull.

Crack!

The whole room exploded.

The massive plastic explosive blast underneath the floor killed all five of the 'Krebs' survivors instantly, blowing a catastrophic hole in the central hull of the vessel. Then, just as Begley had said it would, the tug sank in two distinct sections within seconds.

*

The elderly Home Guard veteran watched the explosion from a safe distance of one mile away, on the deck of a small fishing boat that Conner had arranged for his use that night.

Billy Perry had easily found four of his old East End contacts willing to assist him in a nefarious deed, it was their usual occupation even in wartime. Lots of property went missing during the Blitz from bombed-out houses, and small jeweller's shops did suffer a disproportionate targeting by the Luftwaffe.

He knew men who'd slit a throat for a couple of quid. They'd fought in the last war and would have knifed five Jerrys for free if he'd asked. However, a fair day's pay for an unfair night's work was fit and proper, you wouldn't catch a Labour Member of Parliament doing less. He only wanted his due, which in this particular case, was a large sum.

Apart from the German killing element of the job, the little bastards had been planning to escape. They intended to cudgel him, take his gun, then shoot him and the others. Mr Duncan had taped and translated their conversations in their specially designed hut. Those huts had been Mr Travers idea originally. Their letters home contained secret messages intending to signal the capture of the Enigma machines. They were spies about to pass vital secrets to the Nazis, and escaping Prisoners of War to boot.

They should already be at the bottom of the Norwegian Sea and were now at the bottom of the North Atlantic, about ten miles west of the Faroe Islands, nobody liked a grass. Their fate was justified and legal, by any standards.

The other thing was; Billy had enjoyed it.

Mr Travers and Mr Duncan were good people to Billy's experienced eyes, and they needed a hand. He thought about Mr Duncan's offer seriously. His beautiful, perfect and sinless daughter had joined up to help the war effort now. He'd enjoyed his time as a fixer at the Savoy. It was profitable and safe, he'd been unsafe enough for long enough in the trenches, long enough for one lifetime. Something called him, though, the siren song drew him on, to do one last bit of harm before his time was up.

He might just say yes.

He'd also heard them refer to him as a *nutzlose alte fotze*, a useless old cunt, he'd showed them useless, the cheeky little buggers. One of his best contacts back in Green Street market was a German, who'd taught him a few swear words over a pint and deal. Old Mr Flowers as he now called himself was a Jew who'd had the wisdom to leave Germany about twenty years previously.

He wouldn't use these lads, the Frasers, again if he could help it, he'd had to hold them back from giving the Jerrys a taste of torture. Billy wasn't averse to a little torture, but only for a purpose, there was no need here. Billy knew a lot of bad lads from the East End, that's why he'd moved his family to Tottenham.

*

Friday 11th April 1941 – Sunbury – Greater London

Archie and Rebecca sat in their staff car outside a

private house in Greater London.

Archie didn't want to do this, not after Jezz's wife and not with the Dempseys to follow. He was only doing this for Rebecca.

"Are you sure you want to do this?" he said to her.

"Yes, I'm sure. Now remember, let me do all the talking. I have to do it myself, don't help, unless she hits me."

"Okay, let's get it done."

Archie and Rebecca left the car, and he followed her up the path to the house, a well-kept semi-detached in Sunbury-on-Thames. She knocked on the door, and a heavily pregnant woman answered, about twenty-five years old, tall and red-haired with a round face and a Celtic look about her.

"Mrs Tarrian?"

"Yes."

"My name is Lieutenant Rochford, my colleague and I are from the War Office, may we come in?"

"Yes, is it about the pension?"

"Yes, that and a bit more."

"Would you like a cup of tea? Baby's asleep upstairs," she said showing them into the living room.

"No, that's fine thank you."

"Do you know how he died? The letter and the other officer who came didn't tell me anything."

"That's exactly why we're here Mrs Tarrian, to explain what we can. Your husband was a member of a special unit that undertook secret missions that I can't tell you about. During a mission, behind enemy lines, he was killed, his body couldn't be recovered. The mission was successful. Sorry, that's the wrong word, and I can't think of the right word, I don't think there is one. What I need to say is that your husband died saving lives, my life, in fact, a shell exploded, and he died shielding me from that, it was the bravest, finest act I've-"

"You must be Rebecca then, and you're Archie?" she said and when they just nodded she carried on talking.

"He told me about you, Archie when he got back from

France. He was cut up when he thought you were dead and pleased as punch when he joined up with you again. He said you were a hero, saved his life twice he said.

"And you Miss, he told me you were the bravest woman he'd ever heard of. Well, I can't believe how small you are. He made you sound about six feet tall, and you're so pretty too, he said you were, well, he said you weren't pretty at all, that's men for you, he probably didn't want me to be jealous."

Archie wondered who else was in the room!

"If he died to save you, then he died for something worthwhile, someone worthwhile, could you come here please."

She made Rebecca sit next to her and gave her a warm and close hug. Rebecca looked appalled as she looked at Archie over her shoulder with a 'get me out of here' look in her eyes, Archie just shrugged.

They left half an hour later, Archie drove around the corner and stopped.

"That went well you know, you did well," he said.

"Bloody hell, that was awful," she said, "all those hugs and I didn't want to see the baby, the baby or the bump, the tears. All I wanted, was to take responsibility for what happened, it was my fault, I just expected her to punch me, and she was nice to me."

"Nice eh!"

"Oh shut up smart arse and drive."

"Did you have to tell her we'd pay off the mortgage? The pension that Conner's arranged would have been enough for the payments."

"Take it out of my 30%," she said referring to the twenty-five million dollars' worth of diamonds that were now in the hands of a reliable Swiss Bank.

"No we'll pay half each, that's fair, just ask me next time."

"There won't be a next time."

"There will be, we'll plant more roses before this is over, I might have to buy them, next time."

"You stole the rose bushes?"

"It was short notice, and I didn't know where any fucking rose shops were, I sneaked a few quid through the victim's letter box a couple of nights later."

"Oh well, that's alright then."

"If you grass me up I'll have to kill you."

She looked at him and turned his head to face hers.

"Oh, you're going to kill someone aren't you?"

"Maybe?"

"Can I help?"

*

Sunday 13th April 1941 – Bletchley Park

Archie and Rebecca returned to Bletchley Park from London early on Sunday morning, the 13th April and went straight to their building.

As usual and as they expected, Mary Driver was there, alone. She was in the small kitchen, retching over the sink. There was nothing they could do about that.

Archie made tea for all three of them, and they sat in the private room. Mary knew what they were going to talk about.

"I have to keep the baby you know," she said.

"We know that, of course, you do," Archie agreed.

"I'll have to leave, go away, find another job, the baby will always be a bastard, you know how people talk. I can't even tell my mum and dad they'll… "

"Shh," said Rebecca, placing her hand on Mary's.

"Spud's baby will never be illegitimate," said Archie pulling papers from his briefcase.

"You and Spud, Jeremiah… Jerry were married secretly in Greenwich six weeks before he left England, Rebecca and I were the only witnesses, we had no time for any photographs."

"Bridesmaid!" said Rebecca.

"Bridesmaid and best man then. The marriage certificate is genuine, and service records reflect that too."

"How on earth?"

"Mary, new identities and background papers are being

created all the time, you just have to know the right people. In your case, it's even in the real Registrars handwriting and has your signatures in the original register. Rebecca's artistic copying ability is even more useful than we thought," he smiled.

Mary couldn't speak as she took in the implications.

"I don't know how to thank you, I'll be able to go home and... "

"Sorry Mary, you're not going anywhere," Archie said, "you'll have to stay here, we can't do without you. Your mum can help, there's a posting letter here that'll give your dad a job as caretaker at the Manor. There's a small house nearby that you and they can use as quarters."

"It's a miracle, sir, it's an absolute miracle. Rebecca, I don't know how to thank you, you could babysit," she smiled cheekily.

"Oh No!" said Rebecca wrinkling her nose in genuine disgust, "we can manage miracles, but not that!"

Mary burst out laughing. Archie was glad it was over, this niceness was making him uncomfortable. Killing was much easier, and he still had Joe Dempsey's Mum and Dad to see.

Chapter 2

Friday 18th April 1941 - Hevlyn Mansions

Conner returned late from his leave and arranged to meet Archie and Rebecca at Hevlyn Mansions on Friday the 18th of April. Conner was wearing a Major's uniform and had brought new tailor-made sets of Captain's uniforms for Rebecca and Archie.

Archie was happy.

"I know I once suggested just promoting ourselves, but this is a bit obvious isn't it?" he said.

"Nonsense, Churchill, Gubbins, and Bracken are extremely pleased with us, we'll get no medals and little thanks, we get this instead. Gubbins is acting Brigadier now. Besides, people will pay more attention to you, you'll see that, and you're going to need it. Everything has been, or will be, earned. Now, sorry I can't stay I have a meeting with Bracken and some recruitment to do," Conner said and left.

Archie said he'd stay the night in the flat and do some thinking. He'd expected Rebecca to stay too, and when she insisted on returning to Bletchley that evening, he wanted to change his mind. He couldn't, it would be too obvious that he wanted, needed her companionship.

When Rebecca had gone, he phoned Victoria, he'd had the telephone number for months and resisted. He needed something that he didn't have, and he felt lonely. He wasn't lonely, but he felt it. He'd never had better friends in his life, and he was killing them one by one. Victoria might do the trick for one night, she was all things to all men, just not all things to Archie.

*

Monday 21st April 1941 – Whitehall

Conner sat in their small, now abandoned office in Whitehall and assessed the two young men in front of him. They were brothers, almost twins in looks, barely a year apart in age.

The eldest, George Flowers said, "Listen, sir, don't go on about the Jewish thing, we're East End boys more than anything else. If you give me a choice of job, I'd be a number nine for the Hammers and Henry here'd be a number six, we ain't got that choice.

"Our dad's a decent man, and he said he wasn't gonna slice a piece of our skin off just cos God told him to. He always said God had better things to do than worry about havin' a beard or a funny 'at on. We learned the old language and German cos a lot of our kin could speak it, we don't use it or need it now.

"Sure, they called us Jew boys in school sometimes, there was a jock, a taffy and loads of paddies an' all, every kid had a name o' some kind.

"That recruitment gadgie offered us jobs as interpreters, that's a cissy job. Our whole family comes here, and this country lets us stay here nice and safe, so we offer to translate what Jerry's sayin' as he runs towards you shooting.

"He says he's going to kill you, sir," we can do a lot better than that.

"If we have kids, and I hope we live long enough to do that, I don't want my son walkin' into the Anne Boleyn for a pint before the game and telling them how proud he was of his dad cos he interpreted German and wrote stuff down. Only a wanker would do that, pardon my language, sir. I want him to walk in there with his chest pumped out knowing his dad was somebody and not havin' to say a word about it, cos every man in there knew it.

"We've got relatives who've been murdered by Jerry, we know that for a fact, we're big lads and can do Jerry some real harm, so that's what we'll do. We reckon we're as English as anybody. This is a great, free country and we'll fight to keep it that way for ourselves, not for any God who lets all this happen in the first place.

"As you know, our old man knows Billy well and says he's a proper geezer and Billy says you and yours are sound blokes. We've had the old commando training already, and we'll hook up with you if you'll have us, but we aim to kill and help kill Jerry wherever we see him and the sooner, the better."

Henry and the eloquent George Flowers, formerly known as Blum before their family left the town of Ulm in Southern Germany, had just joined the Chosen Men.

William 'Billy' Perry had also agreed to join as Sergeant Quartermaster and was most welcome.

*

Friday 25th April 1941 – Evening – Holloway – North London

Captain Archie Travers went personally to see Joe Dempsey's parents in Holloway, North London. Ben Dempsey was with him and had arranged the time and place, late on a Friday night when his parents had finished their work shifts.

Conner had sent the formal letter as soon as he'd returned to England. As Archie expected, he had done the paperwork on the ship returning from the Lofoten raid.

The house was in a terrace that backed on to the main railway line, it was a bigger than usual terrace with a small garden and gate next to the pavement.

Joe's Mum and Dad were there, a middle-aged couple, who had put on their Sunday best clothes just to see Captain Travers. The guilt began growing even earlier than expected. A young girl was also there, no older than twenty, maybe only sixteen, she was stunningly beautiful, the same size and shape as Rebecca, but immaculately groomed, perfectly made up, yet not overdone. Ben introduced her as Oona, Joe's fiancée.

'Fucking hell, why did I agree to do this? Now, don't stare at Oona, don't even look in fact, that's it, look at Ben's mum.'

"Would you like a cup of tea, Captain Travers?" said Mrs Dempsey.

'She is gorgeous, oh God, help me.'

"Yes, thank you, that would be lovely Mrs Dempsey," he said.

'Those eyes, blue, deep blue and she's looking right at me.

Stop it, please.'

The tea arrived, the best china, a small lace tablecloth, and biscuits.

'She has the most beautiful pale freckles on her nose.'

He spoke, as gently and resolutely as he could, explaining exactly who he was, or rather, who he was pretending to be.

'Look at her lips smiling at me. Don't smile at me. Her hands, even her hands look perfect, just the way she's holding them, fingers linked in front of her.'

Joe and Ben were fine young men who had volunteered for special duties, recommended by Jerry Murphy, whose mum they knew.

'That dimple on her chin, that slim, elegant neck. I swear I can smell her perfume from here. Don't breathe in through your nose, don't inhale, that's it.'

Joe had bravely given his life to save others. Joe's dad was impassive, deeply moved, and refusing to show it, his wife had a tear in her eye and Ben sat next to her with his arm around her. The Dempsey's had produced two sons to be proud of, as brave and strong as any men he'd known.

Oona had tied her dark blonde hair in a ponytail and the slightest movement of her head as she listened made it swing from side to side. A shorter piece of hair at the front came loose, falling across her forehead, she swept it back delicately with one well shaped white fingernail and tucked it behind one perfect ear.

'No, don't, stop it.'

Oona just continued looking at Archie with her piercing eyes. She wore a plain white blouse with a grey top and skirt, it looked like her Sunday best. However, she'd had it all adjusted to fit, just a little too small for her and perfection came from that. The blouse, tight and the skirt, tighter, with heels, but not too high.

'Oh no, she wants me, I know that look now. Oh God, I can feel a semi coming on. She must know I want her too, she has to know that look, she must see it every day. Fucking hell, she is beautiful, a thing of great beauty.'

Mr Dempsey spoke, "Thank you, Captain Travers, sir, thank you for coming to see us, Joe told us what a good man you were."

'She's smiling at me again, don't smile at me, please don't smile at me...'

"You were such a nice man he said, serious and deadly, you still managed to be nice."

Archie now had a raging hard on, so hard he thought he might come right then in his pants.

'I've got to get out of here.'

He began to stand up, grateful for the briefcase he carried and placing it in front of his crotch.

'I have to get out of here right now. I've got to go.'

"I apologise, Mr and Mrs Dempsey, there's such a lot to do," he said tapping his briefcase.

"Oh yes, we understand, there's just one thing I need to ask," Mrs Dempsey began.

"Yes, anything at all," he said without thinking.

"Can you promise you'll keep my Ben safe?"

"I'm sorry Mrs Dempsey, I just can't promise that."

There he was, the world's best liar and he couldn't tell one old woman, one little white lie to keep her happy.

Ben looked at Archie and said, "I'll stay here tonight if that's okay, sir."

"Yes, of course," said a relieved Archie.

"And I'll walk you home later," Ben said to Oona.

"Oh that's okay, Captain Travers can give me a lift, it's a couple of miles walk, but only five minutes in a car," she answered with a lightly Irish voice. A softly accented, whispered voice that seemed to have an echo within it. It was like that violin music he'd heard, a sound that made the hairs on the back of your neck stand up and took your breath away at the same time.

It was an invitation, he thought.

No, it was stronger than that, it was a summoning, that he just couldn't deny, he had to follow it, even if it led to Hell itself.

Oona walked out of the house and towards his car,

slightly ahead of Archie at first, he could see her small hips swaying slightly in the tight skirt, how did women do that? He walked more quickly to avoid that view of her and still managed to discreetly rearrange his erection while behind her. Having caught up with her, she'd slowed down making it easier for him, he could now smell her perfume more distinctly, it was unusual, fresh and natural and only served to reaffirm his erection.

In the confines of his car, her scent was even stronger, and he breathed it in deeply.

"You smell very nice, is it your aftershave?" she said, looking straight ahead.

"I did put some on this morning, your perfume is lovely too."

"I'm not wearing any," she replied turning to smile directly at him.

That was it, she'd snared him effortlessly with one smile and one superficially innocent, yet predatory, question. They talked, laughed and fenced with words while he drove, she was so young yet so bright, possessing such grace and poise as he'd never imagined could exist. She was the 'Man Ray' photograph made flesh. He was enraptured in just a few short minutes. He'd have to work meticulously and deliberately to plan how best to get away with fucking her, and he knew he had plenty of time and patience to work out precisely how and when.

He had to park his car at the wrong end of the narrow, dark one-way street that she said led to her parent's house, small, well-worn terraces directly facing the street with no front gardens. They talked a little more while sat in the car.

"I'll walk you to the door, Oona," he said.

As they walked to her house, the clear moonlight showed a series of shabby front doors and alleyways on the left. Despite the blackout, he could see a little bomb damage to houses on the right. The war was touching everyone, he felt sorry for Oona living in such a rundown, unsafe area, she deserved better.

He'd never know how he dared, but as they walked

those few steps, he took her hand and she took his. In doing so, one of her fingers lightly stroked the sensitive skin on his left wrist just next to the palm of the hand. He held her hand tightly, vicelike and drew her into an alleyway pushing her back firmly up against a wall, leaning his face down towards hers.

"You just smell so good," he said inhaling deeply.

On tip toes, she stretched her small frame up towards him and grabbed him by the rear of his neck pulling her face up to his. She kissed him deeply, he returned her kiss roughly and urgently, their tongues and saliva mixing, each tasted exactly as the other wanted and needed.

He started to pull at her skirt, she reached down and found his stiff cock, rock hard even through his trousers.

"Oh Jesus, you're too big for me," she said, "fuck me anyway, I'm wet enough already."

He kissed her, and she bit his tongue, not too hard, enough to know she meant what she said, as she undid his trousers pulling at his cock.

"Oh Jesus," she said.

Her skirt was already around her waist, but her knickers were tight and awkward, he crouched down in front of her, pulling then tearing them off and pushing her legs apart. Her pussy was fully shaven, he'd not seen that before, well-trimmed yes, but not fully shaven. Her labia and clitoris were prominent and engorged. He held the sides of her vagina apart with his left hand and began to caress her with his tongue, working two fingers inside her, as Victoria had taught him.

"Oh yes," she said, "yes, yes, don't stop. Oh God."

Less than a minute later, she came.

"Fuck, yes, yes, yes, yes," she panted as her moisture soaked his two fingers. A little ran down his wrist as he pushed his fingers firmly upwards and into the sweet spot at the inside front of her vagina. Her muscles gripped and rippled his fingers tightly, holding them inside her as she came, she was tight and getting tighter. He half wondered whether she could take his cock, then he stood up, and only seconds later he was inside her.

"Oh fucking hell, you are so tight," he said.

"I've never been so wet, you made me this wet. Oh, Jesus, you're too big, no don't stop, you're stretching me, it's good, oh fucking hell, it's all in isn't it, don't stop, fuck me, fuck me hard. Fuck me really hard, oh God yes I'm coming again, don't stop, yes, yes, keep going, don't stop, I want you to come inside me, come on give it to me."

Archie rammed her upwards into the wall, holding her legs off the ground.

"Fucking hell," he swore at her as he came, still thrusting as he did so and she came again too, shuddering and shaking and gripping his cock tightly.

"I don't know how you did that, oh that was the best ever," she said panting and kissing him at the same time.

"Your pussy is so tight and so wet it feels like you have another pair of hands inside you."

"I have to fuck you again, I just have to, can I?" she almost pleaded.

"We could do it again right now," he said, "thrusting his still hard cock inside her."

"No, wait, you have to give me a break, I think I've scraped and bruised my back on the wall."

He put her down gently and looked directly into her smiling eyes, eyes can smile, he knew that now. Her face was flushed, and she was perspiring just a little at the hairline.

"You, are the most beautiful thing I have ever seen, in my entire life," he said as his cock slid out of her.

Somehow, she managed to smile even more, more wickedly. She went straight down onto her haunches and started licking his wet cock. She licked and sucked the end of it, she licked it all over sucking all the fresh moisture, his and hers, from it. She pulled his trousers further down, licked his balls and nibbled them with her teeth while still stroking his cock. She spat saliva on the palm of her hand and worked it onto the head of his cock. Then she lifted his balls and stuck her tongue underneath them, reaching as far as his anus to flick the opening with her tongue.

"I'm coming again, fuck, that is so good," he said, "I'm coming, I'm coming now, don't stop," he said panting.

She moved her tongue away from his balls and took as much of his cock in her mouth as she could manage. She let his sperm shoot into her mouth and worked his cock like an udder with her lips and tongue, squeezing and pulling until he was empty. She stood up, still gripping his cock and stretched as far as she could up to his face, opened her mouth and put out her tongue showing him his sperm mixed with her spit. She shut her mouth, made a gulping noise, then French kissed him again.

"Fucking hell," he said.

"That was exceptional, wasn't it? How big is your cock, it's so wide too, where has that cock been all my life?"

"Where have you been all mine? Let me take you back to my flat right now."

"No, not now, my Dad's expecting me home by ten as usual and I'm supposed to be grieving; so are you."

"Sorry, it slipped my mind, I must have been distracted by something. Tomorrow then, I'll collect you from the end of this street."

"No, Finsbury Park Station tomorrow morning, at say, ten o'clock?"

"Yes that's great, I'll take you for something to eat or shopping, I seem to owe you a pair of knickers."

"You will not, you'll take me back to your flat and fuck me so hard I can't walk straight!"

"If you insist."

She pecked him on the lips gently, pulled her skirt back down then rearranged her hair and the rest of her clothing.

"Walk me the rest of the way home now," she told him, "I might get attacked... again."

Archie just looked at her and breathed in. In the semi-darkness of the pale moonlight, he could make out her features and could feel the wide eyes she held him with. He kissed her on the lips, no more than a peck, then on the end of her nose, then each eyelid. He gently stroked the length of each eyebrow with his thumbs and traced the outline of each ear then kissed his way from her forehead back to her lips, then finally wiped a small gagging tear from each of her eyes.

"That's… that's absolute heaven, who taught you that?" she asked.

"*You* just did," he said and kissed her gently again.

Archie watched her go inside her door, shaking his head, breathless and trying to rearrange his thoughts and feelings into something coherent.

Once inside, Oona locked the door behind her, shouted a hello and goodnight to her mum and dad and went straight upstairs to her room. That was just as well, Archie's kisses had smeared her lipstick and makeup, her eyes still watered from taking too much of his cock in her mouth. Her hair was a mess where he'd grabbed and held it. She checked her vagina for blood, it was red and engorged still, she had managed to take all of his cock without damaging herself. The tip of his cock had just touched parts inside her that she didn't know she had.

She'd given her first hand job aged fourteen and her first blowjob aged fifteen, she'd waited until she was sixteen before having penetrative sex and she'd done it a lot since then. She usually achieved orgasm quickly, never as fast as that though and never more than once. He'd done things with his tongue and fingers that no one else had ever thought of, not that way. She felt empty, though, not from any sense of shame or guilt, she just needed him inside her again, properly and for longer, much longer.

She'd wash properly early in the morning, she needed his scent and taste to stay on her for the night, and she'd be at her best for him tomorrow.

She hoped she wouldn't fall in love with him, it might already be too late, he was a wealthy upper-class gentleman and an officer, a Captain, he was way above her. Even if that were all it was, she'd enjoy being used by him. She went to sleep with her legs wrapped around one of her pillows and dreamed of Captain Archie Travers.

Twenty minutes later, Archie still sat in his car at the end of the street. For a few moments, he'd forgotten how to drive, the automatic movements you made without thinking had all gone. He concentrated hard, found the interior light and turned it on. As he studied each instrument, handle, and part, carefully, he recognised them, and the knowledge of their function slowly came back to him.

Then he realised he'd forgotten who he was. He looked at his hands, turning them around, then twisted the rear-view mirror so he could look at his face. He looked at his uniform and knew it was 1941. He took out his wallet and read his army identity card, working out who he was. He was Archie Travers, no longer Teddy Austin, Teddy knew how to drive, it was someone else who didn't.

The dim headlights of a passing car distracted him, and he fully returned to his present time and identity, although the unease and self-doubt remained.

He'd never seen Oona before, he'd known her for less than an hour, and he ached from the lack of her presence. The feeling was strangely familiar, he'd ached for Oona before he'd ever met her.

*

That evening at the flat he phoned the Savoy at eleven o'clock, then sat in the chair and forced his brain to think about the war, its progress and what he could do next. He needed to do something, he needed to find a replacement for the *'Krebs'* as the last action the team had undertaken.

Nothing was going well, the Atlantic Convoys were taking heavy losses from submarines. The enigma work would eventually help, but we needed another way to stop the U-Boats. Strike at their base perhaps, as Rebecca had told them to.

Yugoslavia and Greece were nearly gone, Crete would be next, maybe Malta. Erwin Rommel was in the North African desert with the best equipment and men; that was going badly for the 8th Army, always reactive and never yet successfully proactive.

Wherever we could outnumber the enemy three or four to one, like Operation Claymore, we could win, any other time we'd lost. Yes, the losses were valiant in places, and we were retreating and evacuating more stylishly, but a first real win seemed far away. The New Zealanders got every shit job going and did it well, maybe he could acquire a couple as replacements; if there were any left, after Crete.

Roosevelt had signed the Lease-Lend Act in March, which meant the British could use the United States as a weapons factory and pay later. Getting the stuff across the Atlantic Ocean was still the problem. The Act was another significant step away from true neutrality, though, and Churchill was playing his cards well. Roosevelt was dealing him favourably from a fixed deck. You wouldn't bankroll someone else's war unless you knew they were going to win, would you?

The bombing of Germany was continuing ferociously and bloody right too. London and other big cities had taken a terrible pounding, Liverpool, Glasgow, Plymouth, Bristol, Coventry all much worse than the official reports. People weren't stupid, no, they were stupid, just not that stupid and even stupid people deserved the truth sometimes, perhaps.

Our bombing and radar were better than the Germans, we need to make sure it stays that way.

St. Nazaire would be worthwhile, but it wasn't the time for that yet. Besides it was virtually a suicide mission for those involved.

Radar it was then, he'd think that through while he slept.

*

Friday 25th April 1941 – St. Nazaire – German Occupied France

Just before midnight, French time, on the 25th of April 1941, Major Rodolf Von Rundstedt, the Head of Wehrmacht Security in St. Nazaire sat in his office. He was waiting for the prisoners to arrive. Those two animals deserved execution, he knew that. They'd gone too far this time, and it became his problem.

As Head of Security, one of his jobs was ensuring the work on building the U-Boat pens and dry dock, proceeded, to a high standard and on time. He'd risen well and as planned since his exploits in Calais and the rest of the Battle for France. In St. Nazaire, he had gently persuaded French Engineers to assist and manage the building project, with workers who needed to be kept happy and productive, not slave labour, Poles, Czechs or Jews. His methods were soft and worked, there had been no sign of enemy agent activity since the escape last year.

This pair of bastards had put all his subtlety at risk, there were brothels they could use, they could have found someone blind and ugly to screw, and their commander had already warned them. Dolf had found a beautiful young French girl to work as his secretary, who was discreet and a great comfort to him. She'd told him he had to stop those two, and he knew she was right.

This time, they'd slit a throat and mutilated the body of a fourteen-year-old when they'd done with her.

They arrived in his office, dishevelled, but not bruised and accompanied by two guards.

"You two are leaving tomorrow, you are being transferred to an SS unit in the East, you'll spend the night in the cells, any questions?" He said tapping the butt of the Luger that lay on his desk.

"No, sir."

"Take them away."

He knew they deserved to die, he also knew that some of his men would disagree. Most wouldn't want to see a fellow German hung in France, we did that to others, not to our own.

Dolf sighed and went upstairs to his rooms and got back into bed with his naked secretary, Claudine.

"It's done. They have 'confessed' every bad deed they've done in St. Nazaire. The victims will be compensated. You will arrange for it to be dealt with by the Maire and the Church."

"Thank you," she said as she began to arouse him.

"Make sure they know I require peaceful cooperation in return. Make sure they know I don't do anything without a price of my own."

She'd typed out the movement orders that afternoon, memorising the names, dates and places of birth as well as serial numbers. It was Gottlieb and Gerolf as she'd expected, no risk was taken tonight, and the British would have the information they had very specifically asked for.

Chapter 3

26th April 1941 - Finsbury Park - London

Rebecca arrived at Finsbury Park Station at 0955 on the 26th April, fresh from visiting her parents in Peterborough. Those visits were always slightly awkward, not unpleasant, it was just, well, she didn't fit into her family properly. She'd have to wait for Begley and Mary Murphy's train to arrive, then they'd go to see Spud's mum. It was a surprise when Begley offered to go with them, but he'd known Spud's mum from childhood. He owed her more than the bowls of soup she'd given him when he was hungry, which was nearly every day. Since he'd helped with the explosive crackers at Christmas time he'd been willing to speak to them, before that he hadn't dared say a word to anyone in Mary's team.

Explaining about the secret wedding and baby wouldn't be easy, but she, as a bridesmaid, would make an excellent witness. She thought she'd pay Archie a surprise visit at the flat that afternoon and they'd do some thinking together. She'd told Archie that she and Mary would speak to Spud's mum without him. They knew how much he was dreading the visit to the Dempseys. She wanted to spare him some of the deceit involved.

The absence of bombing the previous night meant the area was calm, so she sat on a bench enjoying the morning sunshine. Unwilling to forgo some thinking time, she began going through the previous week's intelligence, sifting and boxing it in her mind.

A very attractive young girl walking towards the station caught Rebecca's eye. She looked no more than sixteen, and she's just had sex, Rebecca thought. How can she walk like that? She just oozes confidence, she looks about the same size and weight as me, why doesn't my body move like that?

As the girl walked past her, the hairs on the back of her neck stood on end. '*Archie?*'

Archie's car pulled up nearby and, through the sparse number of people, she saw the girl get in the passenger seat. If Archie had used any peripheral vision at all he would have seen Rebecca, this morning his eyes saw only the beautiful young girl and he drove straight off.

I'll have to do my own thinking today then, she thought disappointedly.

*

Archie collected Oona at the station at ten o'clock, he'd been early and driven past three times before he saw her. She was as beautiful as he remembered. She'd tied her hair in a ponytail again, nothing distracted him from her perfect face. He hoped he looked his best for her too, he had his best fresh uniform on.

"Your perfume smells great again," he told her.

"I'm not wearing any. Honestly, I can't wear it, it brings me out in a rash. Besides, the right scent for a woman is none at all."

"Who told you that?"

"No one, I've never said it before. You're the only person who's ever mentioned my scent."

"I've read those words somewhere, that's all."

As well as her beauty, she just looked like she wanted to have sex, or had just had sex, great sex. Some hormonal property like Rebecca had told him about, no, don't think about Rebecca. Rebecca was just like a fucking *machine*, Oona was, well, just like a *fucking* machine.

He just knew someone as beautiful as Oona would never have looked at him as a Private, he had to maintain the act all the time, he was posh, that's what she wanted, that's what he'd be.

He just couldn't figure out why she was with Joe, and he could hardly ask.

The drive back to Hevlyn Mansions was perilous, she kept making him laugh as he made her, she also kept stroking his erection through his trousers at every set of traffic lights.

He'd enjoyed other women, his time with Victoria was

excellent, the best sex he'd ever had or could imagine. When he'd seen her that last time it was the best yet, still not enough, though. Ten minutes with Oona had shown him that.

As soon as they entered his flat, he just picked her up and carried her into the bedroom, their clothes were fully off this time and very quickly. Her body was tiny, firm and curvy, he'd never even imagined such perfection. He kissed her body everywhere and licked and fucked her with his tongue, he paid particular attention to her anus. He hadn't known it was such a sensitive spot, and her freshly shaven pussy was delicious.

When, after losing count of the orgasms she had, he did eventually fuck her properly, her juices gushed out of her onto his cock, balls, and bed.

"Oh Jesus, now that was the best ever," she said, "on top, you were even deeper inside me."

He stayed inside her for two hours, they stopped for half an hour to eat the meal the Savoy had delivered early that morning. He finally remembered to ask what her surname was, it was Lainne, pronounced Lane she said. After that, he stayed inside her for another two hours.

She rolled him over until she was on top of him, pinning him down, she transfixed him with those blue eyes and long eyelashes.

"I'm going to lick your balls and suck your cock until you come all over my face," she said.

He was in love, he was spellbound, he would do anything for her, he would do anything *to* her! She was perfect and they'd only just begun to explore each other.

She felt the same, although neither knew quite what to do about it.

*

On that same Saturday afternoon, after saying goodbye to Begley and Mary Murphy at Finsbury Park Station, Rebecca waited there all afternoon, she wasn't completely sure why. She sat on various benches, had cups of tea in different cafes, walked, stood, waited, read her book, anything to pass the time.

Eventually, around half past six, Archie's car pulled up, she stepped back into the crowd, she needn't have, his eyes were still enthralled by the girl, who left the car and blew him a kiss.

The girl walked back the way she'd come that morning.

Rebecca followed her, discreetly, her training helped, but, as usual, nobody noticed her anyway.

*

On his return to the flat, Archie sat in the thinking chair. He'd talked with Ben the previous day about his childhood in North London. Innocent questions which enabled him to probe deeper into Nipper's background and the children's home where he'd lived for a time.

"Funny you should ask about that, sir," Ben had said, "I asked around, and it's even worse than me and Joe thought. The place is closed now thank God, those kids were treated as bad as anything you can imagine. Boys and girls, rape, buggery and worse. Some kids just up and disappeared, ran away and disappeared, dead more like. I tell you if it weren't closed now then a few of us local boys who've got firearms now would go right up there."

"Fucking hell," said Archie.

"That's not the worst of it, Nipper had the nouse to run and fend for himself. You see, it was his own mum and dad that put him in there. They sold him, they fucking sold him to the home, sir," he said shaking his head and looking down, "and they say he had a sister too, Alice, two or three years older than him, they sold her an' all. Nobody knows where she is. Just another disappearance. The only good thing was his mum and dad drank themselves to death on the cash."

"Jesus wept."

"No he didn't, sir, that's another trouble, some of his lot were in on it too!"

"You know Ben, sometimes I'm glad I sold my soul to the Devil. I wasn't using it much, he gave me a fair price, and I know where I stand."

Friday 2nd May 1941 – London

The morning of Friday the 2nd of May came, Archie had worked and planned hastily. Rebecca sensed that and worried that she'd not seen him eating for a couple of days. She asked him if he needed any help, she said she'd go with him, she knew he was planning something.

"Not today," he'd said and asked her not to ask him any questions. He thanked her when she agreed not to.

The drive south from Bletchley was easy in the daylight, and he wasn't tired, just hungry. He stopped off briefly at the flat to collect his old kit and made his way by car to Holborn, reaching there before five o'clock.

He walked around the area in his Captain's uniform, seeing what it felt like. People hurried by in the rush hour, leaving work on time, aiming for the railway and tube stations. Young women gave him admiring glances as he stood there, office workers in bowler-hats and spinsters paid him no heed. No one would recognise him now. He took up a position opposite the offices of a large and reputable firm of Accountants, Betteridge, and Co, a building he knew well.

He saw his target leaving and followed him around the corner of the large office building, towards the spot where he regularly parked his car, in the one space reserved for him. Archie waited a few seconds; not too close or quick, leave time for him to get angry and distracted.

When Archie rounded the corner, he found the man, Mr Charles Betteridge, the owner of the firm and the building, fuming at the Army vehicle blocking his car into its space.

"I'm terribly sorry old chap, I'll shift it in a minute," he said.

"You'll move it now, young man," he replied, "bloody cheek, don't you know who I am?"

"I know exactly who you are. Do you know who I am?" he said in reply.

"No, I bloody don't-" Betteridge's voice trailed off as the chloroform took his breath away, Archie had the old man in the boot of his car even before he was fully unconscious. The smell would linger, though, he'd have to explore using something odourless, the SOE boffins would know.

Betteridge came to, at ten o'clock that night, when Archie threw a cup of water in his face. Archie had topped up the Chloroform handkerchief twice until everything was ready. He wore his old private's uniform.

Betteridge found he was tied with thin rope to a wooden chair and gagged. He could see he was under smoke-blackened dirty brick arches that looked like a railway bridge lit by a couple of large oil lamps.

He looked much older now than Archie remembered, about mid-fifties, he'd seemed early forties when he'd last seen him. He was still a handsome man, though, trim and well groomed, elegant even.

If only I smoked I could blow it in his face, Archie thought, as he sat opposite him.

"Well Mr Betteridge, do you recognise me at all now?" Archie said removing the gag.

Betteridge shook his head.

"Let me jog your memory then," he said calmly and politely. He'd decided to be Conner tonight, to see if he could pull it off.

"You recall a young man, called Simon, Simon Seabury?"

Betteridge shook his head again.

"Oh, you'll have to do better than that, old chap. You once had a young gentleman friend and his name was Simon Seabury."

Archie took the fear in his eyes as a 'Yes'.

"You and he were close, he liked you, you spoiled him, he liked you a lot in fact. You became very close, as close as any two men could. He loved you, you know that; he told me so."

Archie paused for effect and continued serenely.

"You took him to a party one night, he was looking forward to it."

Betteridge shook his head.

"He came back from that party in a terrible state didn't

he?"

No reply.

"He came back, from that party, in a terrible state, did he not?"

Betteridge nodded.

"You, and six of your… associates buggered him to Hell and back that night, he did not consent to that, am I correct?"

No reply.

"Am I correct?"

Betteridge nodded, sobbing now.

"He told me what had happened that night, exactly what happened, do you want me to repeat it?"

Betteridge shook his head, still sobbing, maybe he was remorseful, no, and I don't care if he is, Archie thought.

"We worked together and shared the same lodgings. I left him alone that next morning when I went to work. I told him I'd sort it out, but I couldn't, I didn't know what to do, I was nobody, and Simon was nobody. When I got home that night, he'd hung himself, the doctors found his guts hanging out of his arse.

"We went to the same school. He was only seventeen years old, and he was my only friend in the whole world."

He let that sink in.

"The problem you have, Mr Betteridge, is, I used to be nobody. Now I'm somebody, and you're, well, you're nobody at all.

"So, what I need you to do, old chap, is to give me the names, addresses and well, occupations of the six gentlemen involved and we'll say no more about it. Simple really."

Archie got up and walked slowly over to Betteridge, using Dolf's knife to cut the rope holding his right wrist to the chair. He gave him a pen and notebook, a small ledger ironically, and placed it in his lap.

"Now, the thing is, old chap, it's possible that you might try and trick me. I'm awfully sorry to think so badly of you, but you will write the names down, and I will have to check them thoroughly before I let you go. They must be right the first time, or you may well starve to death while you're waiting for me to return."

Betteridge nodded, Archie walked circles around him slowly, looking over his shoulder as he wrote the first two identities down promptly and the next two more hesitantly, then stopped altogether.

"Oh Dear, Oh Dear, your handwriting is dreadful, old boy, what does that say?"

Betteridge corrected his shaky handwriting, he still had only four names.

"I'm going to have to provide you with a little incentive, a little flattery, a little attention, some grooming perhaps, yes some grooming. Please don't make me do this," he said holding the knife over his still tied left hand briefly before slicing off the tip of his left pinkie.

Betteridge gurgled rather than screamed, then he began writing the next two names. Archie looked over his shoulder, he'd recognised the first two names, but was aghast at the last two.

"Thank you so much, Mr Betteridge that's very civilised of you, very civil indeed. Now, old bean, if you could just mark an X next to the chap who did the fisting... there you are, that wasn't so bad was it?" he said as Betteridge put a large X by the second last name.

Archie took the notebook and placed it in his recently emptied kitbag which he slung over his shoulder and casually walked away from Betteridge. He went to a large metal door in the hard brick wall, which he swung open and climbed through. He turned, looking back at Betteridge.

"Oh I say old bean, the bit about coming back for you after I'd checked the names," he said, as he lit a match, "I lied."

He dropped the match into the crumpled papers and kindling piled just inside then shut the furnace door.

The fire would start slowly, he needed Betteridge to see his death coming. One of Begley's unique recipe firebombs would explode in ten minutes, that was to incinerate the body and any evidence; Betteridge would be long dead by then, suffocated after choking. Archie just needed to know that he'd suffered, he didn't need to watch. He walked away slowly and calmly, again whistling that two minutes' worth of violin that he just couldn't get out of his head.

Archie waited in his car until he was certain the device had worked properly, the fuel he'd placed there and the built in airflows in the floor and chimney of the furnace would ensure a thorough job. It was considerate of Jerry to provide an abundance of empty killing ground in the disused, half bombed areas in the East End, Plaistow this time.

Fire and eternal damnation for Betteridge then, God just didn't like poofs, did he?

*

That was another of Archie's God's seemingly infinite flaws, he hated all poofs, most were perfectly decent chaps. Alan was one of the best men he'd ever met, a bit eccentric yes, but look at what Archie did for a hobby. The ones on his list were certainly not decent, not at all.

Archie's God also had very poor taste, in fact, his God was a bit of a cunt, a lot of a cunt actually, with a little arsehole thrown in too. Archie resolved to tell him just that, in the unlikely event of ever meeting him.

Poof was a poor word too, it implied some camp hilarity. Alan was neither camp nor hilarious and certainly not effeminate, Archie had been running with him, Alan had slowed down to let him keep up. Archie might just pip him in 800 yards, in long distance, he'd easily run Archie into an early grave. There just wasn't a usable word for a normal chap who fancied other men. Archie didn't fancy fat women or tall women, and that didn't cause any slurs to be cast on his character. He was a sucker for the small elfin ones, though, Victoria and Oona, especially Oona, even Rebecca was elfin just not a woman, well not in a sexual sense.

He thought he might tell Rebecca about tonight. He

might have to, if she asked the right question, he'd already planned for that eventuality.

The torture troubled him too, he'd expected to take a whole finger at least, but when it came to it, he'd flinched at the end of a pinkie. Luckily he knew the names would be correct after Betteridge had written the first two, they'd been on his list already after his talk with Ben about Nipper and he'd already done some research of his own.

*

He'd changed his clothes by the time he got home. He had a bath and thoroughly cleaned his hands, sniffing them for the scent of death and looking closely at his eyes in the mirror. He didn't eat, he had a cup of tea, he sat in the chair, then went to bed. He didn't sleep at first, then slept poorly and woke early. He had another bath, another thorough hand wash, he still couldn't eat.

He got in his car and was at Finsbury Park Station earlier than ten, so was Oona. She got in the car and this time, she risked a long kiss before he set off.

He smiled at her gratefully, he was Archie again, and somehow held back the tears of relief that he felt welling up in the small remaining fragment of his soul.

*

Saturday the 3rd May 1941 - Finsbury Park Station

Lieutenant Rebecca Rochford sat on a bench near Finsbury Park Station, she'd stayed in a small local hotel in North London the night before. She watched the girl arrive at the station much earlier than previously and do some window shopping, looking at clothes shops, but not going inside, why did women do that? You went into a shop, found something functional that fitted and bought it. There was no need for a ceremony to accompany the act. Then she realised the girl was wearing the same clothes as the previous Saturday. Archie wouldn't notice, she'd heard men never noticed that detail, Rebecca didn't see why they should, but the girl would know, and she'd care.

Rebecca, having worn some civilian clothes today and what amounted to a minor disguise, a blonde wig, risked a walk past Archie's car as the girl got in. Oh No! He has that look! The girl leaned towards him, gave him a lingering kiss on the lips, he smiled broadly in a way Rebecca knew she'd never made him smile, and the look was gone. Oh no! She said to herself, how could I even think that of him? She felt guilt and shame again for the second time in her life, at least feeling guilt and shame, was feeling something.

*

On Sunday the 4th May 1941, Archie drove to the Manor, for once he didn't want to. He wanted to spend every waking hour with Oona, they'd talked as well as fucked for six hours the previous day, although she had to leave and couldn't stay a night with him. She claimed she couldn't explain it to her parents, a Saturday out with her friends from work would be okay, not a late or overnight stay. She worked every Sunday in a small dressmaking factory. That was the only thing he didn't love about Oona, she had to leave. She wasn't lying, he could tell, there was something she wasn't telling him, though, she was holding something back.

There was still a war on; the war was making him into somebody, and he needed to be somebody for Oona; that thought sustained him.

The Manor was quiet on Sunday, and he was pleased to find Nipper in the garden.

"Begley's working on some secret and dangerous concoction," Nipper explained. "I've never had a garden before, it's not normal obviously, you can sit in it and listen; hear things you've never heard. There's birds and flowers and things, and you can think."

Nipper looked well, well fed and well, content. Archie hadn't seen that particular Nipper before.

"I need some advice from you, Nipper, we need a new Sergeant," Archie said.

"You need Ben," he said, "me and Begley had a chat and it needs to be Ben, for his sake as well as him being next in line."

Archie wondered how Nipper had worked that out, he

was dead right.

"I've spoken to Smudger, and he agrees, it would have been Tarrian, but well..."

"You are right, Nipper, remind me to ask your advice more often, mate."

"When you have the team meeting you 'aven't told us about yet, you need to wait for me and Begley to speak up first, Smudger'll do the rest. We don't want Ben doin' anything daft, like refusin' just cos his big brother acted the clown once. That Begley thinks I'm his apprentice, by the way, he's mine," he winked at Archie, "I'll keep him as sweet as Spud done."

"I don't know what I'd do without you, mate," said Archie being Teddy again, briefly.

"You wouldn't last five minutes! And those two new lads are just fine, I can tell a wrong un in five minutes, and they're sound, even if they don't like us northern lads," he said.

"Northern?"

"Holloway. I ain't no Spurs fan either it's the Gunners for me."

"One last thing Nipper. You don't have to say a word, and we'll never talk of it again unless you want to, I've done some research on a Children's Home... in the north."

Nipper looked down at the grass silently.

"If you ever need to talk, about anything, anytime, you speak to me, that's an order, alright?" Archie continued.

"Sometime maybe."

"Anytime," Archie squeezed the boy's shoulder warmly and left. Over his shoulder, he said with a smile, "I love you, Nipper."

"I love you too, sir," he replied.

*

The team meeting went well. Mary Murphy sat in on it, everyone knew her circumstances now. They added her to the list of people they'd die for.

Conner let Archie handle the meeting and sat to one side as Archie did his best to impersonate him. Rebecca sat next to him, very close in fact, he didn't mind.

Ben accepted the appreciation of his peers and was now Sergeant Dempsey; Nipper, Begley, Hospital and Henry would be his men, Smudger took the rest. They were still a man short and needed the right man not just the next man.

They discussed the next planned Operation due to take place in May.

Conner then introduced William 'Billy' Perry as a new Sergeant Quartermaster. One look at Billy had told them all they needed to know about him. In a uniform and even at nearly fifty years old now, he looked deadly and, if he was Conner and Archie's man, that was enough.

The ranks spoke to Billy about the equipment they needed and some items that they just plain wanted. They'd get all of it. Begley's list was straightforward enough, there was nothing legal on it, that wouldn't stop Billy.

Finally, Archie and Conner let Rebecca announce that Spencer Ward would undergo specialist medical training between Operations, she'd seen him reading medical texts in his spare time. Spencer would profit from the war too, Rebecca insisted on paying for it herself.

"That went exceptionally well," said Conner.

"We need to talk about Smudger," said Archie with Rebecca close by and nodding agreement, "we can't face another Mrs Tarrian."

Chapter 4

Saturday 10th May 1941 - Finsbury Park Station

On Saturday 10th of May 1941, Rebecca reached Finsbury Park Station early in the morning, she'd stayed overnight again in the same small local hotel. The previous day she'd followed the girl from her home to her work. The girl left very early in the morning at five o'clock. Dressed shabbily in trousers and plain shoes, she'd gone to her work as a cleaner in a local factory. The factory made clothing, uniforms, as far as Rebecca could find out. The girl walked the three miles to and from her job, on top of a ten hour day. Although the factory was on a bus route, she didn't use the bus. The walk made Rebecca's weaker ankle throb a little, after a long day it must have been exhausting, and the young girl did it even in the late drizzle that day.

This morning, Rebecca just wore her uniform, the disguise from the previous occasion might not do the trick twice, she'd have to plan better next time.

As she half expected, the girl was there at nine o'clock and window shopping. This time, the girl went into one, a small dress shop and Rebecca followed her. The girl asked to try on a short-sleeved summer frock, priced at fifteen shillings and sixpence. Rebecca looked at some plain sensible skirts while watching the girl leave the changing room and look at herself in the full-length mirror. She was beautiful, and the dress fitted perfectly.

The elderly shop owner sniffed a little when the girl said she didn't have enough money with her today and would come back another time after she'd been to the bank.

"Maybe next Saturday," she said.

The girl left the shop, still looking at the window display longingly.

Rebecca approached the owner, spoke to her, placed something on the counter then went to leave the shop, just before opening the door, she said.

"Now! Before she goes. Please."

Rebecca went straight to her hotel, checked out and drove to the cottage.

The owner called the girl back inside the shop, explaining the price on the dress was a mistake, it was five shillings and sixpence, not fifteen.

"I get more confused now I'm older," she said, "would you like me to put it by for you or do you have enough with you today?"

"Do you know, I do have enough money with me. In fact, could I wear it now, please? It's such a lovely day."

The girl did hurry on the way out, just in case the owner suddenly became less confused.

Oona couldn't figure out what had just happened, but she felt exhilarated in the new dress and the early May sunshine.

She didn't have to wait too long for Archie, he was fifteen minutes early.

"What a lovely dress," he said, "is it new?"

"No, I've had it for ages," she said and gave him a deep and lingering kiss then stared into his eyes.

"I'm going to fuck your brains out today if you're lucky I might talk to you as well."

They did talk, a lot, and he was still very lucky.

*

Saturday 17th May 1941 – Wissant- Occupied France

At midnight and with the moon nearly full, the Chosen Men and Rebecca paddled carefully ashore just east of the small town of Wissant near Calais.

Archie was concerned that his choice of target might be reckless, but revenge always helped him to focus better so he went with his instinct. The others were enthusiastic about the plan and the target too.

Reconnaissance photographs from two months previously had shown the Germans erecting a small radar station near the shore. The same sandy beach he'd ran along nearly a year ago. The radar station would be complete by now and would likely contain the latest

German equipment. Taken there by submarine, they'd sneak in, Rebecca would assess what they found and steal some if she could, they'd blow up the rest. Once that part of the mission was complete, the gear safely on its way to the sub, they then had carte blanche to cause mayhem for fifteen minutes maximum then leave. The sub would stay as long as possible although they might have to motor the dinghies to Dover, the Channel was calm enough tonight.

SOE had done little publicly since Claymore, and a front page news story of a short, sharp raid on the French Coast would be useful items for the BBC and newspapers.

The extra incentive for the trip was a small SS Staging Post and Barracks in the fields behind the beach. About a hundred men, ten tanks, and ten half-tracks. This wasn't going to be a battle, just a hit and run, the tanks' engines would take twenty minutes to warm up, and they'd be long gone by then. Conner had somehow obtained two 'Hickmans' a prototype hand-held antitank gun from the Americans. Smudger had already nicknamed it the Hitman, he and Begley would use them on the tanks as an experiment. The gun fired what was called a rocket-borne shaped charge projectile, and Begley was madly in love with it. Archie allowed Begley and Smudger to fire two rounds each for practice. That went well, although they only had fourteen more projectiles. Begley said he could make a better one, and there was a fair chance he'd blow himself up firing it, but that didn't stop him.

Begley was familiar with the principle of a shaped charge. He called it a 'Munro' and explained it targeted an explosive blast on a specific area; on a safe, in a bank, for example, in theory obviously.

Once ashore, and without words or sound, they cut through the barbed wire on the beach and the Radar Compound's basic security fencing. Nipper took one guard with a knife then Rebecca the other with the silenced Luger, simultaneously. The station was empty and unused yet but contained pristine examples of the latest German equipment. Two pieces were small enough to dismantle easily and bring back as well as manuals, gold dust to the right boffin.

As planned, three men brought the equipment to the submarine. Begley allowed Nipper, as his apprentice he thought, to set the slow fused charges. Duncan insisted Nipper go back with the gear, he'd already got his Jerry.

As expected, Rebecca refused to go back with the equipment so she, Archie, Conner, Smudger, Begley, Ben, George and Henry stayed to assist in the experiment. Hospital stayed behind just in case.

They found the staging post immediately. It was a wide space behind barbed wire, with the front gate wide open and the tarmac empty apart from two huge Panzer IV tanks. They were the biggest that Archie or Conner had seen in person. The tanks were next to one remaining hut, complete with bright lights and singing coming from inside.

Where eight tanks and ten half-tracks had gone was an intrigue that could wait; they'd found the easiest target they could hope for. They sneaked into the compound, Conner set the men and Rebecca in firing positions then positioned himself to watch their backs. Archie stayed about an inch from Rebecca.

Smudger and Begley took aim and when Conner shouted, "Go!" they fired, and the Panzers erupted in flames. The light the flames gave off made the crews, who rushed headlong and heedless from the hut, easy targets for the Flowers boys, Ben, and Rebecca. Nearly all the Germans fell dead almost immediately, and much to her annoyance Rebecca's Thompson jammed just as she was about to fire at the last one, a dishevelled officer who fell down, dead drunk. Rebecca had allowed Ben and the Flowers boys to shoot first, she knew they had the same need to kill, as she had. Determined to kill her German, Rebecca took her Luger out and marched calmly over to the officer and stood on his chest taking aim.

"Wait, wait, he's a prisoner, he's an officer, we can use him, we can get him back easily in this state," Archie said, with an urgency that she couldn't ignore.

Rebecca sighed, reluctantly moving her boot from his chest, drew that leg back and kicked him in the balls as hard as she could. He didn't notice at all.

"Oh fucking hell, I think I've broken my ankle again!" she said, limping painfully then bursting into a sprint back to the beach, "only kidding," she shouted over her shoulder.

"Archie!" said Conner, so he ran after her, knowing what he meant, the rest followed as fast as they could with the prisoner and Ben carrying a bundle.

"I'm glad she's on our side!" said George to Henry, just before the slow charges exploded in the distance.

*

The submarine had gone, they knew that might happen and would find out later it had drawn some German Patrol Boat activity away from them, probably saving their lives.

It was a tight squeeze on the two remaining boats, Henry and George straddled the comatose German officer, which worked well.

Archie sat with Rebecca at the front of their boat, willing the white cliffs closer, and only an hour later they arrived safely in Dover.

Wringing wet, they clambered and dragged themselves up the stone steps of their small berth to the quayside. Conner confirmed the safe return of the others with the SOE officers waiting on shore.

"No bacon sandwiches, this time, Smudger," Conner said.

"What a fucking liberty, I'm starving," said Smudger.

"What on earth have you got there Ben?" said Archie, spotting Ben carrying a large wooden box.

"A crate of beer."

"Where the fuck did you get a crate of beer?"

"In Jerrys' hut, sir, there was two pissed French girls in there as well, they weren't my type so I grabbed the beer instead, it's that Stella stuff you like an' all."

They all sat down, soaked with salt water from the

spray of the dinghies, on stone bollards, barrels, crates, the hard floor of the dock and Rebecca on the German SS Officer, pissing themselves laughing. Archie was nearly in tears.

"I'm sorry about the ankle joke, you did look so worried," Rebecca said to Archie.

"That's okay, in fact, you can have the first beer," he said handing her his Swiss Army knife, a present from Conner, and one of the bottles.

"Thank you, you are a good sport," she said opening the bottle to find half its contents spraying all over her face. She did look daggers at Archie, but she did laugh too.

"Must have been the motion of the dinghy, how could I know?" Archie said deadpan-faced. "Somebody get my knife back, that officer might wake up in a minute."

She laughed then giggled like a schoolgirl, she drank the rest of her lager and most of Archie's too, he didn't mind one bit. He was alive, they all were, he hadn't killed any of his own men today, and he was still somebody.

An officer and two guards approached the group as they laughed.

"Excuse me, young lady, you appear to be sitting on my prisoner," the SOE Officer said.

"Not yet he's not, we'll have fifteen minutes first; Archie, Rebecca?" said Conner.

Archie and Rebecca woke the SS Officer and took him aside from the rest of the group. Archie gave him water then Rebecca did most of the talking, fingering her silenced Luger. Archie just played with Dolf's knife while cradling the Mauser in his lap.

Archie did some pointing, shrugging and talking, Conner style.

After fifteen minutes, they shook hands, the prisoner saluted Rebecca disconsolately, and all three walked wearily back to the waiting SOE transport.

"Treat him well," Archie told the waiting guards and officer, "I've made him some promises we'll have to keep. He'll co-operate with a debrief, and I'll see him in a week."

Conner nodded to the officer in a *'just do what my Captain said'* manner.

When the prisoner was out of sight and hearing, Archie spoke quietly to the SOE Officer.

"Have you got a secure line to Gubbins?"

"I can get one."

"Can you get me to it immediately, we know where those Panzers have gone," he said to Conner.

"Where?"

"Russia!"

*

It was late that morning when they finally returned to the Manor; the men could sleep all they needed now, after a well-earned full English breakfast cooked by Maud, Mary Murphy's mum.

Archie, Conner, and Rebecca joined in the breakfast, although Archie joined late. He'd been to see Billy and handed him Rebecca's jammed Thompson.

"Can you have a look at this Billy and make sure it never jams again or get another that won't, please, I can't lose that girl."

"I'll do it meself, and it won't leave my sight until it's next in her hands."

"Thanks, Billy."

"Good to see you back, son."

*

They turned on the BBC Radio News at midday, hoping perhaps to hear the news of a raid on France. The first story on the news was the bombing of the Chamber of the House of Commons.

"That happened a week ago!" said Archie.

"They're officially announcing it now," said Conner.

"Nobody noticed I suppose?"

There was nothing about their raid.

"Our German officer's information probably meant we have to keep that story out of the press," said Rebecca.

"Will we ever get any credit?" asked Smudger.

"Lennard, you can have credit or two more slices of

bacon, which is it?" said Maud Driver.

"I'll have the bacon thanks, Maud."

*

Conner, Archie, and Rebecca went to their cottage. Conner had insisted that Rebecca move into the small third bedroom, he wanted them to be near so he could take care of them and they could take care of him too. He also knew he'd have to go away soon, and his superiors had strongly advised him to take fewer personal risks. He shouldn't have gone to Wissant, but he'd promised the men and wouldn't break that pledge.

Tired as they were, they were home and safe so sleep could wait a little longer.

"Rebecca, how on earth did you get the officer to talk so soon?" Conner said.

"Well, Archie taught me well, the officer knew the war was over for him, and if he ever went back to Germany, he'd be disgraced after last night. He had pictures of a wife and children in his wallet. He had a choice of full co-operation immediately, or we'd take him back to Wissant and dump him on the beach.

"Archie asked if his balls were sore," she giggled, and they smiled with her, "then Archie showed him the SS knife and rifle and told him what I'd done in France. He'd heard rumours of what had happened to the Germans near St. Nazaire, I was notorious for a short while, and he knew I wasn't lying. He recognised the rifle too, Archie's friend, Dolf, is in St. Nazaire, a Major in Security now.

"Then I just told him if his information was useful, he'd go to a comfortable prison camp in Canada and get a new identity for him and his family when the war was over.

"He laughed and said the war was already over and told us about Russia, *'Barbarossa'*, he called it.

"What do we make of that?" Conner said looking at Rebecca, then Rebecca just elbowed Archie.

"Well," began Archie, "he couldn't believe that Hitler was starting another war when this one wasn't finished yet. There'll be no invasion attempt now, and the Blitz will have to stop. The Luftwaffe bombers have to move east to support any attack. They'll keep us on our toes with the occasional raid.

"He thinks it'll be early June when they start the attack, that's far too late. That's five to six months to take all Western Russia before the winter sets in, have these people never heard of Napoleon? Russia is just too big, the Germans have just lost the war.

"Churchill will tell the Russians of course, Stalin may not believe him and think we're bullshitting just to get him to attack Germany first. In purely objective numerical terms, we can sit back and wait for the Russians to do all the fighting and dying for us. The problem is, once they've taken Germany they won't stop till they get to the Channel and maybe not then. Stalin will end up killing more people than Hitler."

"Probably already has," said Conner.

"By the way," said Rebecca, "the Panzers were unserviceable waiting for repair."

"So we need to keep doing what we're doing to make sure we get to Western Europe first," said Conner.

"We still need the Americans though, and we need to work on the Nazi Superweapons," Archie added.

Conner thought for a few minutes then said.

"I need to go to Switzerland and America. That meeting we had last year with John Anderson about Tube Alloys, was next to useless, they won't tell us anything and won't let us meet the boffins. I've found more information out for myself, I wish we'd kept the bloody French papers now."

"They do agree that Heisenberg is the key figure, and you can control him?" Archie asked.

"Yes, I'm seeing him in Switzerland next week and then going to the United States to gauge what stage they're at. There's another thing… I've been *'advised'* not to engage in any more operational work, someone somewhere thinks I can't be risked."

"They're right, we've just decided that Heisenberg is the most important thing we're doing, and only you can do it,"

Archie said.

"Absolutely," added Rebecca.

"That's final then," said Archie.

"Let me tell the men then, please," Conner said.

"Can we take on the Rockets now?" Archie asked.

"That's still a definite no, I'm afraid," Conner said,

"Will you have time to do me a favour when you're in Switzerland?"

"Yes, certainly."

"And America, please."

*

22nd May 1941 – Switzerland

On the 22nd May 1941 Conner, as the son of a wealthy Swiss Banker, began his trip to Switzerland and the United States, it would take two months in total. He'd consciously left the team safe in the hands of Archie and Rebecca. England was a less dangerous place, the full blitz ended on the 11th of May just as Archie predicted, nothing had happened in Russia yet, but it would.

Switzerland went well, Alex gave as detailed and demanding a briefing as he ever had. Things to read, to do, people to meet, things that must not happen.

Heisenberg complained again that work on nuclear fission or weapons in Germany was under-resourced and undervalued. He thought there was no chance of any results before 1948. He would tell Fritz Todt, the German Minister of Armaments it would be 1946, of course.

Conner took some time for himself in Switzerland and enjoyed the company of an old female friend or two.

His trip to America was fruitful too, his connections and friends in the scientific community enabled him to work out that the United States Nuclear Programme was continuing apace. Over a hundred of the best nuclear physics brains in the United States had left their jobs and gone to work somewhere secret. The Government was diverting money and expertise from other unrelated, worthy research and projects, you could only reach one conclusion.

He did the favours that Archie had asked of him. He didn't think it would work in practice although it was better than any plan he had.

The strangest item was that Alex had insisted that he read a theoretical paper written by a boy aged fourteen, Joshua Lederberg, a genius from New Jersey. The American Institute Science Laboratory, coincidentally funded by a Swiss banker, had arranged his research position and funding. Conner could buy the boy the time to think and see what his genius would produce. That research paper had uncannily close links to the favours that Archie had discussed with him. How on earth, two people who'd never met, on two different continents, could be linked to an elderly Swiss Banker, albeit a very astute one, he just couldn't fathom.

Preserving, freezing and raising the dead was something out of fiction, Frankenstein. You could imagine it, write and theorise about it, but doing it was impossible.

Alex answered some questions directly, and other times he'd say that he knew the answer and Conner must find his own. Conner just knew he'd get no answer if he asked, this time, so he stayed silent.

He also remained silent when Alex asked too many questions about Archie, his name, his background, his family, his education, his roots, his training. He didn't know the answers, he no longer knew Teddy, he knew Archie and what he was now, not what he had been. Archie didn't talk about it, and he didn't ask.

*

Saturday the 24th of May – London

Archie hadn't seen Oona for two weeks, he could have driven to London easily in midweek, but Oona only had Saturdays off. He couldn't wait to see her, he ached from her absence, like holding your breath for too long.

At nine o'clock that morning, Rebecca was at Finsbury Park Station, wearing a different set of clothes and a hat this time. Very cunning, she thought, as she sat on a bench, just to the left of the station entrance, watching the direction from which the girl usually walked.

"Hello, do you mind if I sit here," said an Irish female voice from behind her.

"No, that's fine," said Rebecca beginning to feel uncomfortable.

"I'm just waiting for a friend, he won't be here for a while, but you know that, don't you?"

"Do I?"

"You must be Rebecca, I'm Oona, you don't match the description, and you're so pretty. Thank you for the dress by the way. It took me a time to work it out properly, but, when you weren't here last Saturday, it all sort of fell into place. He doesn't need you looking after him, you know."

"I suddenly feel very stupid," said Rebecca

Oona smiled, "and you're not used to that, are you?"

"No, not at all, never, in fact."

"That's all right, don't feel bad, if I wrote down all the stupid things I've done I could fill a book."

"Did he notice the dress?"

"Yes, he did, straight away, I thought he would, he keeps wanting to buy me things, I won't let him, though, I can't let him think I want his money or anything like that."

"What do you want then?"

"Just him… forever."

"What did he tell you about me?"

"Oh, nothing… sorry, I don't mean that badly, he's never mentioned anyone except Ben Dempsey or anything about his work at all."

"So how do you know who I am?"

"So… you don't know who I am either then?"

"No, he hasn't told anyone about you."

"Ah right, I can see it now. I was Joe Dempsey's fiancée, that's how I know who you are, and you can see why we're not exactly shouting our affair from the rooftops."

"Oh, I'm sorry."

"Don't be, I'd swap my whole life for one hour with Archie."

"So would I… just not in the same way as you, not at

all."

"He's the most dangerous man I've ever met, yet he makes me feel safe. You're quite dangerous yourself, aren't you? I thought you might be going to kill me; you're not, are you?"

"No, I just want to help you make him happy, I messed up one relationship for him… it's difficult to explain. I do need something in return."

"That sounds interesting."

"I've done something else that's a bit stupid."

"Yes?"

"I've agreed to buy a dress shop, the one you saw me in, and well, the trouble is I know nothing about dresses, not a thing. I hoped you might run it for me."

"I don't know anything about dresses."

"Oh yes, you do. You know how to wear one."

"I suppose so, I don't get too much practice, and you've seen me walking to work."

"Yes, sorry about that, I had to make sure… to find out… to be certain that you were… well, good enough for him."

"And?"

"Oh yes, definitely."

"I'm not so sure, I'm going to try my hardest. So you want me to run a dress shop, and presumably, you'll pay me. It'll be better money than the cleaning job, and you won't keep touching me up like my boss does now."

"Yes and there's a small flat above the shop which you can live in too, not as swanky as his flat, but you'll like it."

"So you give me a job, dresses, money and a place to live? What on earth can I give you in return?"

"Well I need quite a few things, and you have to promise never to tell anyone, especially Archie."

"Try me?"

"I need you to teach me how to walk like you do."

"Oh, I see it now. I do see it now."

Chapter 5

Saturday 24th of May 1941 - Finsbury Park

Archie collected Oona from Finsbury Park Station, they were both early again, they kissed as urgently and powerfully as they had that first time and he drove off. He didn't know how he'd ever live without that feeling of exhilaration she gave him. It was the difference between being alive and dead, he'd never felt more alive than in her presence.

"Pull in here now," she said grabbing the wheel of the car and swerving into a wide alley, then told him to stop behind a parked lorry.

"Don't move a muscle," she told him while undoing his flies and freeing up the erection that was almost permanent in her presence. She worked so urgently and expertly with her mouth that he came in less than a minute. She milked his cock like an udder, swallowed and brought her face to his, kissing him again, looking straight into his eyes.

"Now if you're not ready to fuck me as soon as we get in the flat, I'll have to kill you."

"Don't worry, if I'm not ready, I'll kill myself!"

He was ready, although they also talked, laughed, hugged, and caressed. He lost himself in her deep blue eyes and scent again, wishing he still had a soul so he could just give it to her.

*

He'd been to the best perfume shops in London and sniffed everything possible, he still couldn't find a match. She must be wearing some and not telling him, she just wouldn't let him buy her anything, maybe that was why.

*

As the days went by, Archie was still disturbed by Betteridge's killing. Not the killing itself, which he easily justified. He'd killed Germans, they were the enemy, and it was what you did in war. The three other murders were his personal war. If he was allowed to fight his country's war, then he could fight his own war, he could live with that balance.

The trouble was, his list was just getting longer. He'd put the two Germans, Gerolf and Gottlieb from St. Nazaire on the list, he knew now exactly who and roughly where they were. That would take time, patience, planning, execution and Rebecca. She deserved her balance too.

He had a list of another six now, two were for Nipper as well, still his to do, his sin to commit.

*

Friday 30th May 1941 – Hevlyn Mansions

Archie asked Rebecca if she'd come to the flat with him on Friday the 30th of May. She said she'd love to, and would leave early on Saturday morning as she had business to attend to. He appreciated that; he could still see Oona as planned. He wanted Rebecca to meet Oona, he just wasn't sure how it should happen.

They ate a light meal which Archie prepared, then talked over a small glass of wine.

"You need to talk about who you killed last week?" she asked.

"Yes, I do. I can't arrange the thoughts correctly in my head."

"Can we use the chair?"

"Yes, please."

She took her shoes off and sat on his lap, she was worried he might not let her.

"Just talk, I'll tell you if you're lying to yourself," she said.

Not for the first time he wondered how she did that, sometimes she knew just what he needed, even when he didn't.

He told her the full story in every detail he could muster, every scintilla of truth, no hint of vacillation and left the pure, dirty facts for her to judge as she saw fit.

"Well, everything you did to Betteridge was fully justified," she said, "he got what he deserved, you're not worried about that, though. When you started killing, you had a short list so you thought you could do it and put it away in a box... like I do. You're worried that once you start killing bad people, you won't know when to stop. You know you won't ever run out of bad people.

"Adopt a religious perspective for a second," she continued, "we know it's complete balderdash, so bear with me please."

"Okay, carry on."

"There's hundreds of different religions, from worshipping a tree or a cow to the invisible man. They all expound a form of morality or ethics, a set of rules for behaviour. Those rules, daft or otherwise, prove acceptable to let's say, ninety-nine percent of the world's population. Even an atheist would concede there're two or three fair points in the Ten Commandments."

"I'm with you so far."

"Okay, let's consider that each set of rules has a set of incentives and disincentives accompanying them. Heaven and Hell. Stick to the rules, you go to Heaven, break the rules enough, you go to Hell.

"So, each person you've killed was going to Hell for rule breaking according to ninety-nine percent of the world's population. You've merely hastened that process and therefore, in their moral judgement, you've done nothing wrong.

"The only person fit to judge you is yourself. I'll help if you let me.

"When you've done enough you'll stop, you'll know when. Something will probably happen that makes you stop. You won't change, you'll still be who you are, you'll just stop.

"Thousands of people are dying every day in the war, they die every day in peace, if some who deserve it, die as well, it just doesn't matter.

"Look at me, last year I wanted to kill every German person in the world, now I just want to kill every German soldier!"

"So what do I do now?" Archie said.

"You need to let me help you."

*

Wednesday 4ᵗʰ June 1941 – Evening – Barnet – North London

Archie and Rebecca drove south from the cottage and reached the northern outskirts of London, near Barnet. Archie had changed into his old Private's uniform, and Rebecca wore the clothes she'd left France in; she half wondered if this was why she'd insisted on keeping them.

To his teams, they were on an internal Top Secret mission, no one would ask any questions.

Archie had refused to eat all day, so Rebecca did too, the hunger and the clothes put her in the correct frame of mind, St. Nazaire, she could see why he did it now.

They'd scouted the old cottage already, one of a terrace of three set two hundred yards down a side road. One cottage was vacant, one only occupied at weekends.

Father Aloysious would be alone, he had no friends now and no longer associated with his former peers.

He'd been the Roman Catholic Chaplain to the Royal Holloway Children's Home. He was a strict disciplinarian and enjoyed meting out corporal punishment. He also had his favourites, those he treated well, who worshipped him, until he raped them, that was. Nipper would have been one of his targets. Another of his targets had been an altar boy, from a good family, with a father bold enough to punch him unconscious in front of his congregation during Sunday Mass.

Private sin, against orphans, received no punishment, but public retribution shamed his colleagues too and couldn't be tolerated. He was obliged to retire, albeit with a generous stipend. Archie had a more suitable punishment in mind.

While they all knew what he was and ostracised him, none of those peers had considered for one second that they might report his crimes. Perhaps he'd been to confession, said a couple of Hail Marys and that ensured his eternal salvation.

He was elderly, late seventies and lived on his own. Physically, the subduing and killing would be easy, the actual torture wouldn't. They'd already agreed they needed the man to talk.

The old fool opened the front door when they knocked. Archie just bundled him over onto his back, and he banged his head on the hard tiling floor, which subdued him neatly. They shut the door and dragged him into the living room. Archie tied his hands to a couple of the exposed dark wooden beams that supported the ceiling and roof of the small cottage. It was well furnished with an open, unlit fireplace, bookcases packed with books and a well-stocked antique drinks cabinet. His former employers were keeping him well in his retirement. Archie and Rebecca stood in front of him and waited briefly while he regained his senses.

"Hello, Father," Archie said, "I won't waste any time, I'm a busy man as you can imagine. I need you to recall a party you went to with a Mr Betteridge. It was years ago, but you should easily recall a young man who was abused by Mr Betteridge, yourself and five other men. I need their names if you'd be so very kind."

"I don't have the slightest idea what you're talking about," he replied, with more than a hint of arrogance and indignation.

Oh good, he's a cunt, that should help, Archie thought.

"I'm glad you're so blasé about this Father, you've just made my job much easier," Archie said as he took a hammer from his backpack.

Then, with one heavy and well-aimed blow, broke his right knee. He screamed in a high-pitched and pathetic wail.

"You can scream as much as you like Father," he said, "no-one can hear you, we tested the acoustics of the area earlier this week, we're not amateurs, you should know."

He then broke his other knee so the priest slumped where he was, held up only by the rope bindings that

Archie had tied around his wrists.

He screamed again.

"You should listen, Father, I told you that was a waste of time."

"We're wasting time," Rebecca said, "let me have him," then started to slice at the belt of his trousers with her own SOE knife. The belt sliced easily under the pressure of the strong, razor-sharp blade. Billy Perry could maintain a knife as well as a gun. She pulled his trousers down to his ruined knees and reached for his pathetic cock.

"Okay, Okay, let me talk, let me talk," he pleaded, crying.

He gave them the names, all of them, exactly as Betteridge had.

"Well done, very well done indeed. The trouble is, old chap, you've given us names we already know. Now we know what an honest man you are, we have a few more questions."

"I won't say more, I'll die first."

"No you won't, you'll die very slowly indeed," said Rebecca, who reached up and sliced off one of his fingers, so easily, it scared Archie a bit.

"Oh Sweet Jesus, stop, stop," he pleaded.

Rebecca tapped the end of his freshly exposed penis with the bloody knife blade.

"Let's talk about the Royal Holloway Children's Home then," she said.

Father Aloysious talked a lot.

Archie struggled to write it all down, and when he was done, he had what he wanted. Names, descriptions, and sins. Rebecca looked sick, physically ill, she was still holding up well, though.

"Okay, we need to finish him off now and go," Archie concluded.

"Okay," said Rebecca.

She reached up to his slumped head, grabbed him by the hair, raising his face and stretching his neck muscles to expose his jugular vein and severed it delicately. He died, gurgling and spluttering and not instantly, she withdrew the knife slowly and deliberately, hardly any of his blood went onto her gloves. She then calmly did the same to his dick, severing it and letting it drop to the floor.

Archie then took two huge nails from his pack, tent peg sized, hammering one through the palm of each hand and into the wooden beams.

"I want all of his former colleagues to know exactly why this happened. That's important, they need to know that this was not buried, not confessed and most definitely not forgiven."

They washed the blood from their gloves in the kitchen as best they could then checked each other for tell-tale stains and left.

*

Once they were back at the flat in Victoria, he let her have the first bath, she noticed he had two bath gowns now. While he was washing, she made a cup of tea and a snack for them. He ate it and drank the tea, he was Archie again. She asked if she could sit on his lap in the thinking chair, he said yes, of course, she did so, and they talked.

They had two names now who might know something about Nipper's sister, Father Aloysious didn't like little girls, only boys, but he knew who did.

Archie took Rebecca to bed, and they embraced all night, they each needed the comfort of the other, and the unshared, unfulfilled arousal was pleasant and calming.

The following day they were able to discuss their next move against the persons on their list, then placed it in a box to be opened later. Their other war could come first now.

*

Saturday 21ˢᵗ June 1941 – The Norwegian Coast – Florolandet

Two weeks later and nearly midnight on Saturday the 21ˢᵗ June 1941, two 70-foot Vosper Motor Torpedo boats approached the coast of Norway. They were near the island of Florolandet, much further south than the Lofoten Islands. Florolandet had a short runway on its south-west side and a small harbour about a mile further east. The facilities provided supplies for German U-boats in the North Atlantic and Arctic waters. If they could delay one U-boat for one hour and it missed one ship in one convoy that was a worthwhile risk. Decoded message intercepts had helped select this as a soft target.

These are hard lands and harder waters even in summer, Archie thought. No wonder the Vikings were so fearsome, only the fittest would survive here, the weak would find no forgiveness in these elements.

Archie, the Chosen Men, Rebecca and Billy, this time, had set off that morning from Muckleflugga Shore Station on the Island of Unst in the Shetlands. Smudger called it *Fucklemylugga*, which he described as a new sex act he'd just invented. Something to do with a female refusing to provide oral sex to a boyfriend then offering a very unsatisfactory alternative.

A powerful, fast tug towed them most of the way to Norway to conserve their fuel for the return journey.

The second boat would drop a small party near the landing strip which was fifty yards from the shore. Smudger and Begley would use the Hitmen to do damage to any aircraft and buildings. They'd used six more projectiles for practice, then Begley had made more of his own! Archie purchased some specialist machine tools for the Manor workshop which was now a passable small arms factory. Anything Archie couldn't buy, Billy could acquire by other means.

The first boat was to simultaneously torpedo whatever was in the small harbour, then they'd both return immediately. A quick hit and run plan, the second boat might not even need to land a party. If the sea was calm enough, they could use the four heavy machine guns and the Hitmen from the deck.

The boats were wooden, though, perfect for the speed they needed, poor for defence if attacked.

Each boat carried extra fuel instead of their usual depth charges, they would need to burn a lot more for a speedy getaway of about forty miles per hour. A return trip of about two hundred and fifty miles should take six to seven hours depending on wind and currents, a tug could collect them if they ran out of fuel.

This time, Archie had insisted that he was the officer in charge from beginning to end. That way he could make sure it all went better than Claymore, it also meant he was responsible for anything that went wrong.

Each boat had a Captain and Engineer on board, Archie's Chosen Men performed any other duties. He'd made himself an acting Major for this job, just to be sure his word was law.

"How did you get to be a Major so young?" the English Captain asked Archie.

"Dead men's shoes," he said.

The Royal Navy crewed the first boat, two Norwegian Naval men, who knew the waters well, crewed the second. Following a prearranged signal, the second boat veered left to take the shore party to the rocks near the landing strip, the sea was just too choppy for a decent shot at long range.

The first boat continued eastwards for another mile and positioned itself to face the harbour entrance. The harbour was so small and narrow that any torpedoes fired through the entrance were bound to hit something.

Archie and Rebecca stayed on board the first boat. As soon as they heard the explosions to their west, they would fire their torpedoes in two salvos. The target would be aflame and visible for the second salvo so they might then have a chance to aim better.

At the designated time, 0030, Archie and Rebecca heard two small explosions and saw flames shoot upwards to their west. That was their cue, and they fired their first two torpedoes into the harbour entrance and concentrated on what they might have hit.

"Looks like only a couple of trawlers in there, sir, bad luck," said the Navy Captain looking through his binoculars.

"Let's fire the other two anyway, I'm sure there's more

in there, we might as well give him a big mess to clear up, it's a long way to come for nothing," said Archie.

They fired the other salvo and immediately turned the boat around to go back west along the shoreline. As they left, a thundering explosion lit up the sky.

"Christ! That was ammunition, my torpedoes can't do that. You must have tremendous night vision," said the Captain.

I must have tremendous bloody luck, thought Archie. They'd hit a small supply vessel loaded with fuel and ammunition.

As they passed the second boat, the Captain saw that it was sitting low in the water, but not sinking.

"She's run aground, sir," came the shout.

"Get as close as you can, safely," the Captain called to the Engineer.

As they motored slowly closer to the other boat, they heard some exchange of gunfire between the boat and shore. Once closer they saw Billy and the two Norwegians using three of the machine guns, raking the shoreline to protect the two returning dinghies.

Archie saw Smudger climbing back on the second boat to start using the last machine gun; firing back to the shore. They positioned their boat so the second one shielded it, they couldn't risk a hit on the first boat now.

"Get them all on this one quickly. Come on quickly!" Archie shouted. "That's an order!"

He saw Smudger take a hit and go down, he was a big enough target, the shots ceased suddenly, and there was no more firing from the shore. He saw Billy move across the length of the boat towards Smudger.

The returning men were the centre of Archie's attention, counting them as they came aboard, three missing and only two of his still on that boat. He jumped across from one deck to the other, making sure he landed near Smudger and Billy.

"He's sorted now, sir, gimme a hand with him, he's a big un," Billy shouted.

It took Billy, Archie, and the Norwegian engineer to lift Smudger up, the Captain continued to fire intermittently at the shore, looking for any movement there and keeping German heads down.

Between them, they hauled him on the other boat to three pairs of waiting hands. Archie and Billy got on board easily, the Engineer was next and last came the Captain.

"Who's missing?" Archie asked.

"Moley, sir," one voice said.

"Does anybody know where he is?"

"In the water, sir."

"I think he took a bullet in the shoulder."

"He's a strong swimmer, sir."

"Does... anybody... know... where... he... is?" Archie stressed each word separately.

"No, sir," a few voices said reluctantly.

Archie crouched down, thought for perhaps ten seconds, listening intently as well as thinking, he heard only one more rifle shot firing from the shore towards the boat.

"Go now, Captain, fast as you can, please," he ordered.

The boat was overloaded now and still made a reasonable speed. Archie went round each man shaking hands with everyone before he sat down in a sheltered spot. Rebecca sat next to him, leaning on him, with his arm around her. They talked and stayed where they were, she offered him some chocolate, but he refused.

"You're not going to kill someone, are you?" Rebecca said.

"No, I'm sea sick, and I've told you I can't swim, I'm afraid I might puke. Could you sit a bit closer please?"

No one interrupted them except Lieutenant Thorson, the Norwegian Acting Captain, who approached them tentatively.

"May I speak Major?" he said.

"Of course, you may, anything. I know you risked your boat and more to get closer to my men, and I'm grateful for that."

"That is it, Major, my friend and I, we are a sailor without a boat and an engineer without the engine, and the Norwegian Navy is very small."

"Yes."

"And we, well… we have heard stories from your men, about you and your… Skjaldmaer, your Shieldmaiden."

"Yes," said Archie.

Rebecca giggled inappropriately.

"We wish to join you, I can sail anything, Baldr can fix any machine, we can kill Germans too, please, as many as possible."

Archie laughed out loud.

"Speak to me onshore and I'll give you a telephone number to call. My Shieldmaiden and I will be pleased to talk to you back at our base."

The Norwegian smiled and went to take his turn at the helm.

"What's a Shieldmaiden?" asked Rebecca.

"I haven't got the foggiest idea, it sounds great, though."

"I'll look it up when we get back," she said and went to sleep with her head on his shoulder. They stayed where they were until they reached Sumburgh harbour in the southernmost part of Shetland. The journey took too long, against the wind and tidal streams, they slowed down to conserve fuel, so it was ten o'clock before they reached the Shetlands.

They'd been out of radio contact for the whole journey.

"I say, you'll never guess what happened while you were away?" said the loud voice of an excited officer on the quayside as they disembarked.

"The Germans invaded Russia," said Rebecca, before walking calmly away.

"How does she do that?" Smudger said.

Archie just smiled.

He gave his contact details to the Norwegians. They had impressed him with their strength in everything he needed from them, quietly expressed, no bravado, just determination.

There was a landing strip near the harbour, where a waiting transport plane would take them back to RAF Akeman Street, a short drive from Bletchley. They could have gone by boat and truck, Archie had used Conner's voice to pull some strings.

In the aircraft, Hospital had a closer look at Smudger's shoulder wound, which was slight, he'd also banged and cut his head on the way down, so he'd bandaged it tightly.

"I'm all right," Smudger said, "I think I've twisted me ankle, though, it's fucking killing me."

"You big tart!" said Rebecca, leaving everyone in stitches.

Smudger was seemingly dumbstruck.

"Honestly, I have never heard such bad language in all my life," he said.

"Honestly?" said Rebecca.

"No, not really," conceded Smudger, laughing.

Archie glanced at Billy, who gave the slightest raising of one eyebrow and the briefest of nods before he closed his eyes and slept.

'Okay, that's one more lost, but one saved today.'

Moley was dead, Archie was sure of that. The Chosen Men accepted the loss, just as they accepted their survival. Smudger could still make a joke, and they could still laugh at it. Archie wanted to join in the laughter and didn't. He didn't mind the men laughing, so he stayed where he was and pretended to be asleep, one more step further away from his friends.

I had to leave Moley, I had to leave him, they know that don't they, don't they?

*

Wednesday 25th June 1941 – The Dress Shop – Holloway

It was the middle of summer before the shop purchase was final, and Rebecca was certain the flat above was suitably ready for Oona.

Oona had arranged for two young friends to work as sales assistants. It was easy to find two attractive and sensible young locals who were happy to have a better job than the garment factory, she knew they wouldn't let her down. The flat, one bedroom and a kitchen living room combination, was a palace to Oona, and she could still stay close to the people she called her mum and dad. The shop wouldn't make a fortune, and Rebecca told her not to worry.

Rebecca came to London for the reopening of the shop, she didn't want to, but Oona insisted. Rebecca had never felt more awkward in her life during opening hours, but that wasn't why Oona had insisted.

After the shop had closed, Oona bought fish and chips for her and Rebecca, and they shared some bottles of cold beer. Then they'd talked and talked, and talked some more while Oona plucked Rebecca's eyebrows properly for her. She painted her nails too; they were still short, and Oona explained it would help her stop biting them. You can still fire a gun with longer nails she said, not too long of course, medium would still work okay. They'd work on her hair next she thought; she knew you couldn't walk like a woman unless you looked and felt like one and that would take time.

"How do you know you can fire a gun with longer fingernails?" Rebecca said, slightly tipsy now.

"There's a man I used to call father who knew about guns, he showed me how, I don't call him father anymore," she hoped Rebecca might not remember that in the morning.

"You do know I'll never tell Archie what I'm doing for you?" Rebecca said.

"And I'll never tell a soul what I'm doing for you, Rebecca."

"If he asks we'll have to tell him of course until then it won't hurt him. Can we be best friends, Oona?"

"Oh no, we'll be sisters, Rebecca."

"I'd like that."

"So would I."

*

66

Friday 27th June 1941 – Bletchley Park

At 0930 in the morning, the two teams and others from Bletchley Park gathered for the planting of another rose bush. Conner wasn't there, and Alan played the *Flowers of the Forest* again, no *Molly Malone* this time. Siggy did the honours for Moley, they'd been mates for a while.

Moley was an only child, single and his parents were dead. Archie could do with a few more like that. Siggy was the eldest of five, and his parents were in their forties, I'd better not kill him then, thought Archie.

Rebecca linked her hand around Archie's elbow, and nobody stared. Archie didn't cry this time. He still had Rebecca's handkerchief in his pocket just in case, he'd kept it, he planned to always keep it.

Smudger was there too, in a huge wheelchair, his ankle was in a cast; Hospital told him not to put any weight on the ankle. Archie had known immediately that it was a bad break and would keep him out of front-line duties. That would be an awkward conversation later, the doctors hadn't told him that yet.

*

After the planting, Archie and Rebecca had talked together in the private room of Building Thirteen.

"Norway, I need to know if I did okay?" he asked.

"Yes, of course, you did."

"Was I as good as Conner though?"

"Archie, you were Conner, didn't you know? You were Conner with Aloysious as well, and I was you! That's partly why he left us alone, didn't you know?"

"How do you do that? How do you always know? Thank you. Do you want to come down to London with me?"

"No, no you need some time on your own. I'll be okay at the cottage alone, I'm a Shieldmaiden, remember."

Before he left, he spoke privately to Mary Murphy.

"Have you done something to Rebecca's hair?" he asked.

"No, she still won't let me near it," she replied, "and I haven't touched the eyebrows either; if you want to know, then why don't *you* ask her?"

"Why don't *you*?"

"I'm a woman Archie, go out there now, be a man and ask her if she's done something with her eyebrows."

"You're joking."

"Oh God, why are men so brave and talented at some things and bloody useless at others?"

"You don't think she's found a man, do you?"

"Don't be so stupid, she's already got one, you idiot."

"Who?" he said.

"Oh just go home," she said.

Chapter 6

Saturday 28th June 1941 - Finsbury Park

Archie collected Oona from the station as usual, just before 1000. They hadn't been able to see each other for two whole weeks. She gave him a small peck on the lips after she got in the car and asked if they could go shopping today. She suggested having a meal in a restaurant because she could spend the night with him and not leave until Sunday evening. They went shopping, and she bought him a hat, a medium brimmed straw-coloured Panama Trilby style one.

"You can wear it when I take you on a picnic," she said.

They ate at the Savoy, he insisted on paying; talked her through it and she bluffed well, she was flawlessly and elegantly dressed.

In the afternoon, he took her back to his flat, she sat on his lap in the thinking chair, they talked, laughed, hugged and caressed.

"I just want to luxuriate in your presence, we don't need to do anything other than exist," he told her.

They had a bath, drank a bottle of wine and enjoyed more talking and laughing. They went to bed, early and naked, they talked and breathed, each inhaling the intoxicating rapturous scent of the other and felt exhilarated and gloriously alive. They went to sleep, hugging and woke in the same position. Restraining their lust was a test which they passed.

"This is forever you know," he said.

"Yes I know," she replied, snuggling even closer to him and gripping him even tighter.

It was everything, everything that ever was and everything that ever would be. Stardust.

In the morning she woke him with a passionate kiss, pushing her tongue into his mouth. She was naked apart from the black silk stockings and suspender belt she'd bought to wear for him. She'd put fresh makeup and lipstick on for him and took his hand.

"Come with me I want to try something," she said, then took him into the bathroom. She made him stand on a towel while she kneeled in front of him, lathered his balls and groin with his shaving soap, and then shaved him carefully with his own razor. He found he was aroused beyond belief.

"Now, you freshen yourself up as quickly as you can, don't forget to brush your teeth and I'll be waiting for you on the bed, be quick or I might start without you!" she said then left him.

He was back in the bedroom in ten minutes, although his erection had faded, the sight of her on the bed waiting called him back to attention.

"I told you to be quick," she said, "ten minutes is not quick, now come here."

She sat on the edge of their bed and made him stand in front of her while she licked every inch of his now hairless groin. Archie couldn't believe how pleasurable, delicate and yet more intense the feeling was. She could pay attention to four or five different areas at the same time, using her lips, her fingers, her palms, her nails, her tongue, her teeth, her saliva, her throat and throat muscles. When she took him to the few seconds just before he could no longer hold back his orgasm, she grabbed his buttocks tightly. At the same time, she pushed her head forward and took his cock deep into her throat. Her nose touched his stomach, and her tongue touched his balls, all at the same time. Her beautiful piercing eyes never left his face for a single moment and held tears where the act had made her eyes water. He exploded down her throat.

"Fucking hell that was unbelievable," he gasped, his legs reduced to jelly.

"Tell me what you want me to do, you choose, anything," he said.

She stood up and kissed him deeply.

"Okay, but you have to promise you won't think I'm a dirty bitch."

"I already think-" he started to say before she put a finger on his lips.

"I want you to fuck me in the bum, I enjoy it when you touch and lick me there, and your finger feels good in there when you're tonguing me. I want to try it with you, I've made sure I'm nice and clean, and I've used some Vaseline so I'm ready for you."

Archie lowered her gently down onto the bed and pushed her legs apart and back until they were behind her elbows and her hands were holding her cheeks open for him.

He knelt down beside the bed and licked her everywhere, she was freshly shaven too, and he brought her close to orgasm three times with his tongue and fingers. Then, after he'd stretched her with one, two then three fingers, he slowly pushed his cock deeply into her anus while still playing with her moist pussy and clitoris. He thrust his cock slowly and then rhythmically into her, matching that rhythm with his thumb on her clitoris. She gasped with each thrust and her forehead and eyes creased with pleasure that was close to, yet not quite pain. He pinned her legs back now, releasing her hands from her cheeks and watched her biting her index finger.

"I'm coming, don't stop, that's it, that's it, fuck... "

When she'd caught her breath and calmed down, some five minutes later, he kissed her gently on the lips, the nose, the eyes, and the forehead. Then anywhere else he could reach while still leaving his cock inside her.

"Did you like that then?" he asked cheekily with a broad smile and a little well deserved smugness.

"God, yes, it was a whole different coming, I can't describe it properly, it was fucking brilliant Archie."

"Tell me what else you want Oona, anything."

"Well, right now I need a rest and a mug of tea, but I want that again later as well."

*

Monday 30th June 1941 - The Manor

Archie sat in the Manor garden, on a warm summer day

under a cloudless, deep blue sky, a day off, almost.

No one to kill or be killed, a day to breathe, to feel warmth, to feel safety, to not feel hunger or desire, a day to relax, a day to not do something.

A day to not think, to feel while awake, the ease that only a dreamless sleep gave you, a day a man like Archie would always seek, and never truly have.

A day for no guilt, no shame, no responsibility, a day as a child, the child he'd never been. Then the sudden, burning, excruciating and all-consuming need for Oona's presence almost broke him apart.

Nipper approached him, interrupting the silent longing.

"Archie, about Moley?"

"Yes, mate."

"No-one blames you. Not one of us wanted to leave him behind, but every one of us needed you to tell us we had to. We knew it, we just needed you to do it for us. We hate you for doin' it to him, we love you for doin' it for us. I can't explain it any better, boss."

"And?"

"And you said anytime I wanted to talk."

"And this is anytime isn't it."

"You know, I know you know, there are things I just bury, they're gone, nothing I can do now. I bury them things to survive, this new life helps, killing Jerry helps, I bury them along with my whole family, God help me, that's how I deal with it.

"Well, I found out that one of my old... acquaintances, shall we say, died suddenly and a bit horribly, sliced and served up a treat you might say."

"And how did that make you feel."

"Satisfied."

"My favourite feeling, Freddie, and you?"

"Mine too."

"Who was it by the way?"

"A priest, Father Aloysious."

"Never heard of him," said Archie.

"Thought you wouldn't have. Do you... need a hand

with anything?"

"No, there are some things a man does for others, some things he has to do on his own. I ask enough of you already. You'll know when I need you, trust me, you'll know."

"I trust you, boss."

*

Tuesday 1st July 1941 – The Manor

Archie spoke to the two Norwegians, Lieutenant Asgeir Thorson, and Sergeant Baldr Odenson, at the Manor. Rebecca sat next to him, and he'd asked Nipper to sit in as well. Archie asked about background and experience, they had all the qualities he needed. They'd been to school together in Stavanger, which they described as the easy part of Norway.

They could have been brothers or cousins, both six foot exactly, dark hair, handsome, intense dark brown eyes under thick eyebrows and flared nostrils. They both had large, strong hands, put an axe in them and you had a Viking Raider leaping off a longboat on the English coastline a few hundred years ago.

"You've changed your names since you left Norway, why was that?" Archie said.

"We wanted to make sure the Germans couldn't target our families back home if they found out we were with the British," said Asgeir, "my new name means Spear of God, Son of Thor."

"And Baldr was the God of beauty, innocence, joy and peace. He was also the second son of a God who made every object on earth swear never to hurt Baldr, which is useful, you can imagine. The only thing that refused to swear was mistletoe, so he was killed by an arrow made of mistletoe or something, it's not a reliable story. So I am Baldr, son of Odin."

"Do you believe in those Gods then?" Archie asked.

"No, of course not, it's all bollocks, that's a word Nipper taught us, they are good names for warriors, yes?"

"What do you think, Nipper?" asked Archie.

"Fine by me, boss. As for the mistletoe, you know me, if

73

I saw any I'd probably eat it."

"No, no it's poisonous," said Asgeir.

"You've never tasted my mum's cooking, mate, come to think of it neither did I much," said Nipper.

He laughed, and they laughed with him.

Rebecca asked one last question, "What's a good name for a Viking Shieldmaiden?"

The two Vikings looked at each for a second, then nodded, and said, "Rebecca, of course."

*

Saturday 5th July 1941 – Hevlyn Mansions

The next weekend, Archie collected Oona, but not quite as usual. She was quiet, seemed preoccupied, and he could sense doubt in her. He panicked, he wanted to be sick. If it was over, he didn't know what he'd do.

They drove silently to the flat and once inside she said.

"Archie, we need to talk, I need to tell you something. Can we sit in the chair?"

"Of course, we can," he said, welcoming her onto his lap and holding her delicately as if she were the finest crystal and might shatter if he touched her too firmly.

"Remember when you told me about the Germans bombing Dublin at the end of May, and asked how I felt?"

"Yes."

"I'm not from Dublin, like I told you, I'm from Belfast."

"I know that, you've softened your accent so you fit in better over here, it's still more Belfast Catholic than Dublin."

"Okay, smart arse, just let me talk, and you listen. My name is Oona Lainne, and I was born in Belfast, 20 years ago.

"My family were Republicans, my father and three brothers were all IRA men, well they were killers, and they killed who they were told to kill, or hurt who they were told to hurt.

"They didn't do anything else, nothing public, no meetings, no marches, no flags, *'sleeper soldiers'* they called themselves. Every Sunday we went to church and every

Sunday my father would walk back alone, he'd walk a different way to us. Maybe three, four times a year, he'd have a note and a package and then there'd be a killing. It might be a Tan, an army man, a tout, a copper or just an ordinary Proddy. Children would talk about killings like that at school and think it was great and funny. So I was secretly proud of him, I loved my father, I loved my family.

"We knew we had a cousin who'd been killed by the Brits, and I figured that's why we did it, had to do it, and it was right. I saw how he was training my brothers for the same, then I saw how he was training me too.

"My own father wanted me to kill who I was told to kill, he taught me how to use a gun, taught me how to shoot and other things too. He wanted me to lure young men to their deaths.

"But... well... that's not the worst of it, the worst thing is, I wanted to do it, I didn't know anything else, you do what you're told in that family, that's the way it was.

"So, I did it, I did it once, a soldier, no more than a boy, he'd done nothing wrong other than wearing the uniform. I tricked him into coming with me down an alleyway then my father and Donal, my eldest brother, did it. They did it, and I watched. They cut him up, savagely, like a pack of animals, before they finished him off and strung him up on a tree.

"When it was done, I couldn't see what that boy had done to deserve that. If he'd personally killed my cousin then maybe, but he'd done nothing.

"I started asking questions, and slowly, you realise that everyone seemed to have a cousin the Brits killed. Then I found out my cousin blew himself up with his own bomb, the stupid eejit. He killed two of his friends who were with him. No Brits ever got near him, the useless bastard, not exactly a heroic end for any of them.

"So I asked more questions and worked out some answers for myself. Sure, there were Brits and Proddies who didn't like me, they thought I didn't like them, so why *would* they like me!

"It was hard to understand, being so young, I was being made into something I didn't want to be, it was all I knew. I had to try and make plans to get away, not just from the family, the whole fucking place, and the whole religion shit as well.

"Then it came around quite soon, only two months later, another note and package.

"I knew my father too well, so I had to lie to him. I told him I was pregnant, he slapped me, he hit me hard, more than once. He gave me enough money to get to England and told me never to come back. I was sixteen."

"He hit you?"

"Yes."

"Do you want me to kill him?"

"No, no, if it came to it I'd do it myself, he taught me how, after all, he's dead to me now anyway, they all are. I'm ashamed that I once loved them.

"My life only started when I arrived in England, I'd found out about Mr and Mrs Cronin, I call them my parents now. Their only son, Michael, had been with my cousin when he blew himself up. They'd left Belfast to get away from all that shite, and they took me in. They still go to mass and that, but they don't make me do it. They're just decent hardworking people is all, like the Dempsey's.

"I'm lucky, I have a better job now, and I have you, I hope, it was so difficult at first. I didn't know who or what I was, I suppose. So I slept with men, a lot of men. I enjoyed it, and it was an escape, I know now, all that time, I was just looking for you. I went with Joe because I hoped he might make an honest woman of me. I told him I was a virgin, and he believed me so we never... it was a mistake, a lie, and I couldn't have gone through with it. You made me who I am now or, well, who I'm becoming now and I'm starting to like myself again.

"I love you, I love you so much, I have to tell you every bad thing about me, if you don't want me after telling you that, then I don't deserve you."

He held her tightly now, she wasn't crystal, she was

diamond-strong.

"We both have pasts, it's the present and future that matter. I love you now, and I'll love you forever, you could have killed the fucking king, and I'd still love you."

"Show me please," she said, and he took her to his bed and showed her as gently and as carefully and for as long as he could.

When they woke the next morning, he made them a mug of tea and asked if they could stay in bed so he could talk to her. He told her every evil deed he'd ever done; how and why. She didn't speak, just nestled closer and closer to him, gripping him more tightly with each short tale. He told her about his team and his friends, especially Conner and Rebecca, he had many words about Billy too.

"In times of war, the law falls silent," she said finally, "I heard my father say that, and you're fighting two wars, at least two. Archie, I knew you were a killer the first time I saw you, I know that look, but it's different on you, there's a purpose to it, a determination, a meaning. It's the difference between being a murderer and a killer, does that make sense? Oh, I just don't have the right words. I'll stay by your side and love you for as long as I live. If you ask me, I'll help you, I'll understand if you don't want me to. I'd like you to tell me what you do, I'll share it with you if you want or if you just need someone to talk to."

"I'll stop if you ask me to," he said. "We'll go away, South America, anywhere, Mars even."

"Don't be daft, I can't ask you to change what you are, I love what you are, do you love what I am?"

"Yes, every inch, every atom."

"What's an atom?"

"Well, it's a very small part of you."

"Which small part?"

"No, I don't mean that. It's a small part of another part, it's very small, I can't explain it properly. I'll ask, there's someone I can ask, she'll be able to explain it, Rebecca should know how."

"Rebecca sounds brainy," she said, more than a little

mischievously.

Archie was in deep trouble, big, deep trouble, the biggest trouble he would ever encounter in this lifetime. If he'd known that, it might have made him laugh, or scared him to death, or both.

*

Thursday 10th July 1941 – Evening – Putney – London

Archie and Rebecca had decided they needed to make simpler plans for the next encounter. Their next Top Secret training exercise, the second name on their list.

They needed corroboration of the information gained from the late Father Aloysious; to see what else their prey might disclose and then a quick bullet. It needs to look random, a knifing, a robbery, a disappearance, yes a disappearance would be fitting, he'd said. No clues, this time, no warning and no example to others.

The target, this time, was a senior civil servant, Arthur Treadpath, a bowler-hatted paper shifter in the Ministry of Works. He lived in Putney and walked to and from work every day, living on his own in a small flat. His wife had divorced him quietly, shortly after the closure of his previous place of employment, the Royal Holloway Children's Home. It hadn't damaged his career, though; clearly, he had friends in high places. Treadpath had a fondness for choking his partners during the act, he'd choked Simon Seabury with his cock.

Following him home from work and accosting him near the sheltered entrance to his basement flat was easy. Rebecca distracted him while Archie subdued him with Chloroform, he still hadn't found anything better, and they pushed him into the boot of their car.

The furnace building in the East End was still mainly intact, and they took him there for the questioning. They bound and gagged him, then laid him flat on his back and poured water into his mouth, choking him.

He gave them the names they expected in a few seconds, he named the same two as Aloysious had, for Nipper's sister. He also gave the name of the senior Police

Officer, who had protected him during the time of the closure of the Royal Holloway Home. He'd then made sure the son of that Police Officer was a rising star in the Ministry at a young age in a reserved occupation.

When the talking stopped, Archie pistol-whipped him with the butt of his Luger and without further ceremony, they took the bound man to the river in the boot of their car.

Archie parked near the spot Rebecca had selected, a long drop into the deep water, weighted as heavily as they'd made him, the body would never be seen again even at the lowest tide. Rebecca's research was always excellent.

"Shall we finish him off first or let him drown?" she said reaching for the silenced Luger.

"No, he deserves to choke," she answered herself, as she rolled the body off the pier and into the dark.

They walked calmly to the car, Archie was suddenly hungry, having Rebecca there had helped again.

"Alright, what's goin' on here then? Don't you move an inch, sonny boy!" said the voice of an elderly War Reserve Constable, complete with a Brodie helmet and a cocked Canadian Ross rifle pointed straight at Archie.

Archie began his mantra, but before he even got to number one, the Bobby fell dead with a silent bullet from Rebecca's Luger through his face. Archie checked for a pulse or breath and found neither. Rebecca didn't say a word, just sat back in the car and Archie joined her.

"Are you okay?" he said.

"Yes of course I am, it was him or you. He should have noticed me, I hate it now when people don't notice me."

He leaned over and kissed her on the forehead.

"Thank you," she said.

"Anytime, come on let's go, the police never stop looking for a police killer. We have some thinking to do."

Archie drove straight to the cottage.

When they got back they talked briefly, they'd done their thinking silently in the car.

"Do we have to lose the Luger now?" she asked, more worried by the loss of the Luger than the loss of the Bobby.

"No, I can replace the barrel just to be extra safe, I've had a couple of spares for a while, here, I'll show you, takes 5 minutes. You've no idea how many were brought back after the first war. We can melt the guilty barrel in Billy's furnace. It's a million to one they could trace anything to us.

"They'll assume he came on someone or something he shouldn't, they'll look for a local villain, an easy target, that's pretty much all they're good for. They might look for some German spy when they see it's a German bullet, they'll get nowhere, trust me.

"We just need to be more careful next time that's all."

*

Two days later, on Saturday the 12th of July 1941, the British Government and the Russians signed the Anglo-Soviet Agreement to confirm their alliance against Germany.

The BBC proudly announced the signing, as did the newspapers. Nowhere was there a hint of doubt or guilt. They didn't refer to it as a pact with the Devil to fight the Devil, Archie and Rebecca knew exactly what it was, though. They were miles apart that day, yet they felt closer together. They felt just that little bit better about the small death of one small policeman, in one small part of a big Universe.

Who is fit to judge us?

Chapter 7

Tuesday 15th July 1941 - Finsbury Park

Oona closed the shop at half-past five as usual and went upstairs to prepare tea for her and Rebecca when she arrived. She'd never felt better in her life, she loved the shop and choosing pretty dresses that she'd like to wear as a young woman was an easy task. Business was good and making a small profit for Rebecca. That pleased her, she wasn't keen on relying on others, she'd done that as a child, and it hadn't turned out well. She needed to be her own person, even if all she planned was to give that self-reliance to Archie forever. No, she'd give some to Rebecca as well.

Oona remained a little jealous of Rebecca, who got to share parts of Archie that she didn't. She needed Rebecca to keep him safe from harm because she couldn't do that. Rebecca needed Oona to make him happy in ways she couldn't. She was going to teach Rebecca how to make a man happy in that way, though. Right, she thought, I see it now. Rebecca can teach me how to keep him safe, Oona had helped with a killing once and hadn't liked it, she can show me how to kill properly, to help protect Archie, like she does.

She might talk that through with Rebecca. No that wouldn't be fair, she was going to do her eyebrows and hair again tonight, and tomorrow I'll try to show her how to walk again. Rebecca still walked like a man, and she wasn't sure how to stop that.

The back doorbell rang, she was bang on time, Rebecca was always on time.

She went down the narrow stairwell, leading to the door of her flat and opened it with a broad smile.

Two gloved hands pushed her backwards violently, onto the small carpeted stairway she'd just come down, banging her head and knocking her senseless; not unconscious, just dazed.

When she came to fully, she was tied to a kitchen chair with a gag in her mouth. Her oldest brother, Donal, sat facing her. He was smartly dressed in a British Private's uniform, with a pongo's haircut, the kind they laughed at as children. What was going on? Donal was much bigger than she remembered, thicker set and stronger, even if she managed to get loose, he'd be too strong for her and his gaze was pure bloody murder.

"Hello there, long lost sister, you've done well for yourself. You've done well for a whore, who did you fuck to get this job?" he said moving the gag down from her mouth.

"I didn't fuck… " he slapped her hard, he was asking questions but had no interest in the answers.

"Shut up, you shaggin tout bitch, I've seen you with that British Officer in his swanky car, the rich cunt," he laughed at her.

"I've written a nice little letter home to father about that. He'll come over himself and do him proper, naked and tarred with a bullet in his napper and his balls cut off. It's lucky for you I'm here on another job, no contact till it's done, or he'd be over here already."

"Donal, you don't understand, it's…"

He slapped her face quiet again.

"Don't talk to me in your poncey English voice. It took me five minutes to find you, you stupid dumb bitch. A few questions in a boozer that's all. You, bitch, are talking to the man here, not some bog born nobody. We've got friends now, friends with money and guns. They'll beat the Brits and the Russians soon enough, then we'll be the people, not those Shankhill Shits and their Bastard Billy Boys. Window cleaner wanted, no Proddies allowed, we'll see how they like that."

He pulled out a Webley pistol from his tunic.

"This Saturday, Churchill at the Savoy for lunch with his cabinet, just one shade with him, the fat stupid old fool. Oh, I might not get away alright, if I don't I'll still be a fucking legend, my song will be sung for five hundred years. I'll be a martyr, and they'll read my name out in Church. I'll give him that bloody V sign."

'Oh sweet Jesus, he's bloody mental, he means it, what have we become?'

"And if I live, I'll be a fucking prince and father'll be a king. Jerry'll see us right, we've got more money than we could ever spend," he said showing her a wad of notes.

"Yes, look at that ya scanger, have you got any scran here, I'm famished."

The doorbell rang, *'Christ it's Rebecca,'* Oona knew it.

"Who's that?"

"A friend, she'll go away if I don't answer it."

"Is that right? Let's wait and see?"

The doorbell rang again, and he gagged Oona.

"If you even try to shout a warning, I'll kill her and you, understand."

She nodded, certain now, he was going to kill her anyway.

*

Rebecca had walked slowly towards Oona's flat from her hotel and had taken extra time to get ready. She was wearing a skirt and blouse, the blouse was uncomfortably tight, and the three buttons that Oona had told her to keep undone were showing a little cleavage. The skirt was tight too and the heels ridiculously high.

The thing was that dressed this way, you couldn't help but walk like Oona, you couldn't help your bottom moving from side to side in the way Oona's did. She felt something she'd never felt before, she felt desirable. It was a warm day and men were noticing her, one even whistled, she gave him such a sour look, he'd hurried away. She'd plucked her own eyebrows today and styled her own hair, just a middle parting and hanging loose, she'd curled it too, starting about halfway down, reaching shoulder-length. She'd also put mascara on and a dark red lipstick. She wasn't sure about the look and thought she might have overdone it, Oona would know. She'd tried doing this for herself, to impress Oona, she hoped.

*

Donal Lainne went carefully down the stairway and opened the door with his best smile.

"Hello there, I'm Donal, Oona's brother, just visiting, come ahead," he said calling her inside with an open hand.

Rebecca knew instantly something was wrong, but went inside and up the stairs anyway, she went slowly, like a woman.

Donal watched her lustily as she did so, oh yes, he was going to enjoy this!

When Rebecca reached the top of the stairs, she could see Oona tied to the chair in the kitchen area and felt the barrel of Donal's pistol in her back.

"Sit there and shut up," he said, pointing to the second chair in the kitchen.

"Who's this then Oona?" he asked and removed the gag, he was cocky now, almost thinking with his cock.

"Just a friend, she works in the shop sometimes. She's nobody, just let her go."

Rebecca sat in the chair and crossed her legs in the tight skirt, pushed her breasts out and did her best to look terrified.

"Oh no... she doesn't look like nobody to me," he said standing and looming large over them.

"She looks like another English whore to me, I think I'll fuck her in front of you then take you up the Swiss while she watches," then spat in Oona's face.

Rebecca leapt up and smashed his left kneecap with her right stiletto, causing him to fall towards her. As he slipped over and down, she grabbed his head in a firm armlock and twisted it back against the direction of the fall. His own momentum combined with all the malicious force, she was saving for Gottlieb and Gerolf, snapped his neck, killing him instantly. His body slumped at her feet, then, she spat in his face and stamped on his groin with all the force she could muster.

"No-one, fucking no-one, hurts my friends!" She spat on him again and kicked him even harder in his useless dead balls.

She untied Oona gently and hugged her, saying, "it's all right now, everything's all right now," repeatedly until she realised it was her who was crying, and Oona who was hugging her. Donal had picked on possibly the worst target in Europe to threaten with sexual assault.

They sat down, embraced and made each other calm.

"Tell me what happened Oona, then we'll plan what to do about it," she said.

*

Three days later in West Belfast, wearing some plain and old clothes, the two friends sat impatiently in a car, stolen near the Shankhill Road by Oona. Her father had taught her how to steal a car; Rebecca had that training too, but she'd let Oona do it, this task was Oona's burden.

Oona watched from a safe distance in the darkness, as her father and two remaining brothers left their local public house, 'The Merry Ploughboy', after their customary Friday night skinful. She knew the route they would take and precisely when they'd shout a noisy goodbye to the O'Conner's and shamble the final fifty yards to their terraced house. As usual, after several pints and less than several visits to the Gents, at least one would stop for a piss. Then, as usual, the others would stop and join in.

"Now," whispered Oona, and Rebecca took the car gradually and quietly towards the three men, all leaning against a wall, one hand on the wall, the other on their dicks.

They did turn to their left to look over their shoulders, they did hear and see the car approach, they didn't see the two women it contained. They did have time to see the familiar muzzle and handgrip of a Thompson Sub-Machine Gun, Rebecca Rochford's. It was a non-service 1928 model, expertly maintained now by Billy Perry and fitted with a 100 round drum magazine. Firing at 600 rounds a minute, it took ten long seconds for Oona to empty the magazine into the three men. The gun was heavy, but the light recoil was manageable for Oona. At short range all three men were dead in three seconds, she wanted to make certain, though. The empty cartridge casings were still rattling around the inside of the car, and the smoke from the muzzle made them cough, as Rebecca drove off, expertly.

"How did you like the rattle of that Thompson Gun then?" Oona whispered to her dead father and brothers.

They abandoned the stolen car on waste ground a few miles away. Oona used a rag and lighter to explode the petrol tank, they didn't need to, but that's what the Ulstermen would have done.

They crossed a set of playing fields and collected their own car in what Oona said was a safer part of the city. They stowed the gun and the grenades they hadn't needed in the car boot.

Rebecca's warrant and identity card had ensured an untroubled journey to Belfast, and there would be none on the return trip to Liverpool. Gubbins had set up return transport for them from Belfast, and a small ferry that could hoist their car onto its deck was waiting. They'd finished on time and as planned. Archie would have been proud, they had no plans to tell him, though.

*

Gubbins had been grateful to Rebecca for Donal's body. He'd already given extra security to Churchill following a tip-off, from one of his old contacts in Ireland, that a spectacular was about to take place. To catch the would-be assassin beforehand was nothing short of a miracle. Gubbins had served as an Intelligence Officer in Ireland in the 20s and personally collected the body from Oona's flat, late that Tuesday night. The uniform, false papers, and gun might give them clues to their origin and where he was staying in London. He listened to their plan and had personally approved it.

"Can you do that?" Rebecca asked.

"I just have, there's a treasonous plot to kill the British Prime Minister in wartime, it needs to be stopped, not a debate in the House. You'll get nothing in writing, and you'll have to do it all yourselves, but I swear on my sons' lives that I will get you out of any trouble you cause. In extremis, I have *'force majeure'* and a letter from Winston I can use. I haven't got anyone who can do it better or quicker, anyway. With luck, we shall never talk of this again."

*

"Are you okay, Oona?" Rebecca asked once the ferry had started the journey to England.

"Yes, they were dead already, they just didn't know it. I'm glad I didn't have to kill my mother, but I'd have done it if she'd been there too. It was them or me, or worse, Archie and you. It's done now."

"Put it into a box."

"You'll have to teach me how to do that."

"You still have to teach me how to walk."

"The way you acted for Donal before you took him, you've passed lesson one, how to rope a dope."

"I need to rope more than a dope."

"You will, don't worry."

*

Oona called Archie earlier to say she couldn't see him until Sunday this weekend. She needed to do something for Mr and Mrs Cronin, she'd said, and she wasn't lying, he could tell. His dependence on Oona made him feel weak, and when Rebecca had also taken some time away for family business, he was bereft.

He decided to do a good turn and take Mary Murphy out for tea after work on Friday. It went okay, and she'd stopped retching, which was certainly advantageous while eating. Pregnant women and babies were, well, he didn't know what they were, other than awkward and not one of the things he was any use at. He'd have to ask Conner when he got back, he missed him too. He'd done something nice, though, and it felt nice, even if he was just pretending.

*

On Saturday morning, he arranged to go for a run with Alan. After reassuring him that Conner was fine and in no danger, but would be away for a bit, they went for about five miles with Alan slowing his pace to let Archie keep up. Archie couldn't manage talking and keeping up with Alan, so when they finished they sat on the bench near the rose bushes outside his building and drank a mug of tea each.

"We're doing what we can to help the Russians," Alan said, "you'll find that out soon enough anyway, you'll get copies of everything as usual."

"I'm minded to recommend we just let them fight the Germans to the last man on each side. What do you think?"

"Well, there's an irresistible logic to it, but you won't do it."

"Why won't I?"

"Because you won't get away with it, you're a man who makes a delicate calculation for every action he takes."

"I thought that was you, Alan, the mathematician."

"Well, yes and no, I do find myself admitting things I should keep quiet about, it'll get me into trouble one day."

"We all find convention to be restrictive. In my case, the war allows me... no, actively encourages me to break some of the rules I don't agree with. For me that's the real liberation, that doesn't mean I want the war to last forever. Will there be a place for me when this war is over? I don't think so; will I have to find another war, when everyone else wants peace, I just don't know."

"What's your plan, Conner tells me you always have a plan."

"My plan is to survive."

"For how long?"

"Forever."

"Forever!"

"I never said it was a good plan."

Alan laughed, he looked different when he laughed, less intense, less serious, and more handsome.

"Well, I must be off now, I have a special young lady to see in London."

Alan looked at him squinting his eyes slightly.

"It's love isn't it?" he said.

"Oh, you're sharp Alan, yes it is, very much so, I'm

afraid. Lucky to find it where I least expected to. However, if you tell anyone, I'll have to kill you. I can't have my reputation as a licentious rake tarnished in such a manner."

Alan seemed lost in thought.

"You'll find it again Alan. One day, suddenly, out of the blue, you'll wake up, and it'll be there when you least expect it," he said.

"I hope so."

*

That conversation troubled Archie as he drove down to London that afternoon. Alan had a melancholy air about him, he was already on his list of people worth dying for, and it was still a short list. Alan wasn't happy, and he deserved to be. Somehow he knew that when the men in suits didn't need him anymore, they'd throw him away, they'd try and throw Archie away as well.

'We'll see about that.'

*

Around half past seven, at the flat, he got a phone call from Oona. She was back, she was fine, just tired and could he come and get her on Sunday morning. She was lying, he knew she was lying, someone or something had hurt her. He needed to go there right now and help her, then kill whoever had hurt her. He had to sit in the chair and think, he had to calm the rage within him, no one hurts Oona, no one! He had to make a superhuman effort to stay in the chair, she was a strong person, and if he loved her, he had to leave her alone when she asked. If he loved her, he had to stay in that chair and not interfere. He managed to do it, the next person he killed was in for a hard time when it came, though.

*

Oona had a bath in lukewarm water, she still couldn't eat, feeling light-headed and drank a cup of tea which didn't help. She passionately needed Archie there right now, that second, but she couldn't share this with him, for his sake. Jesus, he'd go to Belfast and kill half the city, God help any IRA man who ever lived in the North. He hated draft dodgers anyway, if he knew what they were doing in their spare time, he'd declare war on the whole cowardly Republic too. To hide while another man did your fighting for you was anathema to him. He'd curse them all. She had to do some of her fighting for herself, she'd tell him one day, he'd understand, be proud of her and she wanted that. Yes, I see it now, be yourself for him tomorrow, that's what he needs, be patient for him.

*

Rebecca had dropped Oona in Holloway and driven straight to the cottage, it was late evening when she got there, and she'd had a couple of wake-up pills to manage the journey. She phoned Gubbins to confirm they'd got back safely. He confirmed his men had found where Donal was staying. His hiding place was a gold mine of information. He'd kept the names and addresses of all his contacts, neatly written down. The money he had was all counterfeit, poor quality too, plainly snide. The Nazis had paid Judas with thirty pieces of dross. They also found the letter he'd written to his father, stamped and unposted as yet. He thanked her again.

The wake ups had worked well for the journey. However, as she lay in bed, staring at the ceiling, exhausted and unable to sleep, she cried. She'd cried a few times now, for Tarrian mainly, this was worse, she was crying alone. She intensely needed Archie to be there, just to hug or sit on his lap in the chair. She needed to talk more with Oona, to put things in boxes or learn how to walk. She'd had to leave Oona for Archie tonight, Oona said she'd see him on Sunday, Rebecca knew they needed each other tonight and was sure that's what they'd do.

She'd never felt more alone in her life, even when she'd slept on a damp island in marshland in occupied France, with Germans hunting her, she'd felt better than this. She didn't have a box big enough for the emptiness she felt.

*

Sunday 20th July 1941 – Early morning – Hevlyn Mansions

Archie was surprised to hear a knock on his door at seven am. He was up and brushing his teeth, he rinsed his mouth immediately and answered the door anyway. It was Oona, perfectly happy, perfectly dressed, perfectly made up and perfectly there.

"Sorry, I couldn't wait," she said, "you haven't got any other women in there with you?"

"No, of course not," he said.

"Because I'm going to fuck you, right, now."

She shut the door behind her and pushed him onto the hard wooden floor of the hallway, undoing his robe. She kissed him savagely and sucked his erection briefly just to make sure it was hard enough, she lifted her dress to show she had no knickers on and straddled him.

"Now you see," she said as she rocked back and forth and up and down. "If I do this, to an ordinary cock, it slips out just here," she stopped briefly then started again. "But with you," she paused, "it just keeps going and then back and then forward and then it keeps going and going and... God, that's just right, yes," she collapsed on top of him. "Until it makes me come all over you," she panted, out of breath for a full minute, her pussy still gripping and loosening then gripping his cock.

"I love you by the way," she said.

"I love you too, but I think you've fucked a splinter into my arse," he said.

"Let me see if I can find it for you," she said moving down his body with kisses, inch by inch.

*

Early that same morning Dolf Von Rundstedt woke early, feeling the warmth of Claudine next to him. They'd had the perfect evening, a meal, drinks then some energetic lovemaking. She would do anything he asked of her sexually, and he took full advantage of that last night, insisting that she be ready for anal penetration. She even pretended to enjoy it.

He moved over, towards and on top of her, deciding he wanted to have her one last time before his transfer to Paris. She was moist, she always was, and he entered her easily at the first attempt. He fucked her slowly at first, then faster and roughly, pinning her forcefully to the bed, she'd grown accustomed to that, when he put his hands around her throat, she said no. Only, she couldn't say it, she could only whisper it in a croaky and failing voice as he choked the life out of her. He continued to thrust, even after she stopped moving and came as his hands still gripped her dead throat.

He left the bed and began to wash and shave for the day ahead. He didn't know when he'd first suspected she was a spy. Perhaps during sex when she should have objected and didn't, denied something hurt when he'd intended it to.

Anyway, he had his promotion now, couldn't take her with him and couldn't leave her behind to spy on his successor. He'd already arranged for the discovery of her body in an alley a few days later, her head crudely shaved and a swastika cut into her face. Just another French whore who had lost her protector and paid the price. Her death had been short and easy for her, handing her to the Gestapo would have been infinitely worse, and he couldn't let those bastards know what a fool he'd been.

Paris would be better, and he'd find another French whore there, maybe more than one. Yes two, he thought, at least two.

Chapter 8

Tuesday 22nd July 1941 - Bletchley Park

Archie didn't go back to Bletchley until Tuesday; he'd had to spend two full days with Oona. They couldn't get enough of each other, in or out of bed, or on the floor.

He arrived at midday and went straight into Building Thirteen. Rebecca jumped up from her chair and gave him the biggest hug he'd ever had from anyone, pressing her head into his chest. Archie shrugged his shoulders to the wide-eyed audience staring at them and returned the hug tightly.

When she finally let him go, he asked, "What was that for then?"

"I missed you that's all."

She was up to something, he knew, there was no point asking, he'd find out when she wanted him to.

"Conner's due back tomorrow," she said, "let's celebrate."

*

When Conner returned on Wednesday, everyone was delighted to see him and morale, already high, got even better.

I stood in okay, but he's the real leader, Archie thought, happy to take the second seat again.

Archie had managed to speak to Smudger before Conner returned, that was his to do, his responsibility. It was a difficult conversation, a man of his size and weight with a weak ankle was a liability. He'd walk okay and manage a gentle run on occasion, but on an operation, running, jumping and twisting he was no use at all. He'd still be useful in training, weapons maintenance, and quartermaster duties, Archie had plenty of need for him.

"But you let Miss Rochford go on ops," Smudger said.

"How much did she weigh when you carried her Smudger?"

"About an ounce," he laughed.

"Do you weigh more or less than an ounce?"

"I'll shut up now then, Archie."

"Please."

*

Friday 25th July 1941 – The Manor

On an all too rare, boiling hot day, Archie arranged an impromptu briefing meeting at the Manor. The meeting consisted of eating, drinking and starting the weekend early, occasionally, the war could wait. Young people were being young and having fun, with Billy as quartermaster and master of ceremonies. There was a toast to absent friends, although there were no tears this time. Alan and a few others from his building came, Conner had a long and animated conversation with him, which ended with a firm handshake and a smile.

The men were unsure what to make of Alan's rumoured sexuality, but when Archie and Conner had embraced him warmly while shaking his hand, that was enough for them. The war was changing staid Victorian attitudes to sex, attitudes towards sexuality should change alongside that; England was a free country, whatever that meant.

Archie stayed sober all night and left at 2200 to drive down to London, he just had to see Oona, it had been three nights without her, four counting the one to come. Conner stayed at Bletchley to catch up on intelligence gathered in his absence.

*

Monday 28th July 1941 – Bletchley Park

Archie, Rebecca, and Conner met again early on Monday 28th July, to discuss what their next moves should be. Conner told them what he knew about the Manhattan Project, the American atomic research programme, he was still confident the Americans would join the war and have the atomic bomb before the Germans ever would. They all still needed some action for the team.

Archie raised the subject of the planned raid on St. Nazaire.

"The thing is, on the Florolandet raid, I consciously gave

Rebecca and me the safer jobs, and I need to tell you that. I think, as my life gets better I'm less willing to take risks."

"Oh yeah, like you leaping onto a boat that's under enemy fire to rescue Smudger isn't risky, you are not taking fewer risks, you're the bravest man I've ever heard of!" Rebecca said.

"Bollocks! And besides you don't hear a lot about the bravest of men cos they're all fucking dead."

Oh for heaven's sake, I leave them alone for five minutes, and they've fallen in love, Conner thought, they don't even know it, and I might kill them before they do. What are you asking me to do, Alex?

"Calm down children," he said then explained, "even at the sharp end, war is ninety-nine percent boredom sprinkled with one percent imminent danger or death, danger if you're lucky. For now, we wait, we watch and wait and plan."

Archie still pressed Conner.

"St. Nazaire, it's a half decent plan, it has to be done when the time's right, but it's a suicide mission. Or if you're lucky, a Stalag for years. I'm not going, and I'm not letting you go. You are not going back there."

"It's not up to you," she said.

"It's not up to either of you. I've spoken to Gubbins, and it's an SOE Commando Op only, neither of you is going, maybe some of the men in reserve, he's already decided, and that's final."

Gubbins hadn't decided that, although he would when Conner asked him to, Archie and Rebecca were too important to risk.

"Okay then," they said.

"I love the two Vikings by the way," he said changing the subject sharply.

*

Archie and Rebecca had already decided they would tell Conner about their private war. They were certain he wouldn't stop them doing it, but they were wary of his disapproval. In fact, they sought his approval like two children would of a father or a big brother.

Conner listened carefully, and when they'd finished, he spoke.

"There's more than one war in this world, there's always a war somewhere, always has been, I suppose.

"Have you broken the law? Yes. Have you done wrong? No.

"We're fighting a world war against two evil empires with the help of a third one, who on this earth can judge us if we choose to tackle other evils that we find. No-one, no-one can judge us, other than ourselves.

"By the way, did I ever tell you about my part in the sad demise of those unfortunate German Navy chaps from the Krebs?"

*

Late summer – 1941

The Operational Team became so frustrated at the lack of action during the late summer of 1941 that Conner loaned them to Special Operations Executive from the 20th August to 3rd September. Operation Gauntlet, a joint Canadian, Norwegian and British Commando raid on Spitzbergen in Norway. Compared to previous missions, it was a relatively safe adventure. It ended without a bullet being fired in anger, at least it accustomed the men to working alongside other units and a landing of troops by sea. A real-life training exercise where Lieutenant Asgeir Thorson led the men, as he would do many times from now on. Conner had to get used to taking less personal risks, Archie and Rebecca needed to do the same. The men came back on the first evacuating ship.

It was frustrating, like lively children not allowed to play outside in the sunshine.

The men wanted to live, survive and endure, but without risk, there was guilt inside them that they just couldn't reconcile with their real purpose, which was to kill, or be killed.

The war and the righteous nature of their calling to it were defining their youth.

In war, they were somebody, they were important, and there was a certainty to it.

In war, many individuals chose to engage as little as possible, a few chose to engage as much as possible. Each one of the Chosen Men was one of those few.

Archie could remember that feeling and sometimes yearned for its simplicity. It had been anything but simple at the time, his calling now was to give orders not take them, and he was gradually getting used to it.

*

By the end of August 1941, watching, waiting and planning proved too much for Archie and Rebecca, and they made a move against the next target on their list.

They'd studied the Metropolitan Police Commander Clement Sinclair closely enough to know how dangerous and influential he was. He was in charge of Islington Division, former Special Branch and a veteran of World War One. He had friends, influential friends, and was an apologist for the abuse of children, provided they were common and therefore worthless.

They'd planned the job for nearly two months, it needed perfect timing and execution. They couldn't give a man like Sinclair time to plan, they needed him to rush and be hasty.

*

They went to the offices of the late Mr Treadpath in the Ministry of Works and Buildings. They gave no advance notice of their arrival, but a *Major* and *Captain* from a fictitious section of Military Intelligence entered with predictable ease. His secretary showed them straight into the office of Mr Stuart Sinclair. He was the son of Commander Sinclair and the interim successor to Treadpath.

Mr Sinclair was, of course, delighted to see them, the disappearance of Mr Treadpath was a great mystery, one from which he'd personally benefitted. He couldn't understand why Military Intelligence had any interest, although the police investigation had found nothing so far.

97

People had just disappeared during the Blitz and even the reduced bombing after Barbarossa still resulted in similar instances.

Archie spoke first.

"We are investigating a possible attempt to blackmail Mr Treadpath before his untimely disappearance. Would you have any idea at all what might have been the subject of such an attempt?"

"Oh Goodness, no, I only ever had a working relationship with Mr Treadpath, I never met him before I started work at the Ministry and we never socialised," the younger Sinclair replied.

"Our enquiries have revealed some allegations of poor conduct in a previous capacity in Holloway at a Children's Home," Rebecca added.

"Oh God, really, you can't be serious, some people will make up anything, any story, you know what I mean."

"Oh yes Mr Sinclair, I know exactly what you mean," Archie broke in. "It's a complicated investigation, just when we think we might make some progress we get to a dead end, I fear we may have come to another. Can you think of any member of staff who was close to Mr Treadpath?"

"Oh no, he was a private person. I'm sorry I can't help you there either."

"Thank you for your time, Mr Sinclair," said Archie then shook his hand, it was cold, sweaty and limp, and they left.

"What a disgusting little turd that was. I'd wash my hands if I were you," Rebecca said. Archie did, he wanted to kill Sinclair just for the dismissive look he'd given Rebecca when she'd asked him a question.

Once outside the office building, they walked to the local telephone exchange, where they met Billy Perry.

"It's like you expected, Archie, he phoned his dad, they both know the fucking lot, that tape recording machine thing of Rebecca's worked a treat, and there's more too. We'll talk it through when we see what Smudger gets from

Islington. I fucking hate bent coppers, give me a decent thief anytime."

Billy didn't like coppers on principle, and he hated bent coppers even more. By bent copper, he didn't mean someone who took a couple of quid to look the other way. He meant someone who fitted you up for something you hadn't done, or who gave someone a hiding they hadn't asked for.

The second part of the plan needed to happen quickly.

Archie and Rebecca had carefully approached Billy before they involved him in their plans.

"I wondered when you'd ask, Smudger'll help too, he's got three of his own," Billy had replied with the casual tone of a man accepting a pint of beer from a friend.

"I know some people who'll help if there's a copper involved, they'll want coin, and we won't tell them too much, they'll stand, and they won't run."

*

The Sinclairs drove confidently to the White Horse Public House in Barking later, after dark that same day, as instructed by Archie that afternoon. They parked their car near the pub, and as soon as they did, a local street girl handed them a note telling them to go directly to the Old Rose Public House in Wapping.

The plain-clothes officers, who the father and son knew were following them in an unmarked truck and cars, now no longer knew the final destination for certain. The officers still followed their commander's car, stealthily and at a reasonable distance. The Sinclairs were reassured by the thin light from the blackout slit headlamps of the car behind them as they drove to their new destination. When they arrived at the Old Rose, those following lights were still there.

They entered the pub and two large men frisked them thoroughly and none too gently, a couple of distant relatives of the Frasers. They were then immediately directed to a back room where they saw Archie and Rebecca sitting at a table.

Archie didn't say much, and when he did talk he used a common accent, Rebecca didn't say anything, she just fingered the silenced Luger she held in her lap below the table.

Archie played them a copy of the tape. He wanted the names of anyone involved and would exchange that information and their resignations for his continued silence. Archie particularly wanted the names of those who liked little girls.

Archie knew they'd agreed too readily to everything he asked of them. The Sinclairs knew they had friends nearby, violent and well-armed friends, no doubt. Archie didn't care what they thought they knew. He checked the names, asked a few more questions and said they could go, it had taken about thirty minutes.

Billy came in the back door of the pub and joined them.

"There's three cars and a truck all manned by Special Branch, got stuck in traffic and accidents, caused by some broken glass between here and Barking," he said.

"They're pulling apart the White Horse now," Billy continued, "that'll cost you a bob or two to fix, but that's no problem. They were coming mob handed an' all, pistols, Stens, grenades, two Lewis Guns and dynamite in the lorry. You can't fuckin' trust anyone can you?"

"Do we need to hurry, Billy?"

"Nah, Smudger followed the Sinclairs all the way from Barking, he's sure the other mob all got lost on the way here."

"Thank you, Billy."

"Anytime, Archie. No, I don't mean that, I'm enjoying this a bit too much for me own good. I'm not as young as I used to be you know."

"Who is?"

"Ain't that the truth."

"Do we need to worry about Special Branch at all tonight?" Rebecca asked.

"Nah, that bunch of cunts couldn't find their own dicks in a gent's toilet."

"See if you can get me some Special Branch names anyway," asked Archie.

"No problem," Billy said, folding back the switchblade knife he held in his right hand, but not before wiping a smear of brake fluid from it.

*

The two pieces of excrement, masquerading as pillars of the community, left the vicinity of the Old Rose at high speed. They fully expected the pub to be destroyed during a shooting match between armed Special Branch Officers and Fifth Columnists.

They didn't expect to burst a tyre on broken glass on the Highway road into Central London. They didn't expect the brakes on their car to fail so badly, as they swerved and smashed into a high brick wall on their left. The impact injured both men, not seriously, though, and they saw the cars in front and behind stop to help.

They certainly didn't expect their Good Samaritans to cosh them viciously and repeatedly. Their Samaritans did provide them with several shots of the father's favourite Scotch whisky, leaving behind the bottle with two sets of fingerprints on it. They even allowed the passenger one last cigarette, sadly it set light to the pool of petrol that had formed around the crashed car.

Billy hadn't wanted to use the Frasers again, they were irredeemably evil, but he knew no one would grass on anything that remotely involved them, and this was their Manor. They'd also agreed to do the job for a reasonable price, seeing as it involved a proper bent copper, and as such, they owed him one, whoever he was.

*

The names which the Sinclairs had provided Archie with, were consistent with what they already knew and importantly there was one new name with a penchant for very young girls. Archie and Rebecca knew they were concealing more than they'd given and realised the murderous lengths their enemies would go to to protect themselves and their elite clique. There was no time for torture, and a dual disappearance would raise far too many questions. This needed to be an accident, and Sinclair senior was a known drinker, who frequently drove home from his Golf Club after too many Scotches. An accident was just waiting to happen, especially in the blackout. No one in the White Horse knew about the Old Rose, and Special Branch would find no clue anywhere about the events leading up to the tragic accident.

It was a good day's work by any standards, and Archie felt a sense of satisfaction. He'd eaten that day and hadn't needed to wash afterwards, that was interesting, he'd have to work out why.

*

At the beginning of September, Archie took Conner aside in the garden of the Cottage, and they sat on a bench among the shrubs listening to the stream as it flowed past them.

"Can I talk to you alone? We don't seem to get any time just you and me, and I miss it, you're still my best friend. So much has changed, I'm just not who I used to be, I've grown, but there's a degree of acting a part. Except with Rebecca of course, she doesn't know me as well as you do, from before, from before this all started."

"What's troubling you?"

"It's just, well, what the fuck's going on, Conner? Why did nothing happen in the first twenty years of my life and then a hundred things in the next two? Things just keep happening to me, good and bad, I do a lot of deciding who lives and who dies.

"I've got friends, people to live for and people to die for, and there's still an overwhelming need to survive. I'm just so confident that *I'll* survive that I'm deciding who I need to survive with me. Where does that certainty come from? I can't fathom it, is it just blind luck?

"There's a girl as well, I've not told you about, in London. I love her, and she's separate from all this, and that's partly okay, but I need her with me all the time. I, well, it hurts when she's not there. I told her I'd jack it all in and run away if she asked me to, and I meant it."

"What did she say to that?" Conner asked.

"She said she didn't want to change what I am, and I had something to do and needed to do it."

"She knows you as well as loves you then."

"I suppose so, I told her everything about me, I had to, and I mean everything."

"I think I feel the same sense of doubt. There's more to all of this than I can take in, Alex is asking a lot of me at the moment. I need you to meet him so you can tell me what he's not saying. There's definitely something we're a part of, there have been wars before, but this is the most dangerous time ever in world history. If the wrong side gets the nuclear bomb first, they'll use it and never stop, if the right side gets it, they might use it once and then never again in anger. That's the big important issue. If we do nothing else, we have to do that. There's more than that too. Sometimes, I feel as if I'm moving human chess pieces around a board, and you and Rebecca are just pieces too. Then, I feel that I'm one of the pieces, and someone else is moving me."

"Who's moving you then?" Archie asked.

"Churchill, Bracken, Alex, God or Gods, You?"

"It's not me, is it fate, destiny, the meaning of life then?"

"Which is?"

"I told you already, survival of the fittest, if we're fit enough, then we'll survive, and if we survive long enough, we'll be the fittest. Are we here because we're the best people to be here?"

"Have you just answered your own question then?"

"Could be, if you talk long enough, you're bound to make sense eventually."

"So, we do what we want, do our best at it, survive and see where that leads us."

"Agreed, and next time when we talk, we have to include Rebecca, we're three now not two."

"Bloody right too," said Rebecca, emerging from the cottage behind them.

"See, people are starting to notice me now, and I can still sneak when I want to. Archie, you missed out the most important part. Survival of the fittest is not just the meaning of life, it's the meaning of the Universe. Particle physics, for example, there are two kinds of matter, matter and antimatter, the Big Bang should have produced equal amounts of both, but in the observable Universe, there's more matter than anti-matter. One type of matter outfought or outlived or out-survived, if that's a word, the other; so even at a subatomic level the rule still applies."

"It all makes perfect fucking sense now," said Archie immediately, before Rebecca banged his and Conner's heads together.

"Ouch!" said Conner theatrically. "Right, now you're both here, let's discuss a little favour the Americans have asked of us."

*

10th September 1941 – Bletchley

Mary Murphy sat in bed at her home in the small cottage that her mother and father now lived in. She was there with the baby that she'd given birth to, the day before, a beautiful young girl who was feeding comfortably and healthily from her left breast. She'd been lucky that Molly had taken to the breast easily, some babies just wouldn't and the mother always felt bad about it.

Archie had told her to take as much time off as she needed, she wanted to breastfeed for a month and then switch to the bottle so she could return to work. He'd said he'd find a baby minder for her, someone local and trustworthy.

She needed to look after Spud's daughter, and she needed to look after her team as well; without the team and their purpose what world would there be for Molly?

Billy had brought up a girl on his own and gave plenty of advice, mostly welcome.

Archie knew that one tiny part of Spud was alive in Molly, and that helped him.

*

12th September 1941 – 0400 – The Greenland Coast

Conner, Archie, Rebecca, Hospital, Asgeir and Baldr left the deck of the submarine, HMS Triton again. The moon was almost full, and the night sky was bright with stars, off the coast of Greenland. They were in two smaller than usual semi-rigid dinghies, Archie, Rebecca and Baldr in one, the rest in the other. This was a different operation from usual.

Their target was a Norwegian civilian trawler, the *'Buskoe'*, which was setting up weather stations as close as possible to Canada and the United States. Signal intercepts showed that at least some Germans were among the crew, and they had an Enigma machine on board. The intercepts, obtained over eight weeks, suggested that neither the crew nor the ship had arms or armour. Archie reasoned that proximity to the United States meant it had to stand up to inspection by their coastguard vessels. The Enigma equipment and codebooks would go overboard long before any inspection, though, that was where they came in.

"We're getting closer to the Americans joining in the war, and we need to keep them sweet. We take the risk, a calculated one, they get the prize, this time," Conner had said, and he was coming with them.

They all carried Thompson's strapped to their backs and short miniature crossbows in their hands, that was the risky part. They didn't know if the whole crew was German, they didn't know if the crew had hidden weapons. They assumed so, but they didn't want to kill anyone on board unless they had to. The Americans were to receive the prize and crew intact.

The crossbows contained darts which carried Sodium Thiopental, a new drug that tranquilised the target instantly. Archie had discovered this in his search for a substitute for chloroform. Begley, Billy and Smudger had made the crossbows by hand in the stables workshop.

They worked fine; once! Reloading was a nightmare, you could be dead before you'd reloaded. In the restricted confines of below decks, on a small boat, against a few targets, it should be a workable option.

It reminded Archie painfully of the *'Krebs'*, and that was bad, definitely bad. He'd purposely selected a smaller team, only three in each dinghy. The other men were experts at killing Germans, he just wasn't sure how reliable they were at not killing them and taking them alive.

Rebecca had to be there for the machines and code books; he needed the two Vikings to ensure they wouldn't mistake a German for a Norwegian or vice versa. Five of them should be able to take any five unsuspecting Germans.

They were all wearing experimental protective vests made by Wilkinson, who were working on flak jackets for aircrew. They were layered metal plates contained inside silk material and padding on the inside. Although they would stop a bullet going through your heart or another major organ, you still had arms, legs, groin and head vulnerable. They were heavy and cumbersome in a tight space, and they'd had a small one specially adapted for Rebecca. She was to take the first guard on deck, then stay at the rear.

The team had greeted the vests as a little cowardly when they'd seen them.

"Julius Caesar wore armour while he conquered half the world. When he took it off, a dozen cowardly politicians stabbed him in the back, I know who I want to be," said Archie. "You'll wear it if and when you're ordered to."

The camouflage, this time, was dark, dirty snow, not a colour you would think of, but Rebecca and Penrose knew what they were doing. It worked.

As on the *'Krebs'*, the boats approached the *'Buskoe'* in full darkness as it lay at anchor in MacKenzie Bay. Practice had made the silent approach easy for the smaller number of Chosen Men, and the dinghies feather touched the trawler simultaneously. They put their special ladders in place and Rebecca carefully climbed on the one held steady by Archie. The single lookout on watch was alert, pacing the deck noisily so Rebecca found him easily even in the gloom. She fired, and the dart just gave him time to gasp a deep breath before he slumped sideways. He had no weapon, and she handcuffed his wrists and legs anyway while the others went about their work.

Archie went first, Asgeir and Baldr next then Conner last, as they entered the interior of the trawler silently. Small bulkhead lights gave just enough illumination to see the four doors leading off the only internal walkway. Each man picked one door and Conner made a great show of counting, one, two, three, go, with his hand then each man opened his door carefully to enter his chosen room.

Archie immediately saw two bunks in his room and took his first shot instantly at the lower one and began to reload. The bad light and the awkward nature of the ammunition slowed him down, dangerously. He saw the movement from the top bunk but hadn't seen the hand reach behind the bunk for the pistol hidden there. In shock at seeing the weapon moving to aim at him, he reached for it, intending to grab the barrel with his left hand, anything to stop the bullet heading for his face.

The first shot went through the palm of his left hand, deflecting it into his right shoulder. He pulled his hand away instinctively from the pain, only to see the weapon resume its movement towards his face. Ludicrously, he closed his eyes and ducked as if that would help. He heard the shot, at that range, it nearly deafened him. All he felt was a burning on top of his scalp and the weight of the German falling onto him from the top bunk.

Chapter 9

Friday 12th September 1941 - The Greenland Coast

Archie Travers was in pain, but alive.

He opened his eyes to see Rebecca pushing the German off him.

"Fucking," she said as she kicked the German seaman in the balls, "Bastard," as she aimed and took her second kick, then knelt beside him.

"You'll be fine, you're all right, you'll be fine," she said holding his bloody left hand in her right and staunching the flow of blood from his shoulder with her left. She cradled him in her arms kissing his bleeding head repeatedly.

"Let him go, let me at him, Rebecca, Rebecca let me at him," Hospital shouted at her and then he just pulled her away from him.

Conner grabbed her under the arms and lifted her up.

"Rebecca, the machines, the machines and books, concentrate," he urged her.

*

An hour later, the whole British party was on the deck of the American Coastguard Vessel, *'North Star'*. Five Germans posing as Norwegian Seamen were in custody and bound for secluded internment in the United States.

The team had recovered the Enigma Equipment and papers from the *'Buskoe'*, and Rebecca was explaining it to the bespectacled American boffins. Why did boffins all look like boffins?

The Americans had their prize, the machines, evidence of incursion by the Germans and their precious neutrality remained intact. They did, however, owe Britain a favour and they were one more small step closer to joining in the war; it was worth it, Conner thought.

Conner consciously allowed Rebecca to undertake the on ship liaison with the United States Corps of Intelligence Police. She stood there, a foot smaller than most of the men she stood next to. Calmly explaining and directing their actions like a schoolteacher telling a five-year-old how to read for the first time. Her hands were still bloody from Archie's wounds, and her face and lips were red from where she'd kissed and held him. Two definite streaks running from her eyes downwards showed where her tears had washed some blood away.

When she finished talking, a tall, gentlemanly Captain took one stride forward.

"Thank you very much, little lady," and offered her his hand.

"Don't patronise me, you big lump, don't thank me, thank him," she said, pointing to Archie having his wounds tended on deck by Hospital and the ship's doctor.

"He took two bullets to get you that machine and the crew intact. If they'd killed him, I'd have rammed the whole machine up your backside, and another thing, you bloody Americans better join in this war soon. There's not nearly enough of us Brits, and we could use some help, right, now!" she said poking him three times in the chest.

Archie saw and heard the astonished looks and gasps from the American crew. They'd congregated on deck, oblivious to security protocols, to watch the action.

The officer just looked at Rebecca and smiled warmly.

"Ma'am, I think I've heard of you before," he paused, looked around him, then said loudly.

"Gentlemen, Officer on deck!" he stood to attention saluting Rebecca, as did all present on deck.

Rebecca returned the salute, British style.

"And I shall pass your advice to my father."

Rebecca returned to sit next to Archie, suddenly self-conscious.

"Why has everyone heard of me?" she whispered to Archie.

"It could be the trail of crushed and bloody German groins you've left across the Northern Hemisphere?"

"Oh… and who's his father?"

"Well, the chap you just poked in the chest is Captain Elliot Roosevelt," said Conner.

"Oh… "

"Rebecca?" said Archie.

"What?"

"Thank you for saving my life."

"Promise me you'll stop going in first!"

"I can't do that."

"Yes he can," Conner butted in, "I'm ordering him to, right now."

Archie's wounds weren't serious, the nick on the head and shoulder were superficial, four stitches in the head and eight in the shoulder. Head wounds bled more profusely at first and looked worse.

His left hand was more problematic, the flesh and bone damage would never fully heal. At first, there was no feeling in the whole hand, but after a day of intense concentration, the feeling began to return. His hand would later move and feel almost as normal, his little finger still moved just a little slower than the others. He thought he could conceal that from most people, he knew Oona and Rebecca would notice.

The location of the wound on his hand vexed him, it reminded him uncomfortably of the late Father Aloysious. Was an angry God seeking retribution against him? Was fate repaying his sins?

*

Conner insisted that Archie take two weeks leave, and he did that willingly, this time. He took Oona to a hotel, The Old Swan, near Grasmere in the Lake District, they went on the train and bus and were ordinary people for a while. The air was clean and the scenery lush, with rain, they still went for long walks regardless.

She fussed over him, and he let her, they talked, walked and sat by the log fire in the lounge, read the paper, did the crossword together and made plans for after the war.

She changed the bandages on his hand every day, gently and thoroughly, it made him feel safe. He asked again if she wanted just to run away and never come back, she said no, just as she had before.

"In fact," she said, "if you don't stop asking me, I'll join up and demand to be posted to your unit to look after you properly!"

"I'll shut up then?"

"Yes, you will, and you'll promise me you'll stop going first."

"I promise."

It had to end, it was the best two weeks of his life, then it ended, and he returned to war and reality.

*

Monday 29th September 1941 - Bletchley Park

When Archie returned to Bletchley on Monday the 29th September, Rebecca wasn't there, she'd taken leave to see her parents. Her absence disappointed and hurt him, why couldn't she have gone during his sick leave? He'd been looking forward to seeing and hugging her. Conner asked him to go to SOE and interview some Czechs, to pick two for a job that needed doing next year. He did it, but he just wasn't interested yet, two weeks away had taken the edge off his zeal.

*

Rebecca reached London that midday and went straight to see Oona. Oona met her at the door, and they walked upstairs holding hands, in the living room they just embraced.

"Thank you so much, thank you, thank you, thank you, you saved him for me, and you'd already saved me for him," Oona sobbed.

"Sweet Jesus when I saw the bandages, I nearly died of fright. He told me what you did, he told me what you did to the Americans too. Tell me, tell me, anything, anything you want, it's yours, just say the word, whatever, whenever, I owe you so much, Rebecca."

"Well, there is one thing, but… "

"… I promise never to tell another soul."

*

October 1941 – Bletchley Park

At the beginning of October 1941, an urgent report arrived on Conner's desk. He wasn't surprised to find out that Werner Heisenberg, the head of the German nuclear research team, had travelled to occupied Denmark and met with Nils Bohr in September. Bohr was a Nobel Prize winning Physicist who had remained in Denmark after the outbreak of war. If Heisenberg visited him and decided he had nothing of value to the Reich, maybe the Nazis would leave him alone. Bohr had already played a dangerous game in helping Jews escape the Nazis, and there were always those ready to do harm for its own sake. He needed to keep a close watch on that, Bohr was worth protecting just as Heisenberg was worth using.

He also knew now that Hitler had appointed Reinhard Heydrich, Heisenberg's implacable enemy, as Deputy Reich Protector of Bohemia and Moravia. He would rule with a deadly fist from his base in Prague, he'd ordered more than 90 executions in his first three days there. Heydrich was the worst Nazi imaginable and Conner would need to deal with him permanently if he became a threat to Heisenberg again. Archie had already found a couple of Czechs willing to do the job. Heydrich was vulnerable in Prague, but an assassination would result in appalling reprisals.

The thought of Heydrich reminded Conner he needed to discuss something with Rebecca and Archie. He'd already spoken to Alan about it and still needed more help to undo the knot in his mind.

"I need to talk to you about the Jewish question," Conner said that evening in the cottage.

"Okay," said Archie, briefly looking at Rebecca and not knowing what was coming.

"We know the Germans are killing them," Conner continued, "particularly the SS, that isn't the real problem. The point is, we know the Germans slaughter after they conquer. It might be the mentally ill, the communists, the party leaders, the union leaders, the resistance, homosexuals, priests, liberals, gypsies, slave labourers, Poles, mainly Jews, though.

"What matters is that it's not just individual random unrelated cases. They are systematically rounding up all Jews, men, women, children and sending them by train to concentration camps. Then they are slaughtered like animals, gassed with poison and the bodies burnt. It's not thousands, it's hundreds of thousands, and it'll be millions in time. I can't think of a damn thing we can do about it, apart from what we're already doing to try to stop the Nazis winning."

Archie spoke quickly, he knew his answer already.

"Why do we attack Norway? Will it destroy the Nazi party? No, it's because each small attack we make means that Germany has to station hundreds of thousands of troops there, just in case that's where we attack in force. It obliges them to waste men that then can't fight us elsewhere. That's why we're so glad Hitler attacked Russia if he attacks them he's not attacking us. If he'd sent ten percent of the forces to North Africa that he sent to Russia, he'd have all the oil in the Middle East, seriously! So if he chooses to expend useful resources on killing lots of innocent civilians, should we stop him doing that? Even if we did? Where can we take him on, with a viable invasion? Nowhere! We don't remotely have the capacity for any invasion of Europe. Okay, so what if the Americans joined in, we could take him on in Africa first, then France, north or south or maybe Italy. Can we launch an attack out of thin air in the middle of Germany or Poland or Czechoslovakia? No, we can't!"

"Okay, I know all that," Conner said.

"There're lots of Jewish people in the United States," Archie added, "too right there are. Fortunately, some of them are wealthy and influential, some are brilliant scientists!

"So, if Hitler's wholesale oppression of Jews brings the Americans closer to joining in the war, that's what we need in the long run? It's just another mistake on Hitler's part, and we have to use it to our advantage, ruthlessly and without hesitation. It's not 'nice', but it's all we've got."

"Rebecca?" said Conner.

"I'm with Archie, logic dictates that we're doing all we can, besides they have their own God, and he's not doing a lot to help them is he? Who can criticise *us* for inaction when God does nothing; their God's an even bigger cunt than ours."

"In the meantime, there's some evil on our doorstep we can do something about," said Archie.

"Who is fit to judge us other than ourselves?" Conner asked rhetorically.

*

Friday 31st October 1941 – London

Conner made sure that Rebecca and Archie joined him at the Savoy for another violin recital, wearing their best civilian evening wear. Archie hated the evening suit Conner forced him to wear, then he quietly told him it was for Rebecca, and he agreed to attend without any more fuss. Rebecca arrived at Archie's flat later with a dress on a hanger and a bag with shoes and other items.

"That's a dress," he said.

"Of course, it's a fucking dress you idiot," she said as she went into his bedroom to change.

She came out of the bedroom an hour later.

"It's still a dress," he said, "and it fits, you're wearing heels, and you've got makeup on?"

"Yes."

The dress was a sober colour, a deep dark-blue with a high neckline, just showing some of her shoulder blades. She'd tied her hair back behind her ears, simply and effectively showing her slim neck and face. Someone was teaching her to be a woman.

"You look like… a lady," he nearly said, Oona.

"That is the plan, yes."

"Okay, it'll just take me a while to get used to it, that's all."

The recital was by someone whose name and music could not be recalled afterwards, Archie just hoped for another glimpse of Churchill and made sure Rebecca was okay.

When the recital ended, and the civilian guests had left, Churchill came directly across to where the three of them stood. He shook the hands of Conner and Archie warmly and firmly.

"Nice to see you still here, gentlemen," he said then handed Archie his still smoking cigar, crooked his arm and looked to Rebecca.

"Shall we talk young lady, I've been hearing a lot about you," and led her away from any listening ears.

"I understand you had some minor trouble in France and have been doing your level best to remain in trouble ever since?"

"You could put it that way, sir," she said.

"I also understand that you had a short-lived relationship with a young Irishman, who might have done some harm if you'd not stopped him?"

"You could say that too," she said relaxing a little now.

"I will say no more then, about any events that happened in Belfast shortly after that. You also caused some minor concern with my American cousins; seemingly there was an entire coast guard crew who demanded to sail to England and join the war immediately!"

"Oh yes, I was a bit, well… I was covered in my best friend's blood at the time."

"Captain Roosevelt told his father that he felt ashamed when he met you, you fighting and he not. He was wounded during the Great War you know, invalided out of service, he still joined up again, and you made him feel shame. I have written the greatest begging letters in history to his father, you know. People will see that in time, you made him feel the shame of his son, and that's a powerful force. I just need to let you know you have my gratitude, it's little enough, however, if there is anything you need, you should let me know."

"Well, it's funny you should say that. Some close friends of mine from Bletchley Park have written you a letter. They could use your support, and they're a hundred times more important than me."

"So, the Djinn grants you one wish, and you give it to someone else, that's a very noble act young lady and I will do my best to grant the wish. One final thing," he laughed, "I was told you were a plain girl, you are most certainly not, in fact, you are extremely pretty if you will allow an old man to say so."

"Thank you, sir."

*

"So what did he say then?" Conner asked when she got back to them.

"He said I was pretty, extremely pretty," she said.

"The dirty old man, I'll chin him," said Archie.

"No it wasn't like that, you idiot, he thanked me for the work I'd done and said he'd been told I was a plain girl; who could have told him that?"

"Not me," they said instantly.

They said the words easily enough, then thought about them, finally realising just how attractive she was, when she tried. She was already a dangerous young lady and the danger had just increased tenfold.

As they waited for Conner to finish some business inside the hotel with Bracken, Archie and Rebecca crossed the road outside the Savoy to look at the river from the embankment. Archie kept his hands in his trouser pockets to avoid any temptation to hold her hand. Rebecca put her hand in the crook of his arm anyway.

Archie looked straight ahead.

"You're not pretty you know," he said.

"No?" she said.

"No, you're fucking beautiful."

"Thank you."

"If you tell anyone that I said that, I will never speak to you ever again."

"I'd better not then."

"Ah, here he comes, I'll take you home, make you a cup of tea then I'll sit on your lap and we can plan who to kill next."

"Well, some of that sounds good."

'I'll kill any man who even thinks of laying a finger on her... ever.'

He knew that, with sudden, absolute certainty, then wondered where that certainty came from and where on this earth it would take him.

*

Friday 31st October 1941 – Paris – Wehrmacht HQ

As Deputy Head of Wehrmacht Security in Paris, Dolf had a first class job and a lifestyle to match it. It did irk him that he was not in full charge, he could do a better job than the elderly Von Brander, whose career was merely attributable to his family influence and connections. He wasn't weak, he just wasn't as strong or ruthless as Dolf. The Germans were making the French pay a hefty financial price in reparations for defeat, that wasn't enough for him, they could pay more and Dolf intended to collect exactly what was due to him.

Dolf had a splendid apartment in the centre of Paris, the best food, the best wine, power and his choice of the best whores in France. He wouldn't get close to any of them this time; he had a plan, and he was making the right friends in the right places.

*

November 1941 – Bletchley Park

In mid-November, it was a dry, mild day when Alan approached Rebecca's building, asking if he could speak to her outside, on the seat by the roses.

"We've not seen you for a while in our little thinking club," he said.

"I've been busy with some physical rather than mental activity."

"Oh, I see, sorry."

"Not that, Alan!"

"Oh, sorry again."

"Don't be, the war is making changes to all of us."

"Thank you for what you did with Churchill, we seem to get everything we want now."

"I think you might have got them anyway; Churchill is a man of genuine imagination, he sees things others don't. Besides you're worth helping, you still have lots to do, even after the war."

"Well, just don't get killed or anything daft like that."

"I'm planning not to get killed, and if you ever need anything, we'll all help, Archie, Conner too, you know."

"I'll bear that in mind."

*

Monday 1st December 1941 – Late night - Westminster

Archie Travers' second war resumed. There was no snow, but a heavy and still frost hung in the air around Westminster on a late and dark winter night.

They'd followed their targets, a Bishop and a Member of Parliament, several times during the last two months. They knew they frequented a high-class Molly House in Holborn. Their enquiries, by way of Billy's informants, told them the younger males on the premises were compliant actors, willing to suck an old cock or two for the right price. The proprietor, Mr Marcus Grey, took great pride that his house was an orderly one, where client and provider were safe. However, a measure of his pride came from his knowledge of other houses, which were far from safe.

Grey, was a gregarious and effeminate homosexual. He would talk all day if you let him, however on the subject of other premises, his lips were uncharacteristically sealed to all enquiry by Billy's sources.

The presence of their targets in a brothel didn't offend Archie in the slightest; the fact that they were monumental hypocrites and charlatans did bother him very much. He'd seen the Labour MP first hand in the House of Commons, a self-righteous and pompous champion of the poor and working class. He was the one who had fisted Simon, fisted him to his death, he had to die slowly, painfully and shamefully, without a hint of pity.

Archie didn't go around telling people how they should live, then behave differently himself. He had a penchant for occasionally telling people how they were going to die. There was a world of difference.

Smudger was just too damn big to do any discreet surveillance so Archie, Rebecca, and Billy had taken turns following their prey, silently, patiently and eventually productively.

The pair did frequent a different address, they would travel separately, be present at the same time and leave together unaccompanied after two hours. Billy had seen the children delivered to the address for the night. Aged less than ten, he guessed, only two children, but there were fourteen visitors the night he'd watched. He'd followed them, a boy and a girl on their return journey to a Children's home in West London.

The house was in a quiet mews in Kensington, just off the High Street. Archie had rented a house on the opposite side of the mews and nearer to the main road so they could watch arrivals and departures. They all wore civvies that night; Smudger and Billy kept watch on the house while Archie and Rebecca had followed the Bishop and the MP there. They joined them in the rented house to agree on the exact plan for the evening. Billy and Smudger told them that they'd seen a fresh boy and girl arrive earlier and none too willingly, they'd looked about five or six.

The three others, Rebecca, Billy and Smudger all looked at Archie. His plan involved following their prey when they left, that now involved the rape of two children almost in front of their eyes.

Archie tried to start the mantra, but the words came out without thinking.

"How many are in there?"

"Four or five, no more than that," Billy said.

"The plan's fucked, we go in now. Smudger, you're on the door, these premises are closing tonight."

Chapter 10

Monday 1st December 1941 – Kensington High Street, London.

They ran heedlessly across the mews, not caring if they were seen or heard.

A firm knock on the front door saw it open, and Billy knocked the doorman down with one punch, before coshing him just to make sure he stayed that way. The next person they saw was a woman, and Rebecca just shot her dead with two bullets from her silenced Luger.

They had crossed a line, there was no plan, they were just intent on killing anyone they saw and rescuing the two children. There were only three bedrooms upstairs, they took one each, Rebecca found the MP with his tiny cock in the boy's mouth and shot him dead right through the brain. Archie found the Bishop trying unsuccessfully to rape the girl, pistol whipped him and punched him to death. He was still pounding his dead face with his Webley pistol when Billy pulled him off.

"I think he's had enough…"

Archie's hands throbbed inside his gloves. It felt like he'd broken a couple of fingers on his right hand which had done the most forceful punching, and he could feel dampness and pain in his left palm.

He looked down at the man's ruined features, nose, mouth, teeth, eyeball sockets, all smashed and dripping blood.

He hadn't known he had such violence in him. He already knew what he was capable of to ensure his survival. This was pure savagery, he was berserk with an uncontrollable blood frenzy. He concentrated hard, straining then forcing his focus on what he needed to do next then took that fury, placed it firmly in a box and slammed it shut.

That process appeared to take ten minutes in his mind, however, in reality, it was just the space between two words.

"...son," said Billy.

He regained full control of his mind, he hadn't known he was capable of that either.

The two children were stupefied, barely conscious. Billy found a fifth person hiding under a bed in the third bedroom, the deliveryman who had a half empty bottle of liquid morphine in his pocket. Billy recognised the addictive smell before he even opened the bottle.

They dragged the bodies and delivery man into the kitchen. Billy forced him to swallow the rest of his Morphine until he collapsed on the floor. Then he turned the gas cooker and rings on full. Archie placed a couple of Begley's special slow fuse grenades on the hob.

"Ten Minutes," Billy said choking a little on the gas already.

"Yes," said Archie.

They left the house and drove to Bletchley Park, the cottage, in their two cars; the children lay asleep on the back seats.

The children stayed in the cottage for three nights until Conner found a safe home for them while they waited to go to Canada as orphan evacuees.

*

Archie couldn't look at the children while they were in the cottage, Billy, Smudger and Rebecca looked after them, he stayed on the camp bed in the private room of Building Thirteen.

After everything he'd seen, done and still intended to do. After all that shame and disgust, all that sin, he still couldn't look at the faces of two innocent children who'd done nothing wrong.

He didn't eat for three days until they'd gone from the cottage. He couldn't close his eyes without seeing the Bishops smashed skull and couldn't see that picture without knowing that he'd enjoyed it and wanted to do it again. The MP had died far too easily and painlessly, he regretted that, he deserved much worse.

He'd reopened the wound on his left palm with the force of the beating he'd given the Bishop. As he looked at it in the private room in Building Thirteen, he felt a presence.

I won't pray to you. Do you hear me? Whoever you are, fuck you, if I see you at the gates of Hell itself, and you offer me the Universe, I will not pray to you.

The presence faded.

There were no press reports of the explosion and fire, and no mention of a missing Bishop and MP. Something was wrong, he'd heard tell of the Establishment and only now began to suspect what that term meant.

Fuck you, too.

*

Rebecca took him to the cottage as soon as the children had gone. She made him a cup of tea and a sandwich and ordered him to eat it as they sat at the kitchen table.

As he ate, she fixed her eyes on his.

"Listen to me, listen to me! When you quite righteously beat the Bishop to death, he had a copy of the Bible in his jacket pocket. It fell out as we dragged him downstairs, just for a second it was open on a page. I can see that page as clear as day."

She reached for a pen and paper and wrote; then read aloud.

"Proverbs 22.29. Seest thou a man diligent in his business? He shall stand before kings; he shall not stand before mean men."

She paused and lifted his chin, so she could look him directly in the eyes before she continued.

"To have power and not use it would be the worst crime you could commit; Gods, Kings, and Governments fail, not you. It was a mess, cocked up beyond anything we planned, but we killed five evil people, and two children are safe.

"Put it in a box, Archie, we, I, need you back," she said. "There's something you're not telling me, you don't have to, and I need you back. Please."

She leaned towards him across the narrow kitchen table and gave him the gentlest of kisses on his closed lips. The touch was the lightest imaginable, and she left it there for a full minute, denying the need they felt for more. For the longest of moments, he breathed in through his nose, smelling and tasting her purity. It leeched the sin and guilt from him, he took a deep breath through his nose and became Archie Travers again.

Rebecca looked deeply into his eyes.

"Yes, it's gone," she said, "but if you dare tell anyone I did that I'll never speak to you again."

*

7th December 1941 – Evening - Hevlyn Mansions

Archie had been his new old self for several days and had just enjoyed a weekend in bed with Oona. Sometimes they just didn't bother getting dressed; there was no point. Late on Sunday evening, he got a telephone call. He leapt up, a call at nearly midnight couldn't be good news. It was Conner, the Japanese had attacked the Americans at Pearl Harbour, on Oahu Island, Honolulu, Hawaii.

He thanked Conner and said they'd speak at ten the next morning, he'd rush back to Bletchley first thing.

"We've won, we've won, it'll take time, we're not alone, we've won, and I can keep you safe forever, forever," he told Oona what had happened and hugged her.

"Have you got a plan then?" she said.

"I have a million plans now, my head's bursting with them, the first plan is to love you forever, is that okay?"

"It is."

*

The following day he drove straight to Bletchley, dropping Oona at Finsbury Park on the way. When he arrived, Conner and Rebecca came out of the building, and they embraced, sighing with relief.

Rebecca said, "I got a telegram this morning from a certain American Captain, it said he looked forward to meeting me again soon."

Conner was more sober.

"Remember this, we will win, but we'll lose a bit more first, things will be bad in North Africa and the Far East. We have to make the Americans give priority to Europe, they must fight the Germans as well as the Japanese. Now, my dearest Archie and Rebecca, we do have some serious planning to do."

*

Friday 11ᵗʰ December 1941 – Afternoon – Bletchley Park

At four thirty in the afternoon, Conner had urgently called the operational team into Bletchley Park. It was a bitingly cold winter's day, windless, the daylight had just gone, and he asked the teams to stand outside.

The teams stood in their usual crescent around the rose bushes. The street lights of the Bletchley site giving a ghostly air to proceedings and it began to snow, large heavy flakes that settled immediately.

"Today, I'd like us to take a moment to remember absent friends," he said, paused for a minute's silence then said, "today, we also have new friends."

Three United States Army personnel stepped forward from the darkness into the light. A Lieutenant and two Sergeants, smart and envy-inducing, in their best-tailored uniforms.

"Ladies and Gentlemen, my name is Lieutenant Bradley Anderson, I'm from Brooklyn, that's New York by the way. This is Sergeant James McPherson Lightfoot, he's from Texas, and Sergeant Herschel Davids, he's from Queens, also New York. We've been in your fine country for eighteen months now, guarding the United States Embassy in London. I was here before, one Friday in March and was privileged to be present at another ceremony here. You didn't see me, I was at the back, in the trees. I was too goddam ashamed to stand anywhere else that day.

"The three of us have seen what you and your country have stood against in those eighteen months. Well, I'm here to tell you that a certain Mr Adolf Hitler was obliging and misguided enough to declare war on the United States of America this morning. So we are finally allowed to help. That's all we want to do, just point us in the right direction and we'll kick some German butt," he said looking at Rebecca.

"Although we have heard stories of your exploits, so it may be you want us to target a different part of their anatomy. We have a lot to learn, and we'd like you to teach us if you'll have us."

Everyone shook hands with the Americans, laughing and joking. Conner had done it again, an instant team had formed.

As Embassy guards, they'd learned how to be polite and not too loud, British style. All claimed distant European ancestry, James claimed to be Irish, Scottish, Texan and Apache. Bradley regarded himself as entirely of English ancestry, and Herschel was of Polish and Jewish origin, he just said he was a New Yorker if anyone asked. None were religious, none were pacifists, and none could see why they hadn't joined the war two years ago. They were here in Conner's team with the explicit consent of President Roosevelt, Winston Churchill, and the United States Ambassador and would have volunteered regardless.

No man worth the name could hear the story of Rebecca's escape from France and not want to die for, or with, her; it was as simple and as complicated as that.

That particular tale grew in the telling and, it would later be said, that Churchill related it to Roosevelt over cigars and whisky, one evening. If the full truth were known, any man would die for her twice.

What did you do in the war, Daddy? 'I hid behind a woman who was five two and 7 stone,' was no answer for any man or any nation.

Archie knew the three men's stories already. In reality, the three Americans were among the best-trained killers the United States had ever produced and were attached to the Internal Security Section of their Embassy. They were Military Intelligence from what was then called the Corps of Intelligence Police, an organisation which in the mid-thirties had totalled fewer than 20 personnel.

They were trained spies and killers, but you could hardly give yourself that title as a neutral American in London in 1940-41. Nominally, they guarded the Embassy building and the Ambassador, they'd loathed their inactivity and had never put their skills to any real use. Archie knew he could use and channel that impatience.

They'd also hated working for the previous US Ambassador, Joe Kennedy, with his appeasement stance, and they much preferred working for the current incumbent, John Gilbert Winant.

When the latter had arrived in the UK at the height of the blitz in March 1941, he'd said, "I'm very glad to be here. There is no place I'd rather be at this time than in England."

He'd been having dinner with Churchill when they heard of the Japanese attack on Pearl Harbour. Anderson had been on close protection duty that night and witnessed the drama first hand.

"God help me, I was pleased, I hid it as well as Churchill did," he'd said smiling at Conner. Yes, Archie could use that.

Winant had said that he wanted to do something immediately for Churchill.

"Give me a few men like Anderson," Churchill had said.

"I'll do better," Winant answered, he'd heard Rebecca's story too.

The Americans went to the Manor that night. Asgeir Thorson was to take the lead on the team's contribution to the St. Nazaire Raid, Operation Chariot, in March 1942 and Anderson was to be Second in Command. Conner ordered the team and the new men to get to know each other over the weekend. Nipper and Smudger taught them how to swear properly.

Conner, Archie, and Rebecca gathered in the cottage at six o'clock that night; Conner made everyone a mug of tea, and they sat in the lounge.

"Get it over with then," said Archie, Conner was up to

something big.

"Okay, we fly to Washington on Monday," Conner said, "we're staying until mid-January."

"Who else is going?" said Archie.

"Just us three."

"What?"

"Remember the stuff I made you read on Japan?"

"Yes, it was boring as hell, wasn't it, Rebecca?"

"Well, you'll never guess who turned your thoughts into an Intelligence Threat Assessment?"

"How much did we get right?" asked Rebecca.

"A lot. The Americans want to see us immediately. These people do seem to pay attention to us after the event. Your ability to accurately predict complete disaster knows no bounds, Archie. Gubbins will go later as will Churchill and the top brass. What we do will be off the record, as always."

"So some other bastard can get the credit?" said Archie.

"Probably. However, it will definitely be a bastard with a big army standing behind him."

"Okay, what do we need to bring?"

"Nothing much, ourselves, best uniforms and some paperwork blanks and examples from our Bletchley team. You need to be back by nine o'clock on Monday morning, we go to Bristol Airport from here, they're sending a plane for us!"

"Can I go to London now, is that okay?"

"Yes, that's fine, we'll be away a long time, you go straight there."

He gave Rebecca a hug and a kiss on the forehead and left.

They knew he had a special reason to spend every weekend in London.

*

That weekend with Oona was agony, knowing he'd have to leave and not see her for a month almost made him weep every time she held him.

Oona showed him another side that he'd not seen

clearly before. She had immense strength and resilience, telling him to do everything he had to, for as long as he had to, as long as he came back safe.

She asked lots of questions about the Japanese intelligence he'd worked on, and she always asked the right questions including some he hadn't thought of. In explaining it to her, he could see the events slightly differently. She anticipated what he was going to say and said it first, which could have been annoying, yet never was, given she was invariably right. A bit like Spud, she knew what he wanted and did it without being asked. He knew she could do that in bed, but this was different, shared intuition perhaps.

She also asked him questions about what she called winning the peace and how not to do it. Archie was aware that a childhood spent in Belfast meant you knew how to bear a grudge; for several hundred years, over wars long past.

She'd worked out for herself that there would be superweapons, rockets and huge bombs that would destroy a whole city. Another bigger blitz on London concerned her, nights spent in the Cronin's Anderson Shelter had left scars on her mind.

Archie genuinely wondered if he should give her a job at Bletchley. No, he'd never get any work done at all.

She also asked questions about Rebecca, and when he'd answered them all, she told Archie that he should tell Rebecca everything about her. Women were psychic, Archie decided.

"We'll have Christmas when you get back," she said as she kissed him a final goodbye.

*

Conner, Archie, and Rebecca spent Christmas Day in a five-star hotel in Washington. They'd worked and travelled non-stop since their arrival, everyone wanted a slice of them, and they needed a break. Conner had arranged it all, a family meal he'd said although he acknowledged that one important member of the family was missing, now that

Archie had told them everything about Oona. Rebecca listened and hadn't asked any questions, he hoped she wasn't jealous, she didn't seem so. She seemed to like what he'd said and would usually ask questions, perhaps she was psychic too, probably was, he thought.

The meal, wine, location, and company were first class. You could be anywhere in America and not know there was a war on. You could relax and feel safe; Archie had kept busy, there was an overwhelming number of things to do and see. He was somebody now, in America he was somebody, the biggest and best place and he was still somebody, and he liked it.

Every time he had a second's worth of rest or went to bed he thought of nothing except Oona and his need for her. Keeping in touch was impossible, he'd written a letter, but she couldn't reply, and he couldn't say much other than he loved her and missed her. He'd bought her a special gift, which would be a surprise on his return. He'd take her to the Savoy and get them to serve a Christmas Dinner in January with crackers and all the trimmings. He didn't care if the whole world stared and thought they were mad. He'd make this Christmas her best, even if it were three weeks late.

Rebecca missed Oona too and felt guilty that she had Archie, that day.

Conner had a family and was glad, but someone was missing for him too.

*

Oona spent Christmas morning alone and missed Archie in a punishingly depressive way. She needed him with her that instant, Christmas was a family time, and they'd forsaken their own. Archie had never spoken of his family other than saying he'd left them and never looked back. Their son had gone missing in action, presumed dead, in France, and he was someone else.

She went to the Cronin's house for Christmas Dinner, she'd provided the meat earlier and brought a bottle of wine they wouldn't accept. It was pleasant, she wasn't alone, but she was empty.

She wondered if she could get a job near Bletchley so she could be safe with Archie. No, he'd never get any work done, would he?

She had a glass of wine at home later, the Cronin's had insisted she took the bottle home with her. She went to bed early and tried to count her blessings. She had two of the best friends she'd ever had, she had the best lover and best man she could imagine. She still cried herself to sleep, eager for it to be any day other than Christmas Day.

*

Early on Boxing Day Morning, Oona's sleep was shattered by the smashing down of her front door and several pairs of heavy feet running up her stairs. The door to her bedroom burst open, she just had time to see the dark shapes of three men move towards her before a brutal fist knocked her unconscious.

When Oona awoke, she was groggy and aware of being sat upright on a hard chair. Her eyes were blindfolded and her arms held behind her back by rough metal on her wrists, handcuffs. She was cold and sensed that she was still wearing the thin nightdress she'd worn to bed. Her left arm ached near the shoulder, and a sharp pain at the centre of that ache told her she'd been injected with a needle. She had a drunken feeling in her brain, not caused by the pain in her jaw and she could move her mouth okay, so nothing was broken. The nightdress felt damp, as if water had been splashed on it, it felt torn and was around her hips rather than her knees. Her breasts were sore, but she felt okay elsewhere. She was starving, she'd been unconscious for a long time. She still didn't move, she began to think, to work out what was happening, to look for a chance then take it.

Any thoughts of planning were stopped by what felt like a full bucket of water being thrown over her face. She coughed, spluttered and was glad it had woken her fully and sharpened her brain.

"Right, Miss Lainne, are you sitting comfortably now,

shall we start?" said an Irish accent.

'That's a Proddy accent, I know that a mile off, it's not a friend of father's, what the fuck's going on?'

"Yes, Miss Lainne, it's Boxing Day, we've been up early, and we'd like to get this matter sorted without delay," said another voice, an English one, not London, northern she guessed.

"We know you're a member of a family of Republican murderers, the Lainne's of West Belfast," the Irish voice continued. "We've been watching your family for years, waiting for you to make a mistake."

'That's bollocks, I know that from Rebecca. Gubbins said her family were unknown to any law enforcement bodies or any intelligence units, and he'd checked that personally at the highest levels.'

"Yesterday, you were seen at the house of another Irish family with links to treason, and whose son was involved in acts of treason."

'That's bollocks too, the Cronin's left to escape all that.'

"You were seen carrying a package from that house yesterday, and we want to know where it is."

"That was a bottle of wine," she said.

A hand slapped her in the face, someone else was there, closer, at least three of them then.

She heard the cylinder of a round pistol chamber rolling near her face and the sound of it being cocked.

"We believe you were involved in the murder of a young British soldier, a honey trap; some dirty Catholic hoor lured him to a secluded spot where he was killed by you and your family. We have your bastard father's fingerprints now, and they match those found at the murder scene. We also have a blonde hair found on the uniform of the victim. You wouldn't know any dirty, blonde haired Catholic hoors would you? Your mother was very definite when we... well, when we spoke to her. She definitely said you were a hoor," the Proddy voice continued.

'It must be police, Specials maybe, are they on or off

duty? That makes a big difference.'

She coughed, her mouth was too dry to talk properly, and the coughing gave her a chance to think. She had to gamble, she could be dead in five minutes if she didn't.

She felt the metal of a gun barrel pressing against her right temple. She expected the gun to just click on an empty chamber, they weren't going to finish her that quickly. The noise when it came was loud and right next to her temple. She felt relief and the warmth then the chill of her own urine running down her legs as she pissed herself with fright. The hand slapped her face again.

"You need to speak to a friend of mine, Captain Archie Austin Travers, he'll vouch for me." She was panicking now, that might not work, they wouldn't know Archie.

The Irish voice laughed.

"And where will we find him then, hoor?"

"He's in the United States on Army business."

"You'll have to do better than that, hoor."

"There's a Brigadier Colin Gubbins, you must have heard of him, he'll vouch for me." She needed to increase the risk to her captors. She needed to threaten them.

"Well now, I've heard of him, but how the fuck you would know his like, I don't know."

"Because he's the Head of the Auxiliary Section of Special Operations Executive and I work for him, you stupid fucking cunt!"

The hand slapped her face again.

"Language please, young lady," another Englishman, a Londoner, scum from his accent, she could tell.

"And where would this Brigadier be then?"

"He might be in America too, I'm not sure, contact his office in Baker Street and check if you have to. One thing I am sure of, you'll pay for this, he'll make sure of that, you incompetent fucking idiots."

'In for a penny.'

She had done what they suspected of her, and she knew they'd never prove it in a court of law. She also knew they had another type of court in mind. A Proddy Tan wouldn't be too interested in the rule of law, and a common Irish girl could easily disappear without a trace. She needed to be somebody, somebody with friends.

Her last remark must have hit a nerve, and she heard two people leave the room. It was a big empty one, judging from the echoing sounds, it wasn't a cell or a police interview room. She could still feel the presence of the third man remaining in the room, hearing his breathing and sensing his malice in the hairs on her neck.

A hand jerked her hair sharply backwards, and she felt a face pressing down onto hers. She felt and smelt his bad breath on her, his aftershave was cheap and sickening. He put the thumb of his right hand into her mouth forcing it open, coughed up some phlegm and spat it down her open throat. He forced four of his fingers into her mouth, triggering her gag reflex until she choked and retched. He let go of her hair, and she heard him walk casually out of the room, he was light on his feet for a man.

'Jesus, he's the most dangerous one, he doesn't care if he gets caught, he hurts for the sake of it.'

His rough handling of her hair had loosened the blindfold, and by moving her head back against the top of the chair, she shook it off. She looked around her, this was no police station. It was an empty warehouse with a few wooden chairs, a table and an old, soiled mattress in the corner, with her knickers lying on top of it.

This wasn't where you took someone to ask them questions, this was where you took them to kill them... or worse.

Chapter 11

Friday 26th December 1941 – North London

"Shitting hell, who was supposed to do the address checks?" said Inspector Norman Tennent, the Protestant Northern Irish voice.

"You know we never did any," said Sergeant David Packard, the northern English voice, "you told us just to steam in."

"Well, find some poor sap to take the blame then! No, better still, get round to the station yourself and pull that index card from the address watch list, it was never there, right! Who did you phone to check the address? No that doesn't matter, just make sure whoever took that call from you keeps his fucking mouth shut. We can still get away with this, get her to the Nick and booked in for 0600 this morning, get her cleaned up and I'll get an old gun. We found one at the address this morning, didn't we?" he emphasised his last words.

*

After the incident with Donal, Gubbins had used his connections to flag up Oona's premises and address at every police station in London. Marked for preventive protection and no action without reference to the War Office. Rebecca had known that, had told Oona, and she felt she was safe.

*

Packard disagreed with his boss.

"Let's just shoot the bitch now, she could disappear, or we could sell her on, she'd be worth a few quid. Christ, we could just give her to the Animal."

Tennent slapped him down.

"No, no, no, too many risks, we made a big stink at her address this morning. If she was just a nobody, then okay, not if she's got friends; she can have an accident later if we need. I'll call SOE myself, remember, I do all the talking and make sure your pet Animal hasn't shagged her yet."

*

Lieutenant Jimmy McKay, the SOE Duty Officer that Boxing Day, had spent a dull day, drinking tea and catching up on reports he hadn't read yet. When the phone rang, he knew it must be important although he was sceptical of an Irish police prisoner dropping Gubbins name. However, no one could possibly know he was in America, so that caused him real alarm. When he heard Archie's name, he knew it was important. He knew Rebecca by sight from her training days and had heard of her involvement in several areas. He knew something big had happened in Holloway involving Rebecca and an unidentified female friend. Rebecca had no friends in her time at SOE, if she had a friend now, then that person must be someone special too.

McKay was at Holloway Police Station forty-five minutes later, it was five o'clock in the afternoon, and he brought two armed men with him. He wasn't sure what to expect, so he remained calm when he arrived, all just a cock up, fuss about nothing he expected.

"Inspector Tennent. Now. My agent here. Now," he said as he approached the Sergeant at the front desk. He used an equal measure of calm and threat, copying Gubbins he hoped.

Tennent arrived within seconds in response to the summons and Packard came behind. Tennent had expected to lie before less of an audience, he'd been a liar his whole career so it came easily nevertheless.

"Lieutenant?"

"What are you doing raiding a property that's on your protected list?"

"Some mistake in the records, sir, there's no index card for that address."

"SOE records show otherwise."

"You don't understand, sir, there's no card there now, it must have been misfiled."

"So incompetence abounds in your division does it?"

"A misunderstanding, sir, the girl was seen leaving a suspect house with a package and on searching her address we found a gun, what were we to think?"

"You found a gun?"

"Yes, sir."

"Show me the gun."

"It's in the evidence store, sir."

"Show....me....the....gun," McKay enunciated forcefully.

"Packard, fetch the gun," Tennent ordered.

Two Constables brought Oona from the cells area, wearing just a torn nightdress, barefoot and with a blanket over her shoulders, the bruising on her cheek evident. She'd deliberately refused to clean up.

McKay, shocked, opened his mouth to shout at Tennent, then Oona fell to the floor in a faint.

'That's right, faint, play the little lady card.'

"We have to search people, sir, they can hide things anywhere," said Tennent, "she resisted arrest, and we had found a gun."

McKay's two armed men moved swiftly to pick up Oona and held her closely, making sure they covered her decently with the blanket, the looks they gave the police officers were deadly.

McKay realised he'd begun to reach for his service pistol, but at that same instant, Packard arrived with the gun.

McKay looked at the old gun, dirty and not fired for years, they were lying. They were lying about the gun and the index card. He remembered his interrogation training and the session delivered by Archie; if someone lies to you, make them lie again.

"You found this gun at my agent's address?" he said looking Tennent directly in the eye.

"Yes, sir," said Tennent, and he blinked just once.

"You found this gun at my agent's address?" he said to Packard fixing him with the same stare.

"Yes, sir," said Packard as he looked down just slightly.

He'd pressed them both, to lie to him in front of the audience. He looked at the Desk Sergeant's face behind Tennent and Packard and saw only shame. He wouldn't say a word, though, they were closing ranks, he knew. He saw another man in the office behind the Sergeant, in plainclothes, never had he seen a man look less like a policeman; less like a man. He was skinny, five six, pale faced with dark hair, and rotten teeth that he bared when smiling at him. That wasn't a smile, it was a snarl. He'd remember that face and its utter contempt. He decided to push it one step further.

"Hardly surprising, since I personally left it there," Jimmy said.

Tennent opened his mouth, but he could hardly say he knew McKay was lying, as he had obtained the gun himself less than an hour ago. McKay saw the smallest flicker of a suppressed smile on the face of the Desk Sergeant.

McKay stared forcefully at Tennent and Packard daring them to say anything until he was certain he'd made his point.

"I'll take this, as well as my agent," he said, motioned to his men, and they left the station.

Once in McKay's car, Oona put on her best English voice, learned from Rebecca.

"I'm quite alright you know, I'm just cold and hungry, it's a shame I didn't have any shoes on, I would have liked to have kicked them in the balls on the way out."

"Another time perhaps," said McKay.

"Oh definitely," she said.

"Until then, could you please explain to me what the hell is going on?"

*

26th December 1941 – Paris

Dolf Von Rundstedt had spent a self-indulgent Christmas Day with two of the best French whores in Paris. He packed them off home on Boxing Day, he had to meet Oskar Alber, a Major in the SS Headquarters, and it had to be private.

It hadn't taken long to find that Oskar was ambitious and utterly ruthless, not like Dolf, but they would complement each other's skills well. No one would mistake

Oskar for a man with any pity, his hawk-like features, and pockmarked face was a killer's face, even when he wasn't killing. Dolf could be genuinely charming, he might regret having to kill a man, but he'd still do it without hesitation. Personal gain, self-aggrandisement, and revenge on the French were Dolf's prime motivations, a normal survival of the fittest. Twisted ideology drove Oskar, Dolf would acquire what he needed, then retire in luxury.

Dolf had a respected family name that served him well in his youth, studies and military career. His family had class and were well to do, just not as wealthy as they once had been or as they deserved to be. He intended to rectify that.

They agreed the old and soft Von Brander must go; an assassination would take place, and a suitable man framed, of course. A Jew, who had already disappeared a few days earlier, was being treated well, kept fed and undamaged in the cellar of a private house controlled by Oskar. A British-made gun that Dolf provided from St. Nazaire would do the killing, it was a genuine resistance weapon and would be covered with the Jew's fingerprints.

Dolf would stand in temporarily for Von Brander, and he would personally track down the culprit, thereby leaving him well placed to take over permanently.

The killing of a Senior German Officer would justify the reprisals against the local population that Oskar desired. The not too prompt capture of the Jew by Dolf would justify Oskar's methods.

Dolf wasn't unhappy with the necessary reprisals, but Oskar wanted five hundred deaths to set an example. Dolf persuaded him to settle for a more reasonable two hundred, communists, Jews and other undesirables preferably.

Oskar's superior had repeatedly blocked his constant requests to begin the deportation of Jews from Paris. This disgraceful murder would remove that block and maybe his superior as well. In either event, Oskar could resume his true calling in life, the extermination of helpless people whose existence he didn't favour.

"Whatever did you do with those two animals I sent you from St. Nazaire?" Dolf asked over a glass of excellent white wine.

"Those two pieces of dung, they were useless soldiers, no-one would have them, I had to send them to Buchenwald, they were desperate for guards. They're probably fucking a Jewish corpse right now," Oskar said without a trace of humour and, in truth, he'd intended none.

"Up the arse I expect," said Dolf.

"A *man's* hairy arse too."

Dolf laughed loudly, the joke was funny after all, and he was glad. Glad that Oskar would be so busy killing his hostages and deporting Jews, he wouldn't see what else, of real value was disappearing from Paris.

*

That night, Oona slept on a camp bed at the SOE building in Baker Street. McKay took her to collect her belongings from the flat, and she arranged for the salesgirls to run the shop in her absence. That shop and flat had been her private heaven for such a short time, and that was gone now, she could never return. She explained as much as she dared to McKay, enough to highlight the danger from Tennent and Packard, enough to ensure he'd protect her with his life if needed.

The following night she stayed in a spare SOE bedroom at Bletchley Park. Lieutenant Thorson arranged for one of the Chosen Men to guard her room. She had no clearance to be anywhere near Bletchley Park, but McKay couldn't think of a safer place for her to be, and he had a well justified bad feeling about Tennent and Packard. They were killers, they'd kill to protect themselves. He'd not spoken to Gubbins, he was busy enough in America and nobody knew exactly where Archie and the rest were.

Everyone Oona met was kind, and Nipper was the most talkative of the guardians assigned to her.

"We all knew Archie had a special girl in London," he said, "but he was keeping it quiet, I guess we know why now. Don't worry about Ben, he told me you couldn't find a better man anywhere and if you made Archie happy, then so was he. Billy says if you've tamed Archie then you're even scarier than Captain Rochford, which is pretty flamin' scary I'd have to say."

"What about you Nipper?"

"Me, I'm just glad I ain't a German or a copper. Generally speaking, all women frighten me."

*

Sunday 28th December 1941 – The Manor

Oona enjoyed that she was liked just for being liked by Archie and Rebecca, but she needed to be her own person as well. She couldn't demand to know what happened in their building or anyone else's, so she asked Nipper if he'd take her to the Manor to meet Billy. She knew Billy was close to Archie, a dad even he'd said, maybe speaking to him would make her feel closer to Archie.

Billy was alone in the workshop cleaning Archie's sniper rifle.

"That's his Mauser isn't it?" she said, startling him a little, she had entered quietly. "Goodness, it is a thing of great beauty like he said."

"It is Miss, yes, he has an eye for things of great beauty," he said, "and you must be Oona."

"Yes, and you must be Billy."

"What do you need, Miss?"

"I need you to teach me how to fire and maintain weapons properly and to fight like Rebecca, please."

Billy asked her to pick up a Thompson that he knew was empty.

She picked it up carefully, checked the safety was on, and no bullet was in the chamber. She took the safety off, pointed it at the ground, cocked it and let it click.

"I prefer the pistol grip at the front, you can't hold it properly with the muzzle grip," she said.

"I'll sand down and polish a standard one to fit your

hands."

"You're just going to do it, you're not going to argue with me?"

"Nope."

"Can I ask why not?"

"Because Archie wouldn't want me to, and you'll need to know. You know a bit already, I can see that, and you'll need more. I hear you had a run-in with Special Branch?"

"Yes."

"It was Tennent, Packard, and the Animal, yes?"

"Yes, I know two of the names and I can guess the nickname of the third, how do you know so much?"

"I have unusual sources of information, as Archie would put it."

"And?"

"And they were already on his list, now they're at the top."

"Okay, I see it now."

"And when he's back, the first thing we have to do is stop him going straight there and killing them."

"Can we not kill them then?"

"Oh, we'll kill them alright, Miss, don't you worry, we'll have to, in due course'll be fine, there's no rush. Trouble seems to find the boy easily enough, no need for him to go looking for it."

"I like you, Billy, I think we'll get along just fine."

"Would you like a cuppa, Miss."

"I'll make it, where's the kettle and call me Oona please."

"Oona then, one last question."

"Yes, Billy."

"Did they lay a finger on you?"

"No, one punch," she said tapping the left side of her face, "and a couple of slaps, not in the way you mean."

"Good, if they had, then I'd have to drive him straight down there meself."

*

Friday 9th January 1942 – Over the Atlantic Ocean

Conner, Archie, and Rebecca were on the return flight from the United States to England, Gubbins was with them, and his team had given him a huge file of documents to read. While Archie wanted to speak to him and thank him for all he'd done, he looked like a man who just needed to be alone to think, so he left him that way.

Archie felt strongly that Gubbins should be in sole charge of SOE, not just compromising as one of a group. Like Churchill, he was the right man in the right place at the right time, just let him get on with it.

Archie hoped to be as skilled as that one day and considered the last month's events to see what he could do better. Conner and Rebecca slept, but he needed to get his mind in order, filed and boxed. When he'd done that he could see Oona with nothing else in his mind except a certainty of purpose and certainty of her presence. He had a hundred jobs to do and needed to arrange them in the right order, purpose management, he called it.

He needed to perform each task in the right order, making each task easier and rendering the outcome more certain and controllable. He made a list, full of words, numbers and wavy winding arrows, he'd do it roughly on the plane and then do it more neatly later.

He loved America and its people, the Americans were also a very inventive nation, weapons, drugs, tools, and science. He used his position to secure certain experimental items, new bulletproof vests, for testing purposes with an agreement to provide an evaluation and report. The Americans could invent almost anything, but didn't necessarily think of all the potential uses for those inventions. Archie however, had an extremely fertile imagination.

He also made his expensive private plan for the future, no, all their futures, he'd share that with Rebecca and Conner later then Oona when she was ready. He thought they might just laugh at him. In the meantime, he concentrated on what he'd made of America and what it had made of him.

*

Visiting America was the most empowering and humbling event of Archie's short life. They'd arrived in Washington on Wednesday the 11th of December.

Captain Elliot Roosevelt met them off the plane in Washington, and he tried to salute Rebecca, but she just gave him a big hug to the utter astonishment of all present. Somehow, as with all Rebecca did now, it just worked. For someone who'd once had no emotional interaction at all, she could now get any man to do anything she wanted just by smiling and being who she was, looking like she did.

Captain Roosevelt regained his composure enough to introduce them to Harry Hopkins, who was President Roosevelt's closest adviser. He was the frailest man still standing upright that Archie had ever seen. He'd lost 75% of his stomach through cancer and still worked every hour his God sent him at the White House, advising the President. Doctors had given him four weeks to live, two years previously, and they kept him alive by blood plasma transfusions and a special liquid diet of vitamins and proteins. Archie was inconvenienced by a scratched palm on his left hand.

Archie told him that he was hoping to shake the President's hand and that he was even prouder to shake his, and he meant it.

After the humbling nature of their meeting with Hopkins, who was deeply pro-British, their first meeting with American Intelligence on Friday the 13th December was ego boosting, the relative novices didn't have a clue!

They just thought they could get a thousand people working on a thousand different things, and they'd have a thousand solutions to a thousand problems. They had no concept of using assets wisely and efficiently, no idea how they would identify what was most important and act on it effectively. They'd had enough information to tell them the Japs would make a sneak attack on Pearl Harbour. They just hadn't turned that information into worthwhile intelligence in time to do something about it. That was a familiar flaw to Archie; intelligent people with zero common sense.

Rebecca eased his frustration by pulling out three blank forms that she'd designed from Archie's intuitive intelligence evaluation system. He thought for a minute it might go wrong, but she was irrefutable. She handed one form to each of the three Generals present, then a pen and told them to fill in each section, as she went through the known information before Pearl Harbour.

"And what would you conclude, Gentlemen?" she said.

"That they were going to attack."

"Where?"

"A Major target in the Pacific."

"Which would be?"

"Pearl Harbour."

"And when would you have concluded that?"

"December the 1st, over a week before the attack."

The senior General present who hadn't given his name, sighed, stood up and left the table to gaze out the window.

"All three of you were in France weren't you?" he said without turning round.

"Yes, sir," said Conner.

"And you managed to get out of that hell hole against all the odds, then work this out in what, three months."

"More or less, sir."

"Well, let me tell you, this whole son of a bitch country is still in France, without a goddam map between us."

He paused, he was a huge man, with huge resources and was exasperated.

"How would you like United States Citizenship, promotion and four times your current salary, today?" he said as dry as the desert, his Texan drawl said he came from.

All three stifled a laugh at his joke.

He didn't turn around or move a muscle, "I was not joshing with you, I'm serious, deadly serious."

"We have unfinished business in Europe, sir. We've

made promises we can't break," Conner spoke for all of them,

"I can respect that," the General said, "there are promises I need to keep too. What do we need to do now, what's your best guess?"

"You need to strike at Japan now, whatever the cost, you need to show them they're not safe like we did to Berlin the first chance we got," Conner said.

"A bomber raid from a carrier should work," Rebecca added.

"And?"

"Patton," said Archie.

"That prima donna?"

"He's the last man the Germans will want to see."

"You're the one who read Guderian's mind?"

"Well, I read his book, great people can feel the need to tell everyone how great they are, it doesn't make them any less great, Caesar for example. The lesson I've learned is, we must be prepared to do anything the enemy does, except better... or worse if you take my meaning. Do anything he doesn't want us to, including fighting dirty. Patton will attack the Germans and keep on attacking until he wins. There has to be no hesitation, no half measures, no pity, none, no scruples, no conscience, no sense of right or wrong, just winning."

"And you've done that, haven't you son? No, you don't have to answer that question, that's between you and your soul, that's not for sharing. And you, Conner, what would you say?"

"Europe first, difficult for you, but the Germans are more dangerous scientifically than the Japanese. The Japanese think that placing no value on individual life is a weapon, if the Germans get the big weapon first, they'll use it first, without question."

"Point taken, young man."

He paused again for longer, even his fellow Generals seemed discomforted. You could almost hear his thoughts straining and stretching across space and time, computing facts and information, weighing them, evaluating them, discounting them, including them.

"Okay, we're done," he said almost dismissively, disappointingly.

"You can go now. *You* stay," he said pointing at Archie without looking at him. Nothing had scared Archie for a while, but the feeling of self-doubt returned and took his breath away for just a second.

The General finally turned to look at Archie and sat down.

"I've heard a bunch of stories about you, boy, you and your friends, are they all true?"

"Some stories are true, some are just made up. Sometimes a story is such a good one, it doesn't matter if it's true or not, you just let it be told anyway. All the stories you've heard about Rebecca, Captain Rochford, are entirely accurate. Only half of what you've heard about me is true, the other half is worse!"

"And the truth is?"

"I'm lucky, that's all."

"I like you, boy, you sure you won't work for me?" he said.

"Sorry, sir, it's just, I kind of work for myself at the moment. That's the best situation for me. I'm not that good at following orders. Especially when I know better."

"Amen to that son," he said, fixing Archie's eyes with his own. "Sweet Jesus there's a darkness in you, boy. I could surely use that?"

Archie was tempted, sorely tempted, he could bring Oona, it would be safe, heaven, a haven, they could be whoever they chose to be, be anything they wanted to be. Could he bring Rebecca though? He owed Conner so much, the team, both teams, Churchill, he couldn't let go, not yet.

"It's tempting, sir, but there are things I love, people I love, in England and if I can't save them then what am I selling my soul for? And you can tell I've sold it can't you?"

"Hell yes, mine is long gone, boy, long, long gone."

He paused again for thought.

"We'll meet again, boy, now get the hell outta here before I kidnap you and anyone you've ever loved. My name's Winters, by the way, Harlan Eldridge Winters, people call me *Harsh* behind my back. You need anything, you speak to me."

*

Just after Christmas, on Monday 5th January, the trio had established enough kudos and credibility to secure a meeting in Washington with four unnamed nuclear scientists who were working on something they all knew about, but couldn't discuss. A four-star General accompanied them, and his purpose was that of a guard towards a prisoner.

Conner took the lead and spoke vaguely about Heisenberg and his value to the Germans, the work of Bohr, the heavy water manufacturing capacity in Norway.

Rebecca was keen to show her knowledge on the subject. If she'd taken a different path, she would have been working for Tube Alloys herself. These men were treating her like an idiot and Archie wasn't going to let that go unchallenged.

The scientists just vacillated, they were getting nowhere.

Archie hadn't said a word and just watched the four men carefully. They were tanned, with dry red skin on their noses, they weren't based in Washington then. One had sand under his fingernails, and all wore light summer clothing despite the winter temperature. They had dark bags under their eyes and had unmistakably flown overnight to reach the meeting. They weren't used to the sun by the looks of their peeling noses and were, unusually for boffins, spending time outdoors. They were working on the manufacture and testing of Atomic Weapons. They'd be in a secret location, the middle of nowhere, a desert probably for the security of the research and development. A big desert where a prototype could be tested close to the research. They were working in makeshift laboratories, they hadn't had time to build permanently yet, so they were outside looking at the construction.

They'd flown overnight for 10 hours, maybe 1600 miles at 200mph.

Yes, that was where Archie would build and test.

"When do you expect to finish building the Laboratories in New Mexico?" he said, interrupting a one-sided conversation. You'll have to build a whole town there, I suppose, near Albuquerque or Santa Fe, you'll need an airport," he continued to a stunned silence. "You'll test it at White Sands, I assume."

"What's your game, sonny?" said the General.

Archie told them how he'd worked it out. Then, when the four were busy checking fingernails and scratching their noses, he pulled out a United States of America Tourist map he'd bought from a drugstore and slapped it on the table. He'd already drawn a large X on the Map, slap bang in the middle of New Mexico.

"This Captain sitting here has risked her life to destroy the last Deuterium Oxide in France to make sure our enemies can't have it. She also recovered the research papers that came from at least two of the French Scientists that are working with you.

"So I just thought that if we're here to decide whether Britain should give you access to all our atomic research, you might think it proper to provide us with a measure of respect. You should also consider more carefully the fact that you are not quite as brilliant as you think."

"You're doing the right thing with Heisenberg and get us Nils Bohr if you can, he's a friend of mine as well as a brain," said the eldest of the four men.

"I have relatives in Germany, at least I used to, we do need all your research, please. We'll get there eventually, with your help it'll be sooner, even six months is a crucial amount of time for us, one month even."

"Thank you," said Conner.

"And give my regards to Alex when you see him next."

"I will."

"My apologies for the precious paranoia, it's becoming

contagious and will continue even after we've finished I suspect. Will you support us?"

"Yes, you know we have no real choice," said Conner.

The four scientists and the General rose to leave.

"Could I have a brief word with you alone, General?" Archie said.

The General was unsure, hesitated, then stayed behind. Conner and Rebecca left the room.

"What is it, son?"

Son was better than Sonny.

"The thing is, the short guy with the slight squint is a spy, Russian probably, a communist definitely. It could be straightforward blackmail over his homosexuality, or more probably he has a taste for younger partners, very young partners and the need is being fulfilled by his controllers.

"He never even glanced at Rebecca, but he liked the look of me, I'm afraid. I get that kind of attention sometimes. I've seen that look on his face before.

"He was the only one who wasn't genuinely shocked when I knew where the site was, he already knew it wasn't a secret. He won't actively sabotage anything, he needs it all to work so he can pass on the detail. He's careless and arrogant enough to lead you to his contacts. What you do with the information is up to you. I've no proof, you know I'm right, though, don't you?"

"I know I was told you were one smartass sonofabitch. Are you sure you don't want to work for us?"

Chapter 12

Thursday 8th January 1942 - Washington - USA

Conner, Archie, and Rebecca worked tremendously hard in the United States; the huge distances involved were the most tiring, you could hide all of England in New Mexico.

General Winters agreed not to shoot or kidnap Archie, then insisted on taking him, only him, to the Los Alamos nuclear research site and showing him the security plans. Now he was no longer terrified of him, he liked Winters enormously, he was an American version of Gubbins. Winters trusted him and asked his opinion, which was a proud moment for Archie, he'd stand alongside Winters, anywhere.

On his return to Washington, he was exhausted mentally and physically, just wanting to get home, home to Oona. They could leave a couple of days earlier than the main party, there was no communique to agree, no propaganda to commit, no frills.

Their driver told them he was taking them to the airport via the White House, which was an unwelcome distraction. Archie just wanted to leave, they'd probably have something else they wanted him to read.

He was pleased to see Hopkins waiting for them at the White House; he'd earned the right to delay them.

"This way please, we don't have long," Hopkins said.

Hopkins hurried, Archie thought he might break or collapse, but he just showed them into the Oval Office. The President called them over, he was sitting in his wheelchair behind his desk, alone and drinking a cup of coffee so strong you could smell it from the doorway.

"Ah excellent, you've made it then," he said, "we have two minutes don't we, Harry?"

He looked at the three of them, like a grandfather looking at his son's children, he looked proud.

"Harry tells me you wanted to shake my hand, well let me tell you that's not why you're here. You're here because

I want to shake *your* hands."

He motioned Conner towards him, then Archie and shook their hands. When he finished that, he called Hopkins over to him. Between the two of them, it took about thirty seconds for the President to stand upright, unsteadily, on the metal braces holding his polio wasted legs. His left hand was on his desk, his right arm supported under the armpit by Hopkins.

"There are some things a man must stand up for, Captain Rochford," he said and shook Rebecca's hand gently.

"Good luck and safe journey home," he said as they left his office.

They all had a tear in their eye as they left and tried to hide it from Hopkins.

"He can get you like that, Jeez he does it to me too," Harry said.

*

Saturday 10th January 1942 - 0400 – England

The return flight from the United States took eighteen hours with two stops for refuelling, Archie guessed it was Greenland and Iceland. The United States Air Force Dakota with extra fuel tanks and proper seats, instead of just benches, was luxurious. He closed his eyes and wanted to sleep, but couldn't, he'd lost that skill he realised, that ability to sleep anywhere, anytime. He went over plans in his mind repeatedly. He tried to do the relaxation exercises Conner had taught him, shallow breathing, relaxing each extremity one by one, working inwards until you reached the part of the brain that let you sleep finally. Nothing worked, and he remembered that he hadn't eaten for a day. He knew that feeling, and had no such plans, no plans to kill, but his subconscious was definitely getting his body ready for something.

Something somewhere was wrong. The engine noise changed tone, and the plane dipped to one side, beginning a turn.

Gubbins must have seen something on his face.

"Nearly there," Gubbins said, finally putting his papers aside and then into his briefcase, he hadn't slept either. He left his seat and came to sit next to Archie, blocking him into the window seat from which he could see the beginnings of a fresh dawn. Gubbins didn't say a word, he was up to something.

The plane landed unsteadily with bumps and scrapes of rubber on tarmac and brakes on wheels, then taxied safely to a stop near the main terminal building at Bristol Airport. Archie rose to collect his bags with the others when Gubbins put a restraining hand on his arm.

"Not yet Archie, we need to have a chat when it's quiet."

Conner and Rebecca looked briefly at them, then left.

"See you in a minute then," Conner said. Archie nodded.

When it was quiet on board, and he was sure no one could listen, Gubbins spoke.

"Just listen for a few minutes, your friend Oona is perfectly well and safe, she is perfectly well and safe," he spoke slowly, "understand that first. There has been an incident, though... "

He explained in detail how he'd first met Oona with Rebecca in the flat, the Belfast incident, and then the brush with Special Branch.

"Try to remember that Oona is safe and that you can make sure she stays that way. What I say to you now will never be repeated, so listen carefully. The sectarian issues in Ireland aren't a mere disagreement or dispute, nor a conventional war, they're a blood feud that's lasted for centuries. Where either side sees fit, they'll pursue a vendetta for all time. If they can't kill you, they'll kill your mother or your son, or even your bloody dog; when they've done that, they'll piss and shit on the grave too. The worst of them are bastards beyond belief, and they don't forget. One of the names I gave you, I see you've heard it before, is among the worst. I know him, God help me, I've used his kind. He can't be touched by conventional means, he is protected and knows too much. You, my boy, should not feel bound by convention."

152

Gubbins paused, thinking, before continuing.

"When you do what you must, do it well, finish it thoroughly. If you need to, speak to me and me alone."

"Thank you, sir, and pass my appreciation to Jimmy McKay, I owe you one now," Archie replied, the first words he'd spoken.

Gubbins left, and Archie slowly collected his thoughts and belongings, already postponing all other plans. No wonder Rebecca and Oona seemed psychic, he smiled at that, though, good things sometimes came out of bad. They were friends, he knew they outnumbered him now, and he even smiled at that.

He was serenely calm, which was strange, he should have been angry, angry fit to explode. He was angry, and he'd managed to put the anger away in a box until he needed it. He needed to be calm, and he could make himself so, that pleased him, he'd grown.

When he reached the foot of the short steps leading down from the Dakota, he saw a group of people. Gubbins was there talking to Conner and one young woman in a uniform he didn't recognise, who came running towards him. It was Oona with her dark blonde hair tied back, it was the most beautiful thing he'd ever seen in his life. She did look like some elven princess turned deadly warrior. She flung herself into his arms, and he hugged her tightly, breathing her into his lungs.

"Are you impersonating an officer, young lady?"

"It was Billy's idea, he wanted to make sure I was allowed in, it's Rebecca's, it does fit. Do you forgive me?"

"What for?"

"For Rebecca and me not telling you about... well... me and Rebecca I suppose."

"Nothing to forgive, you looked after each other and me, I couldn't ask for more."

"Archie, have you, you've changed haven't you?"

"Yes, and it makes me love and value you even more, is that okay?"

"Is it okay if I love *you* even more?"

"Yes, in fact, that's compulsory."

"Okay, now let's get you home to the cottage where I can look after you properly," she said taking his hand and leading him away.

"I thought I was looking after you?"

"Don't be daft, besides Billy's been teaching me how to take care of myself."

"Your Irish accent's gone hasn't it? How did you do that?"

"I'm pretending to be Rebecca, remember."

Archie walked calmly to their car, his bag in one hand and Oona in the other. Rebecca looked at him apprehensively, he just smiled at her and gave her a reassuringly warm hug and a kiss on the forehead.

"Billy," he said, then nodded an acknowledgement and shook his hand, he would embarrass Billy if he hugged him or thanked him too much.

In the car, Billy drove, and Conner sat in the front, Archie, Oona, and Rebecca were in the wide back seat. Billy talked first, then Oona, then Rebecca and finally Conner. Archie didn't say a word, he closed his eyes, saying he was tired. When they thought he was asleep, he heard Rebecca say that Gubbins had said he hadn't slept a wink on the plane, spent the whole time writing and they needed to watch him closely. That was true, he listened carefully to every word they said. Taking it all in, arranging it in his mind, forming plans for the short term, today, then tomorrow then the following weeks. He'd have to do this just right.

His body was exhausted, but his mind just wouldn't rest. He remembered Mike, Spotter, and Corp, did he actually kill them, would he really have killed them? Too right, he would, for five minutes with Oona he'd have killed all three of them, for a day, all of Europe, for a year, the world, for a lifetime, the whole Universe.

He still didn't, couldn't, wouldn't sleep.

They reached the cottage at noon, it was damp, miserable and the tenth of January. The fire was roaring,

Billy and Oona made sure everything was ready for them the day before, and Maud Driver had lit the fire that morning. It was warm, welcoming and felt like home. Billy tried to leave, but Archie stopped him.

"You're needed… and wanted, please."

"Yes, sir."

"And don't call me sir, we're way past that, Billy," he said gently and calmly, squeezing the old man's shoulder.

Archie flopped down on the sofa next to Oona, once she'd made the customary pot of tea.

Archie spoke, and they listened, this was his show now.

"Okay, I have a plan," he said, "in three parts, we'll sort the first part now then discuss the rest tomorrow. Oona, you never leave my sight again as long as you live, is that clear?"

She just nodded her agreement, she would argue the details later, they knew that. She'd win the argument, and they knew that too.

"You join the team at Bletchley immediately, and you live here now. You never go back to Holloway, ever. You need a new identity, Conner, can you do that please?"

"Yes, of course."

"What's my new name then?" Oona asked.

"It can stay as Oona, we'll pronounce it as we do now, except we'll spell it U N A, Una, the Irish way, but you'll lose the accent permanently."

"And the surname?"

"It'll be Travers, of course," he said handing her a small leather box which he'd pulled from his bag and opened for her, a solitaire diamond on a plain gold ring.

"If you'll have me? I did plan something more romantic. Honestly, I did. If it doesn't fit or you don't like it, it's Rebecca's fault."

He looked at Rebecca pleadingly for some support.

"Well say something then?" he said to Una.

"She's lost for words, idiot," Rebecca said.

"Is that good?" he replied.

"It's perfect," Una said, "it means unity, Una that is, I

will happily be Una Travers forever."

"Longer," he said then stood up and raised her hands to lift her next to him. He planned to kiss her gently in front of everyone, but his legs gave way, and he collapsed to the floor in a deadweight. It could have gone badly if Billy hadn't moved to cushion his fall and shield his head from hitting the stone hearth of the fireplace.

Una screamed, and Rebecca took over.

"He'll be all right, he just hasn't slept for two days, he won't have eaten either. Conner, did you see him eat anything? He does this sometimes, it helps him think and plan, it reminds him of Calais. He thinks he needs to be desperate to be at his best, he sometimes does it to punish himself so nothing else can. I don't fully understand it, neither does he I suppose? Una, there's cans of Heinz Lentil Soup in the kitchen cupboard, heat then strain it so he can just drink it straight from a mug."

Conner and Billy lifted Archie onto the sofa, sat him upright, and he came to.

"Sorry about that, for a moment I was jumping off a jetty in Calais and Smudger wasn't there, thanks for catching me, Billy."

"Shut up and breathe in and out of this paper bag," said Rebecca, "sorry it's my fault, I should have seen what you were doing, you pushed it too far. You need to learn to ask for help when you need it, you can't do everything yourself. We're a team, you don't have to save the whole fucking world on your own every day!"

A couple of minutes later Una gave Archie his soup in a tin mug. Billy and Conner went into the kitchen, pretending to get something to eat, but actually to avoid the embarrassing sight and sound of Archie getting a right telling off.

Archie drank the soup quickly, it wasn't too hot, just right, Una had topped it up with cold water to take the edge off it. Conner and Billy came back and took him upstairs to his room.

"He needs to sleep for about 24 hours, the big idiot,"

said Rebecca, "lentil soup is his favourite."

"I should have known that?" Una said.

"What, the soup?"

"No, I mean about the desperation, I should know that."

"How could you? He feels it, and you ease it, always. That's why I don't mind him loving you more than me. You take it all out of him, you wash his soul clean, he thinks he doesn't have one, but… "

"Rebecca, you are the best sister I never had, is it okay if I go and sit with him? I promise not to wake him, and I won't fuck him either, I might suck his cock while he's asleep, though, it's been ages."

"Leave it until tomorrow please, these walls are thin, and I'm in the next room… I'm never going to get any sleep am I?"

"Me neither."

*

Una didn't suck his cock although she was sorely tempted, she did sleep with her arms and legs wrapped around him. She did wake him at nine o'clock the next morning and told him to have a bath while she made him breakfast, in bed, she stressed her words.

"You are not to get up yet."

She made a large pile of crisp bacon sandwiches with thick white bread and the hottest strongest tea the British Empire could produce. She served Billy first; he'd slept on the sofa with a weapon next to him just in case. She'd gotten to know him well in a couple of weeks, he'd looked after her like a personal bodyguard from the moment they'd first met. When she'd served Rebecca and Conner, she came down to collect Archie's last, Billy was halfway through his second sandwich and had his mouth full.

"Billy," she said, "when I marry Archie, you're giving me away, alright?" and went back upstairs without giving him a chance to reply.

She dropped off Archie's breakfast then went to have a wash and brush her teeth. When she came back to the bedroom, he'd finished his sandwich.

"Now go and brush your teeth again," she told him.

"Have you eaten?" he asked.

"Yes I had a piece of toast while I was cooking the bacon," she lied, "now go and brush your teeth."

It was stupid, she knew, but she wanted to be hungry too, she needed to be punished a little for not noticing his need, a need that she should have seen to. Perhaps that small act of contrition would help her guilt over taking him for granted.

When he returned to the bedroom, she was naked under the covers waiting for him. He climbed in next to her, there was no need for foreplay, they were both ready. He lay on his left side and she on her right side facing him, she raised her knees, one under his left hip the other on top of his right hip. He entered her easily, slowly and gently. He kissed her forehead, each eyebrow, each eyelid, the point of her nose, her chin, the place on the left of her mouth where her one dimple sometimes showed, her neck and her ears. All the time thrusting gently, slowly and deeply with all the love and infinite patience he held for her. She came with a shivering and shaking climax, and he kissed away a tear that appeared in her eye at the same time.

"Forever," he said.

"Forever," she replied.

They stayed that way for an hour, just enjoying the intimacy and the continued slow, firm deep thrusting. Talking and getting acquainted again, subconsciously removing any possible gaps in the truth that existed between them.

"Tell me something I don't know about you?" she said.

He thought for a moment or two.

"America has changed me. When I was there, it made me realize how big I am, I thought I was somebody here, and that was enough for me. I know now that I could be somebody there as well, it's the biggest pond in the world, and I was a big fish. That sounds bad and big headed, but at the same time, I met a couple of people who made me feel very humble."

He told her about Roosevelt and Hopkins, their perseverance and selflessness in the face of monumental adversity.

He told her about Winters, the much larger than life American General, who scared the living daylights out him, and was his friend now. He told her they could go there now, work and live in safety for all their lives. Once again, he told her that if she asked him to, he'd go there with her.

"No, and don't tempt me again please, you, we, have business to do here. Besides, you weren't born for safety, Billy told me trouble finds you easily enough, no reason to go looking for any. I think you'd find danger, or it would find you, wherever you went. Wherever you are, is as safe as I'll ever be. I'm going to let you get more sleep, I'll wake you later with something to eat. Billy's going to give me away at the wedding, Rebecca as a bridesmaid, Conner as the Best Man, no fuss at all, none. Good that's settled then," she pronounced firmly.

*

Friday 16th January 1942 – Greenwich – London

Una Rochford, the younger sister to Rebecca, born on the 10th January 1922 in Hertford, became Mrs Una Travers at two in the afternoon on Friday the 16th of January 1942, at Greenwich Register Office. It was bitterly cold, all five persons present wore their uniforms, and there was no fuss, just unbreakable love, and friendship.

The ceremony was brief and certainly not legal, the two false identities, birth certificates and proofs of residence invalidated the union, but no one would ever know or care. The oaths that Archie and Una made were binding, for all time, they all knew and cared about that.

Chapter 13

Friday 16th January 1942 – The Manor - Bletchley

After the ceremony in Greenwich, they drove straight to the Manor for drinks and food. Christmas had long passed and would wait until next December, but Archie wanted the whole team to share his joy.

Una insisted on being a Private and starting at the bottom in Building Thirteen.

Billy was still giving her weapons training each evening, he was teaching her how to assemble a Thompson Sub-Machine Gun while blindfolded. He'd adapted one with a smaller grip and shorter butt, especially for her smaller body frame.

He was also quietly showing her how to use Archie's Mauser; she'd demanded to know anything that Rebecca or Archie did, and Billy just said yes. The Mauser was just a little too long for her to use comfortably; she could aim and fire accurately once, not repeatedly or speedily. He said he'd try and find another to adapt especially for her. He'd see what the Americans had, they made guns specifically for women, he'd told her.

She was talented, Billy knew that immediately, tell her once, show her once and she had it. Rebecca was just a little stronger, a little more agile, but give Una a gun, any gun and it was like another limb, it became part of her. Jesus, Archie could pick them, he wouldn't like to see a fight between the two of them. That would never happen, they were like twins separated at birth and by a couple of years. They loved each other as much as they loved that boy. Billy was glad he was past all that, he couldn't handle the women of today, not a chance.

*

Rebecca was getting Una more physically fit and able, able to break a neck with a clean twist applied the right way. Elf defence classes, Smudger had called it, his only clean joke ever as far as Archie could remember, and he helped them tirelessly and patiently. Fortunately for him, neither could reach his neck without a ladder.

"And I've hidden all the fucking ladders just in case!" he'd said.

Archie was teaching her to drive, there were some tasks even the bravest of men shouldn't undertake, but Una told him to teach her, so he had. Fortunately, she was as adept with cars as she was with guns.

Una did leave Archie's sight, but she was either at Bletchley Park, the Manor, the cottage or with Archie. He saw her every day, and she was with him every night. It was bliss, and somehow, her almost constant presence helped him to concentrate better, rather than distract him, and they did get a lot of work done.

*

At the Manor, on the evening after their wedding, Una circulated and mingled well, how did people do that? Archie thought, he couldn't. Gubbins and Jimmy McKay came as well.

Una took Billy aside and held the crook of his arm while he held a bottle of something dark and strong.

"Billy," she said, "thanks for being my dad today, I've never asked, and this isn't the right time I know, but, your daughter Grace, is she… okay?"

"She's fine, she's found herself a nice safe young man, a mechanic, that's what she needed. Not some big dangerous bastard like… well, like a big bastard who was very dangerous."

He managed to avoid naming Archie, but she knew what and who he meant.

"He did the right thing letting her go like he did, she wasn't meant for him, you were, that's it. I don't worry about her at all, that's a good thing. I worry about other people now."

"You're like a father to him you know, and he's the son you never had," she said, "neither of you will ever admit that, don't worry I won't say a word. Thank you, Billy," she said and kissed him on the cheek.

"Now where's that husband of mine?"

Archie had felt uncomfortable being the centre of all the attention that evening, all that goodwill towards him was just making him feel guilty, which of course, he was. He was going to kill these men or more likely, let them be killed while he was safe, and they weren't going to mind one little bit.

Since his return from America, he insisted he drink only tea and water, he needed to be fully aware, always and certainly while Tennent still lived.

He'd been at the Manor at first light the previous Monday morning, only to be cornered by six different questions from six different people. What shall we do about this, what do you think of that, tell me I've done well. Tired and distracted, he found infinite patience for all of that, although he knew that Billy and Smudger had said to give him a break.

He'd learned the trick of sitting on the bench in the Manor garden, it gave shelter from its covered pergola even in the rain. That gave him a little time to think and when they spotted that, at least they only came one at a time.

That night, he sought refuge in the garden again. It was freezing and windless; he liked it, cold sharpened his mind while heat only dulled it.

The frost was heavy, and snow began to fall, thick and deep, settling immediately, this would last all night. No light came from the blacked out Manor windows, but the snow provided its own light, bringing the features and shapes of the bushes and trees to life. There was a silence about snow falling that appealed to him.

"Come here you," said Una, "sneaking off without me."

"You sneaked up on me too."

"That's because I'm a secret elf."

"It's no secret."

"I've brought us one glass of wine for a toast. I know you don't want to drink tonight, but I do want half of one small glass of wine, and I'm not going to have any unless you do."

She'd snared him again, so they shared one small perfect glass of white wine.

"Now, I know you wouldn't let me buy you a ring?" she continued.

"Honestly, I can't wear rings, they irritate my fingers, it's like a form of claustrophobia."

"I don't need you to wear a ring to know you're mine. I have a Christmas present for you, that's all."

She handed him a small brown paper-wrapped parcel. He was a bit puzzled and opened it. It was a book with a green blue and white dust cover, it looked like blue mountains with snow on the top, but he couldn't read the title.

"It's a children's book, I read it a couple of years ago, my childhood was a little short, so it helped to lose myself in a story. Your childhood was a little short too, so I got a copy for you. It's a first edition and Conner had it signed by the author, an old professor of his, he said."

She kissed him on the forehead.

"I give you the gift of the feeling I received from reading the book," she said to him.

"Those are the best words I have ever heard spoken," he said.

"It's like a fairy story, there are elves in it, dwarves, goblins and other people, they fight a huge battle at the end. I can't say more, it'll spoil it."

"Thank you," he said, "and I know this is the wrong time to say it, but there's been no right time. You and Rebecca killed your family to keep me safe, I promise with all my heart I'll keep you safe forever, and I'll give you another family."

"Well, I don't need another family just yet, there's no harm in practicing a little, though. While we're on that subject, you've been the most gentle and careful lover since you came back, and it's been great, but sometimes I just need you to fuck me very hard, rough and very quickly. Right now would be perfect."

"Now those are the second best words I have ever heard spoken."

*

They had the weekend off, nominally, they just stayed in the cottage, snowbound and made plans.

On Monday evening, after a day at the Manor and Bletchley, Conner, Archie, Rebecca, and Una sat eating a tea that Archie had made. Sausage, mash, and gravy, it was his turn, it was technically edible.

"Funny thing happened today," Archie said, once they'd sat down, "Billy got a call from an old mate in Holloway, it was about that Special Branch Sergeant, what was his name, Una?"

"Packard?" Una said.

"Yes, that's him, he's dead, slipped on ice when he was walking home from the pub, banged his head on the pavement. Tragic, but it's an ill wind, as they say."

"And when did this happen?" Conner asked.

"Friday night about ten o'clock," said Archie.

"When you and all your friends and associates were verifiably fifty miles away," Rebecca said.

"Exactly, the level of tragedy depends on your perspective obviously," Archie said as they continued to stare at him.

"What?" he said.

"And who on God's earth would think that a man might suddenly fall and bang his head, on a stone hearth, for example when no-one was there to catch him?" Una said.

All four stifled a giggle, they shouldn't have, they weren't schoolchildren, this was a deadly serious business, but they did laugh and regretted nothing.

*

At the end of January 1942 the preparation for Operation Chariot, the raid on the docks at St. Nazaire, began in earnest.

Asgeir Thorson was in charge of the Chosen Men's role, with Brad Anderson second in command, Archie would handle the training and planning.

Gubbins agreed to let Conner's team take part in the raid as a reserve and rescue vessel. He had enough of his own well trained SOE men, itching for a fight, but having some high calibre seasoned men to spare suited him well. He had, as Conner had asked, forbidden Archie or Rebecca to take part. In fact, they wouldn't even be welcome at the Falmouth embarkation point. He didn't trust Rebecca not to jump on board a ship at the last minute, and he didn't trust Archie not to jump on after her.

Archie didn't like the training and planning. If he wasn't going, he felt that Thorson should be free to make his own decisions, that's what he would have wanted. The team were unhappy to be reserves, they wanted action at the sharp end; the fools. The sharp end of Operation Chariot had a secret pre-determined number for acceptable losses, it was a high number, and he didn't like it.

He didn't like how keen the SOE commandos were either. He felt they were naïve, maybe he was jealous of them, he could just see how many things could go wrong, badly wrong, even if it went well overall.

He had an argument with Rebecca and Una about Nipper, he didn't want him to go.

"He's still a child, I'm going to make him help Billy and Smudger," he'd said.

"No you're not, he has to go with his mates, without them he's nothing, he has to go," Rebecca said.

"If you love him you have to let him go," Una said.

"I don't know why I even started this argument, next time just tell me what to do, it'll save a lot of effort."

Asgeir was pleased that Archie was giving him so much operational leeway, it showed he trusted him. The men saw that confidence, and he needed to adjust to them being his responsibility.

Their task was easy, take a small gunboat from Falmouth to St. Nazaire, towed by a bigger ship, there would be plenty of naval and air support. His boat would provide covering fire when needed, as directed by the command gunboat. They'd also act as a rescue vessel if needed.

"It'll be when needed, not if," Archie warned him.

Asgeir was mainly concerned with the thinking on your feet bit, making quick decisions under fire and then being lucky. All the men who knew Archie were certain he wouldn't die, so the closer they stayed to him the better, but he wasn't coming this time. Asgeir just didn't know if that was a good omen or not. Archie probably wouldn't come again, the Brass judged him to be too important to risk. Asgeir didn't believe in God or Gods, he did believe in omens, though.

He asked Archie what he thought, he replied that he'd once believed he would die alone, without friends or lovers, in England. Archie still feared that fate and was planning to come back whatever happened. That was like Gestumblindi's ancient Norwegian riddles to Asgeir. Archie just assured him that he would die in Norway, definitely not France and probably in a burning longboat. Archie then told him that sometimes he talked complete bollocks, and it became true and sometimes he just talked complete bollocks, sometimes words just appeared from nowhere, like then. Archie was part Viking, Asgeir decided, now that was a good omen.

That conversation was nonsense of course, but it reassured him strangely, he told Briony Samms what Archie had said, and she'd been reassured too.

"He's a man who keeps his promises," she'd said.

He'd been seeing Briony for three months now. Briony was impossibly good looking, almost like Hedy Lamarr, an actress Asgeir had seen in a Clark Gable film. The most attractive quality Briony had, was that she didn't think she was beautiful. She had no airs and graces at all. Although they were already close, the war and their jobs made them keep a protective distance, somewhere between casual and serious.

Asgeir couldn't understand how Archie could court danger so casually, not just in war, how did he find two women as dangerous as Rebecca and Una and keep them both happy in different ways. It was crazy, he was a Berserker with two Shieldmaidens.

*

28th March 1942 – St. Nazaire

Operation Chariot began on the 28th March 1942. The RAF bombed the dry dock and other critical areas in St. Nazaire first, Rebecca had identified and pinpointed them. Then a modified obsolete destroyer, the Campbeltown, packed with explosives and flying a swastika flag, rammed into the main gates of the dry dock. On a delayed timer, it would explode later, closing the dock for the entire war.

Commando raiding parties landed from the Campbeltown and other small vessels. Boats launched torpedoes into the dock and at shipping. The gunboats engaged the German shore batteries, it was mayhem.

The raid would later be judged a great success, it achieved its aims.

Eighty-nine decorations including 5 Victoria Crosses were awarded, and a terrible price was paid.

Of the 622 men involved, only 228 returned to Britain immediately afterward, how many were dead or prisoners of war wouldn't be known until months later.

Asgeir had taken his reserve boat in close to provide fire from its three medium guns and to pick up survivors from sinking vessels. He had to do it, he picked up sixteen survivors who would have drowned or faced capture if lucky.

In doing so, the front gun of his boat took a hit which mangled Herschel Davids to pieces and blew most of him overboard. Ben Dempsey took shrapnel to his jugular and bled to death in Hospital's arms. Siggy Stubbs just disappeared overboard without a trace.

We lost three, and we saved sixteen, Asgeir repeated a hundred times silently on the journey home. It was bad, but if handled well, the bond between the survivors would be stronger, he knew that from experience.

Archie and Rebecca met the returning men at Falmouth, only then did they learn of their three deaths.

Three seemed so few in the context of hundreds missing and dead, but they were his men, three more jobs like that and he'd have no team left.

Archie hated it, he hated doing it. Nevertheless, he calmly shook every hand and told each man and boy that they'd done what they had to, and he was proud of them.

How old was he now? He thought about it and couldn't remember, was he twenty-two or twenty-three, how old was he supposed to be, when was his real birthday? He genuinely couldn't recall, old enough was all he could guess.

Asgeir watched him shake and grip the grimy, bloody hands firmly and slap the backs and could see the bond between them getting stronger, he'd remember that.

Brad wanted to inform Herschel's family, and Asgeir wanted to inform the family of Ben and Siggy. Archie said he had to do Ben Dempsey, he'd done it for Joe, it would have been the worst cowardice had he not.

At least there was a body, this time, he unzipped the bag, Ben was in, he needed to look.

"Sorry mate," was all he could think to say, he had no prayers left in him and no God to listen. "Sorry mate."

"Lucky you talked Una out of coming down with us Rebecca," he said as she held the crook of his arm just like she always did when he needed.

"She'll want to go with you to Ben's, you know," Rebecca said.

"And I'll have to let her, won't I?"

"Yes, you will. I'd like to come, but she'll need to do it without my help."

*

Sunday 5th April 1942 - Holloway

The following Sunday morning, nearly midday, after Mass, Una had said that was best, they went to Ben and Joe's mother and father's home.

It was the worst, dirtiest, lowest thing Archie had ever done in his life. He went there, to see two parents, whose two sons he'd killed. He'd stolen their eldest son's fiancée and taken her as his wife. Their presence together in uniform told them just that, or as near as made no difference.

All of that; and the Dempsey's were nice, they made cups of tea for them in their best china again. Mrs Dempsey hugged Una and Archie told them where and how it had happened; he wasn't supposed to, but the raid was in the papers. They deserved to know that their sons died taking huge risks and trying to save lives. He also told them that he hadn't been there, he'd sent Ben to France to die, and he'd stayed at home.

They stayed for a long hour, then drove away. Archie pulled the car to a sharp halt just around the next corner, got out and vomited on the pavement. Una brought him the water bottle he kept in the car and let him rinse his mouth out.

"Sorry, it's that Earl Grey tea, it's disgusting, but I had to drink it, that's all it is, honestly," he lied.

"I'll drive," she said, "and you'll eat one of the sandwiches I made last night, don't even fucking think about punishing or starving yourself, right."

"Right, your Irish accent's back, you know?"

"For the Dempsey's sake, I'll lose it now."

"You were brilliant in there. You always are, I love you so much."

She drove them away, a curtain at a nearby window twitched, and someone somewhere made a note of a car registration number, its occupants and the house they'd visited.

*

Friday 10th April 1942 - Holloway

Archie asked Nipper and Begley to go the funeral, which he paid for. He even arranged for smart dress uniforms for them, Joe and Ben's parents were as proud as they should have been for their two boys. There was no body in the coffin, just the correct weight. Ben's body was in a deep freezer in Hertford, with blood, blood plasma and tissue samples, one day, one day Archie hoped, someone, somewhere would give Ben another chance. Next to no chance in this lifetime perhaps, but as he'd discovered in the United States, there was always a small chance of virtually anything happening.

*

14th April 1942 – The Manor

In mid-April 1942, there was an early and unusually mild spring day. Archie sat in the garden at the Manor and unexpectedly felt the first real warmth of the sun so far that year. There were Tulips in the borders, white and lemon yellow bloomed first, then the dark blues and a deep red later. Archie had planted the bulbs in September, the blues and reds were 'Mistress of Dark' and there were three more rose bushes in Bletchley Park. For the first time, he'd made something live instead of die.

Conner was away on business relating to Heydrich and Heisenberg, working with SOE and the two Czechs Archie had spoken to last year. He'd not wanted them in the team, too willing to take on a suicide mission, he'd thought, too dangerous. They had the unmistakable scent of bad luck about them.

Nipper joined him in the garden, he'd expected somebody to, there was something in the air that morning.

"Boss, we need to talk, it's Joe and Ben's mum and dad, they're dead!"

"What? How? The funeral was only four days ago, they didn't-"

"There was a robbery at their house, and they was done in," Nipper blurted out.

"I was seen at Ben's funeral, there was loads of locals about, I got a call last night from a mate I keep in touch with, a thief obviously. The word is, the Dempsey's got money, compo for Ben and Joe and it was in the house. Everyone seen that fancy coffin you paid for and there was big money being spent on a stone, and it was supposed to be in the house in cash. There was a break in at night, and they was topped for the cash, floorboards ripped up an' everything. The dad was tied up and tortured to make the mum talk, is what the coppers say.

"The thing is, my mate, well look, he ain't a clean geezer by any means, but he swears there ain't a thief in London that low, but-"

"There is a copper though isn't there?" said Archie.

It was his fault, Archie knew it, he'd marked out the Dempsey's by his visit with Una, how could he have been so stupid. He stood up impulsively as if to do something immediately.

They couldn't prove anything with Packard, they couldn't touch him or any of his people where they were. They were sending him a message, a challenge, provoking him, trying to get him to make a mistake. It was ruthless, shocking and intentionally crude and he decided it wouldn't work. He sat down, calm and composed.

It was still his fault, he'd been far too cocky about Packard, he deserved it, he'd asked for it, the Dempsey's hadn't.

"Yes, Archie, there is a copper that bad, but I ain't saying nothin' else till you swear I can help this time. I mean it, Boss, I was seen, they know me, and they've killed my mate's family. Those bastards still think I'm nobody, I ain't, I'm somebody now."

"You certainly are, Freddie, you're my friend, and you can help this time. They were going to rape and kill Una and they still will if they can. I can barely hold myself back from grabbing a Thompson and driving down there right now."

"Oh no, Archie, we can do much better than that, I've been watching you long enough, and I've got the makings of a plan. And keep calling me Freddie, I ain't no nipper anymore."

*

April 1942 – Paris

By the end of April in Paris, Dolf Von Rundstedt was a happy man, he was the permanent head of Wehrmacht Security in Paris. Von Brander was dead, his assassin caught and executed as planned and perfectly timed.

Oskar had, however, killed the 500 hostages he'd wanted to and that was an unfortunate and inconvenient circumstance. Dolf just hadn't been able to stop him, Oskar was a man with many grudges against many people. Killing was his goal, not the opportunity to profit from it; the compensating consideration was that he was still stupid enough for Dolf to use.

Oskar's superior had been *'recalled'* to Berlin after his predictably inept response to the killing. Oskar was temporarily in charge, which gave Dolf freedom to acquire as much as possible of the wealth in Paris. Gold and jewellery were what he liked best, money had a transient value, after the war, gold was still gold. He'd learned that lesson from his father's mistakes after the first war. He stole art as well, of course, whose purpose was to act as gifts for others, to smooth over administrative difficulties, and ensure allegiances.

He knew this war was lost already, it would take time, eighteen months perhaps, he had to survive as well as possible, and wealth would help.

His current problem was that while Oskar was a valuable tool for him, he was proving to be a provocative slave master. He was causing more resistance incidents, rather than fewer and his tenure was displeasing Berlin. Dolf's contacts had warned him that Reinhard Heydrich could move from Prague to Paris. Heydrich was much more likely to make Dolf disappear than the other way round.

Chapter 14

27th May 1942 - Prague

On the 27th May 1942, Reinhard Heydrich shaved and washed, preparing for the drive from Prague to Berlin to meet Adolf Hitler. Hitler planned to give him a new important role, and a huge number of people would certainly die as a result of his involvement in whatever it was.

Conner sat with Gubbins in Bletchley Park and considered all relevant intelligence on Heydrich and possible permutations for what might follow. He had to decide instantly, his best guess, the least number of deaths, whose deaths, the greater good.

"Do it," he said to Gubbins, "It's too big a risk, if we can't touch the rockets, then we have to delay the bomb as long as possible. The target's London first whichever. I'll bear the guilt."

"Don't worry about the guilt, Conner," said Gubbins, his voice without a trace of reassurance, "there's always enough to go round."

On that same summer's day, Archie sat in the private room of Building Thirteen to ensure no distractions and worried about Conner. He was hiding something important, he couldn't even talk to Archie about, and they'd already shared the deadliest personal secrets. If Archie had changed and grown since Calais, then Conner had too, his trips lasted longer and troubled him more deeply on his return. He knew he was worried about the Prague job, that was just normal worry, this was deeper, subtle, melancholy, an unaccustomed mood. The cottage was home now, but he thought Conner had perhaps spent time at Hevlyn with Victoria. He'd traced her and phoned to check, and she hadn't seen him for months, no one else was closer to him. Conner didn't mind Una and Rebecca living at the cottage, they gave him more cheer than he could.

Una had turned Rebecca into a woman who styled her own hair, put on a little makeup and possessed female poise, she turned heads now, people, men, noticed her. He'd still kill anyone who tried to take advantage of her.

With Conner, it must be Alan, no one important would care if it was, but 1942 was the wrong time. Meanwhile, all he could do was be his best friend and wait for a different year.

*

That same day in Prague, Jan Kubis and Jozef Gabcik, two Czech nationals expertly trained by SOE led a team of brave men. Their task was to kill SS-Obergruppenfuhrer Reinhard Heydrich, the most cynically evil man in Europe, a favourite of Adolf Hitler and architect of the Final Solution to the *'Jewish Problem'*. They'd parachuted into occupied Czechoslovakia five months earlier and remained hidden since, waiting for orders to proceed.

They knew what they were doing and the price of it. Their lives were part of that price so they'd earned the right to make that judgement, take that risk, accept the consequences.

Conner found no such comfort for his decision from his place of safety in the rural English countryside. He couldn't take the risk that Heydrich would damage his work with Heisenberg, he thought rightly that was the biggest of risks.

They did kill Heydrich, he died of blood poisoning from wounds received during the attack, days later, on the 4th of June 1942. The full details of the monumental cock-up would become apparent long after the end of the war.

The Sten gun they'd tried to use to kill him had jammed and failed, the makeshift bomb they used wounded Heydrich and one of his attackers. The German Army massacred their entire team in a church later, following a betrayal by one of their own number. Two of the team took their own lives with their last bullets, rather than face capture. The Germans also killed at least thirteen hundred people in a series of astonishingly brutal reprisals. An entire village destroyed, all the adult males shot, all the women and children sent to concentration camps. All of them murdered, except a few children, deemed Aryan enough to be re-educated, who were adopted by members of the SS.

Most importantly, Heydrich was dead, Conner's conscience was not eased in the slightest.

*

Friday 12th June 1942 – The Manor

Conner approached Archie in the Manor garden, it was blissfully quiet with just a slight hint of apprehension. Conner knew Archie's outline plan for Una's continued safety and approved; he had a detailed schedule, and appropriate patience was in place.

"The Americans want you over there," Conner said.

"Why?"

"They won't say. Winters wants you, just you."

"When?"

"This week."

"Fuck off."

"I'll tell Churchill you said fuck off then?"

"What's it got to do with him?"

"You're going with him, on his plane."

"No, I'm not, I'm not leaving Una, I'm worried enough that she's in Bletchley today, those bastards want her, and I'm not leaving her. Yeah, tell them I'm not going unless she comes too."

"Oh for goodness sake Archie. There's a war on, people leave behind loved ones all the time, for years."

"No, I'm not going until Una's safe."

"Do I have to get Rebecca and Una to speak to you?"

"That's a low trick, you'll get them to gang up on me."

"If I have to."

"I don't care, I'm still not going, just tell the Americans I know what they want me for and she's an expert, tell Winters I said exactly that."

"What do they want then?"

"I haven't got a clue, I'll make something up when we

get there."

"Well, that is your usual modus operandi."

"See, you half believe me already."

*

Wednesday 17th June 1942 – Stranraer – Scotland

Shortly before midnight, acting Major Archie Travers and acting Lieutenant Una Travers sat aboard a Boeing Flying Boat, uncomfortably close to Winston Spencer Churchill as it took off from near Stranraer.

"I'm fuckin shittin' meself," Una said deliberately lapsing into her true Irish accent.

"Don't worry, we'll be fine, he's too busy, he'll ignore us," said Archie.

"Young man, young lady, if you please," Churchill shouted above the engine noise, beckoning them closer, in a tone that would clearly brook no argument.

"Bugger." said Archie through a genuine smile that showed gritted teeth then went towards Churchill with Una and sat down.

"Out with it then!" Churchill said.

"Sir?"

"What do the Americans want from you, of course?"

"Oh that, they swore me to secrecy because I pointed out there was a spy in their version of Tube Alloys, one of the scientists. You're about to formally approve sharing all our research and our scientists with them. They probably just want to me to reassure you that they're safe to share with. They also want to build it all in the States. They've started up a base in New Mexico, Los Alamos according to what they showed me already, they probably won't even admit that to you. You don't need to know."

"And?"

"You know we've got no choice, they've got a million miles of desert to hide it in, where are we going to put it? Chislehurst caves?"

"Well someone did suggest that, briefly!"

"I'll bet. I'll bet it was brief anyway. It's down to resources and safety, they've got more of everything. We should go through the motions of a bit of bluster, then flatter them by agreeing to let them do it. Then, when they're in a good mood, we ask them for something, like five hundred Sherman tanks for North Africa. You know we need to outnumber Rommel three to one, even if we are cracking his codes."

"Anything else, young man?"

"Not at the moment, sir."

"And this charming young Irish girl is?"

"His wife, Una, sir, but I'm English, born in Hertford," Una said.

"She's an all-round expert in many different fields, sir. In fact, whatever the Americans want; she's an expert in it," Archie added.

"Ah, I see it now, your previous work as an Irish Dress Shop Manageress was a deeply undercover disguise," said Churchill smiling.

"Exactly, sir, you see it exactly right," she smiled and fixed him with those dark-blue eyes, daring him to ask another question.

"I'm going to have to watch you two, I can see that; as long as you're on my side, I won't worry too much. In the meantime, I'm off to see the pilot, he's an old friend of mine."

Archie and Una returned to their original seats, they were large and comfortable, the flight would last over 24 hours.

"I think we got away with that," Una said.

"He's letting us get away with it. Now, hold my hand and go to sleep. I'll think about it."

*

Friday 19th June 1942 – Finsbury Park

Freddie Knowles sat in Katy's Café on Seven Sisters Road, Finsbury Park in North London, eating scrambled eggs on toast and a mug of tea. The food was disgusting, a scraping of cheap margarine barely moistened the burnt toast and only the salt he poured on the egg gave the meal any flavour. He loved it, he retained his inborn ability to eat anything that wasn't still alive.

Katy's greasy windows showed a cheerful bright summer's Friday morning in June 1942, and his ankle was giving him gyp. His plaster cast was tight and uncomfortable, try as he might he was rubbish on the crutches.

The man everyone called the Animal, rarely in his presence, though, entered the café boldly, sitting opposite him at his window table.

Freddie was trying to stop shaking, this was going to take real balls, but he remembered he was somebody now.

"Long time no see," the Animal said, "tea, Katy," he added arrogantly with the air of a man who never paid for his tea in Katy's. A typical copper's trick, although he was by no means a real copper.

"I've been busy. After I busted outta the Royal, I had to lay low. The war helped; I was well fuckin' sorted in the army, three square meals every day and a bed with only my cock in it, what more could a young boy want?"

"Different when they start shooting at you, I bet?"

"Fuckin right, France was a right pile of shit; you do that, you come back safe, and they chuck you in Colchester for not bein' dead."

"Yeah, I heard about that, thought about helping you, then thought, Nah! fuckim, he's nuthin' to me."

"I got out okay."

"That posh officer sorted you, the proper posh one, not the other cunt. He fucks you now, does he?"

"Nah, nuthin' like that, I'm just cannon fodder, have you any idea how many of my company's left now? Four, one's a Major, one's a Captain, one's a sergeant and what am I? Still a fucking Private, those other buggers don't even go on ops anymore. Listen, I made fuckin' sure I fell off that rope in training, there's another big job comin' up in August, don't know where, it'll be another suicide job. My luck's running out, so I'm looking to make some better luck for meself."

"Keep talking and keep your voice down, you little turd,

I shouldn't even be talking to the likes of you. You never could keep quiet could yah."

"Listen, you need something, and I can help you get it."

"What can you get me?"

"I can get you the girl you and your friends want and the other one too, on their own, in the cottage and the Manor empty."

"We can get that anytime we want."

"Bollocks. You've known where they are for weeks, you ain't got enough men to take on what they've got, or you'd have done it already. You ain't got enough bad men, bad enough for something this dodgy, have you? Of course, if you're not interested?" he said, rising to leave.

The Animal grabbed his wrist with his familiar strength, like a one-handed Chinese burn, pulling him roughly down into his seat.

"That could be true, we can only get six, maybe seven bad enough and up for it as you say."

"And you don't like the odds either, I know you of old. You like six or seven men onto two women, though. I can get you the exact place and time, they ain't comin' to that shop or Holloway again are they?"

"Okay, suppose I need your help, what do you want? Money?"

"Money? No… a lot of money, yes… and a girl is what I want."

*

Friday 19th June 1942 – Paris

In Paris, that same day, one young man, now an Oberstleutnant, a Lieutenant Colonel in British terms, Rodolf Von Rundstedt, the Head of Wehrmacht Security in Paris, sat in a highly regarded street café. A small, exquisite glass of red wine in his hand, two bodyguards and a fresh young French girl, soon to become his latest whore, sitting next to him. He was a happy, relieved man, he hadn't expected the extremely welcome news of Heydrich's death. Sometimes events just fell into place for Dolf, like Archie letting him go. Dolf's theft, personal aggrandisement, and whoring continued relentlessly. Dolf worked hard and long and played in a similar manner.

Life remained excellent, although he'd recently acquired a need for a foolproof way of avoiding culpability for the 500 French Citizens murdered by Oskar's men. The majority were Jews and Gypsies so held little lasting consequence; sufficient were French-born Gentiles to suggest that a trial in a French Court might happen post-war. He'd need a change of identity, Swiss perhaps, not easy, expensive, yet possible, yes, he'd set that in motion immediately and start building a history.

Two glasses of wine later he took his fresh companion to his apartment, she knew what awaited her and was apprehensive, but the wine had done its work on her and his desire.

She wasn't a full virgin, and her inexperience satisfied him, he stripped and pinned her down on the bed, taking her roughly. She appeared accustomed to roughness, and he enjoyed the pained look on her face and lines on her forehead. The tear in her eye just prompted him to turn her over and take her again. That was definitely a first for her, she squealed with pain, and he liked that. He'd forgotten her name already, but he paid her well, extra even, and he'd taken what he'd paid for.

*

Saturday 20th June 1942 – The United States

Winters had wanted Archie for the reason he'd suspected and couldn't trust the details to an encrypted message or any other pair of eyes or ears. Winters had identified several spies in fact, and he personally gave Archie the details of two connections in England as well. They were small fry, yet disturbingly well placed. Archie would speak to Conner and Gubbins about that, he didn't know who else to trust. Usually, he could intuitively see the machinations and connections clearly and instantly, something different was happening here; it was beyond his comprehension, and he didn't like not knowing.

On support for American handling of Tube Alloys

material, Archie put Winters out of his misery immediately. Of course, he positively wanted it done in the United States, it would be undertaken more effectively and sooner. Conner, Rebecca, and Alan had all confirmed that.

Archie also knew that they were sending Alan to the United States in connection with his work. He told Winters to keep him safe while he was there. He stressed that Alan wasn't a security risk, he was what he was and wasn't open to blackmail.

"In fact," Archie said, "I know at least twelve people who would kill anyone who even thought about calling him a name. And don't even think about trying to keep him in America, he's ours, and we need him."

"Think about this, then," Winters said, "don't answer now, think about it boy, you, your wife, Rebecca, Conner and any fifty people you name, transferred here, tomorrow for life, work for me. It's more money and a better pension, you retire when the war ends. I mean it, boy. Jesus do you feel safer here or not? Whaddya say?"

"You know I can't say yes. I can only say that I'll help you in any way I can. There are things to be done in England, and I have to do them personally, face to face, eye to eye, eye for an eye. There are debts that are owed to me, and I intend to collect them; personally."

"I can respect that, son, think about it anyway."

"I will, thank you, sir."

Archie and Una rose to leave, Archie saluted, as well and sincerely as he ever had. Una moved closer to Winters, took his right hand and put her left hand on the back of his neck, drew his face down to hers and kissed him on the cheek.

He blushed.

"Thank you for trying to save him," she said, "but that's my job."

'Bloody hell, she can do it too. I am in so much trouble.'

"Whatever your answer is," Winters said, "I hear you lost some men recently. I was going to say I had fifty men willing to join you, after that kiss, I've probably got five hundred ready to join you, let me know if you need any help."

"Thank you, sir, I will, we both will."

*

Before they flew back to England, mortally tired and coping with it as only young people can, Churchill summoned them by telegram to Hyde Park, the private residence of the President. There were drinks and a light buffet, talk and many names, high titles and ranks around the exclusive event hosted the President.

The telegram told Archie to make sure he spoke to a General called Eisenhower, he wasn't one Archie had heard of. He didn't know whether to ask someone who he was or try to spot him. The big fish, he thought he was, began to feel small again when a hand tapped him on the shoulder.

"Major Travers, I presume?"

"Yes General, Eisenhower?"

"Just call me Ike, we'll get to know each other well, tell me about Calais, please. How to get back there would be useful too."

"What do you want to know?"

"Well, when nearly everyone else was retreating, you were ordered to fight to the death. How does a man do that and survive?"

"Well, the orders didn't say whose death, I just made sure it was someone else's."

Ike laughed.

When Ike moved on after an hour, Una and Archie stayed together, slightly apart from the dignitaries. For privacy they went outside to a terrace and embraced, overwhelmed by the scale of events around them.

They hadn't made love since they'd arrived, they'd been too busy or too tired, yet they'd become even closer, even more than man and wife, more than lovers. Neither knew the words, neither tried that hard to find the words, the feelings themselves were enough.

"I want to stay here," she said, "I mean it, I've never felt safer, not just from the war, from other things, other dangers. Let's give everyone else a choice, to come here or stay where they are. We could have a family here, I know it, they'd be safe, it's paradise, I love it."

"Okay that's what we'll do then," he answered without the slightest hesitation and took her hands gently into his, kissing her forehead.

"We'll stay, we won't even go back now, we'll stay, I'll speak to Winters tonight."

Just at that second, they saw Churchill approaching them.

"Ah, the two lovebirds together, reminds me of when I was young, youth is wasted on the young, you don't know that yet. I've just come to say to you, that I know the Americans are making you a handsome offer. It is one you should not be afraid to take, do it, make a fresh start, live your lives, do it with my sincerest blessing. No, don't say a word, it's done," waving his cigar dismissively, he turned and left.

"Jesus, did you see him," Una said, shocked, "he looks so tired and so old, we only saw him a few days ago, he's aged ten years."

"He's about to have a heart attack if you ask me," Archie replied, "he has that look. I saw it in a man at work one day; he knows it too, he must have had one before. He won't die, it's not his time, not by a mile, he's pushing himself too hard, though."

"And we know someone who does that don't we?" Una said.

"Yes, we do."

"We have to go back, we can't stay can we?" she said softly, whispering, needing to say the words and half hoping he might not hear.

"No, we can't stay, if he can do it, we have to as well, we have to stay where he is."

"It was a nice dream."

"One day, we'll have the universe and all the time in it."

"Not today, though?"

"No, not today" he sighed.

The following morning, Churchill was up early as was his usual habit. Before breakfast, the President invited him into his private rooms. Roosevelt sat at his desk with a tape recorder.

"Apologies for the early start, there's something you need to hear," he said then switched the tape recorder on, and Churchill listened earnestly.

*

Tuesday 23rd June 1942 – The Manor

As soon as he was back at the Manor, Archie spoke to Brad Anderson. He asked him to talk to Winters team and get a couple of men from him, or anyone else he knew who was already in England.

"You choose," he said, "they don't have to be the best, they have to be the best for our team, you know what I mean, they have to fit in."

He had the same conversation with Asgeir Thorson, suggesting a couple of the commandos they'd rescued from the sea off St. Nazaire. Again he told him to make it his choice and feel trusted to do so, as Brad had been.

The truth was that Archie couldn't stomach choosing four more people to die. He'd seen how Conner had reacted to the Heydrich killing and wanted to avoid some of that extra guilt. He felt like a coward, but they were proud he'd asked them.

Brad chose Mickey Tully, a 22-year-old US Ranger of Scottish descent, who he knew and was already in England, although he had little experience, Brad trusted him. He was affable and normal if a little too enthusiastic.

Winters recommended three of his men who were flying over for security duty at their Embassy. Brad asked for the biggest, Gabriel "Gabe" Hunnicutt, he was six foot eight inches tall, even bigger than Smudger and wider too. Archie had worried what Smudger would turn his surname into, and when he saw the size of him, he'd felt sure he wouldn't dare; he did.

He was concerned that any dispute between them would register on the Richter scale, Gabe only laughed like a drain which still registered on the scale. Gabe was what Brad called a backwoodsman, who had killed his first Grizzly Bear aged five or some such nonsense and could survive for 3 months living off the land if he had to. Gabe was probably the most silent man Archie had ever met and rarely spoke unless he had something important to say.

Asgeir chose two New Zealanders who'd been with SOE, they were among those rescued from the water in France and felt a debt to the team. Asgeir told Archie he could use that debt, and he knew what he meant.

They were close friends, more than six foot and muscled with strange tattoos on their forearms, Ta Moko they called it.

Brayden Chester and Roebuck Castle; they'd been in Greece, Crete, North Africa then St. Nazaire and survived. They were pushing their luck, though, they were a pair of men who watched backs and took only carefully calculated risks. He liked all four of them, despite half hoping they'd be dull, uninteresting cannon fodder he wouldn't mind killing.

However and sadly, he liked them instantly, and would try his best to take a step back from caring about them and make that somebody else's job, Brad or Asgeir's.

Hospital's medical training was continuing fast, between any other duties he had. It would typically take a certain number of years to qualify as a doctor, in war everything was faster, less red tape, less fuss, do what works rather than what's usual.

In any event, the precise qualification didn't matter; whether he could save a life or fix an injury did.

The only other issue that Archie insisted on was *'Future Planning.'* Archie wanted blood and tissue samples taken from every team member, and he wanted any bodies frozen and preserved as well as possible. He knew there was no way to raise the dead, but he knew there would be. He knew that one day, scientists would be able to take cells from one human body and make another identical body, a foetus at least, that would grow into a body. It wouldn't have memories, it would have life, though, a life that hadn't been taken too soon by Archie.

Archie made Hospital take the samples from everyone and preserved them in a deep-freeze inside a bomb shelter in Hertford.

They had a chance, a slim one, and the best he could manage.

After discussions with Doc Ward, Archie paid for each team member to have a full medical and fitness check at the best facility in Harley Street. Each man was subject to checks that even Doc couldn't fathom, they were hypnotised at one stage, and their brain waves measured primitively. The team thought it was so daft that Archie volunteered to go first, then put his foot down. The Doctors would conduct the tests regularly, and Archie introduced a new diet regime for the men.

Archie also banned smoking, but when that caused a near mutiny, he stepped back and just banned it inside all the buildings.

"If any of these things make you one percent better, that one percent could save your life or mine, so just do it," he'd insisted. Archie was incrementally becoming the leader of the team, taking decisions that Conner would once have, and people accepted it, so he just carried on. He was changing again, he knew it, he just wasn't sure what he was changing into.

He felt an overwhelming sense of responsibility towards the team and could do nothing to change that, so he sought as much control as he possibly could, even over the smallest detail. He knew he'd kill some of them, but badly needed to be certain he'd done everything he could to save them.

Archie continued to keep a diary so his future self might read it and know who he was. That was quite mad, he thought, so he told Rebecca and Una about it. They'd have noticed anyway, and they told him he was definitely mad, then kept their own diaries. It would never work, never in a million years, but he needed to do his best.

Chapter 15

Friday 3rd July 1942 – The Manor

Archie was working late with Begley and Billy on new booby trap designs, Archie had no end of devious ideas they could make a reality. He'd done that for several days, and Una had Rebecca drop her at the Manor so she could make him a sandwich then make sure he ate it. She brought a huge pile of sandwiches to the workshop, she found homemade raspberry jam in the kitchen cupboard, so she made doorsteps for three.

"It's Friday evening, it's July, the sun's still shining, I'm giving you one more hour then I'm taking you home. You need some rest," she scolded him then went to sit in the garden and wait. She had no actual rest in mind for him.

She sat on the bench under the pergola remembering how she'd demanded he fuck her right there on their wedding night.

'Yes, we'll have more of that tonight, maybe in the car on the way home.'

Her train of thought, which was beginning to arouse her internally, was interrupted by Freddie Knowles hobbling awkwardly towards her, and he joined her nervously.

She was a thing of great beauty, and he worshipped the ground she walked on. In a different life, he might have stood a remote chance.

"Hello, Miss," he said.

"Yes, Freddie, and please call me Una."

"Okay… Una, I was wondering, well thinking, I tried for ages to get the lads to stop calling me Nipper, and they just kept on doing it. The more I complained, the more they did it, so I just gave up, then suddenly they started calling me Freddie just like I wanted. Did you…?"

"I told them to do it, I told them you were a man and deserved a man's name."

"You did that, for me?"

"Of course, Rebecca and I were talking, and we've decided you need to shave that fluffy moustache off. If you shave properly every day for a month, it'll grow back thicker. I'll do something with your hair as well, Monday after work if you want, come to the cottage, yes, we'll do it then. It'll be our little secret, don't worry."

Maybe, just maybe, one day, with some help from the right people, Freddie thought.

*

The following Sunday morning it was still bright and clear. Archie had sought out Alan and arranged to go for an early morning run. Archie was getting just a little closer to Alan's full pace which pleased him. It wasn't his distance or natural style, so he'd set a target of getting closer each time they ran.

When they'd finished, they sat on the wooden bench that he'd placed near the rose bushes outside Building Thirteen and talked. Some innocent questioning about Conner produced no clues about his behaviour. Only a liar of Archie's talent could have seen that Alan was subtly evading the question, and he chose not to set his usual traps. Archie just asked him if he'd mind giving him some tissue samples and explained why.

"Yes, of course," Alan said, "it's a logical extension of my paper on the thinking machine. If you build two thinking machines, they can communicate. Then you build a machine that talks to a brain which is just a very complicated machine. You could take the information from an old brain, store that information in a machine then transfer it to a new brain in a new body. It's possible you could also fill a human brain with entirely new information."

"Absolutely," said Archie, "so how soon can you build this machine?"

"That's the tricky part; it would be the size of England, but I do like your thinking." Alan paused for a few seconds then said, almost to himself, "Morphogenesis, yes, I must think about that, later, when I have time."

*

There was one machine they could build; SOE had given Archie the small gunboat they'd used for St. Nazaire. They renamed it *'The Serpent'* although Asgeir had the words *'Orm Hinn Langi'* in Old Norse painted alongside the English name.

Rebecca painted two perfect copies of ancient Viking style dragon heads on the bowsprit and matching tails on the stern. She discovered, surprisingly, that her artistic ability extended to painting. No longer just a boat, it was their boat, another part of their home, it was a lucky boat. They'd use it for their part in the raid on Dieppe, Operation Jubilee, due to take place in the August of 1942.

The Serpent only had two medium guns now, one amidships, one astern. Asgeir decided that replacing the shattered front gun with another was a bad omen and wanted to install torpedo capability instead. He understood torpedoes and wanted the flexibility they would give his armament.

Begley and Asgeir argued about it, Begley wanted a new medium gun, probably because he knew he'd get to fire it, but not the torpedoes.

Archie went to sit in the Manor garden and just waited for them to come and see him. It didn't take long, they came together which was a positive sign, and Archie knew he'd go with what the boat Captain wanted. Begley, however, was an *'original'* and Archie needed to respect his status.

He let them talk, a discussion not an argument.

"Those Lewis Guns, Billy lifted last week, how many were there?" Archie asked.

"Six," Begley answered.

"Could you fit all six of them into a bracket that would fire them all simultaneously? Three banks of two, like spots on a dice?"

"Easy."

"Could you make the bracket small?"

"Easy."

"Because we do need the torpedoes as Asgeir said."

"Right."

"If you made your bracket small enough it'd fit between the torpedo tubes and one man, you obviously, could fire it?"

"I'll start now," said Begley and ran off.

"Thanks, Boss," he shouted over his shoulder.

"Thanks, Archie," Asgeir added smiling.

Begley and Billy fitted both, leaving room for only four torpedoes, but still capable of delivering serious head on damage against a bigger opponent. The deck mounting for the medium cannon held the six Lewis Guns foraged from the RAF inside Begley's contraption.

"They was in a wreck, and nobody wanted them," Billy had already explained, the new boxes of ammunition were less legitimately explained. Begley had made a small, sturdy bracket that held the deck firmly and fired all six at once. Begley insisted on tracer ammunition and by pure coincidence that was what Billy had found.

"The serpent shall be the smallest, but she doth have breath of fire and mortal poison in her bite," said Rebecca when Archie showed her the finished article.

He looked at her and asked who'd said that. She didn't seem to hear him, so he just kissed her on the forehead.

"Thank you, sorry I was miles away, what did you say?"

"It's not important."

Archie had planned his section of Operation Jubilee down to the last detail. His instrument of thought matched the risks against potential gains, even if no one else was doing it. He needed to keep it straightforward, the main plan had too many components and logistic complications that could go wrong. He offered his team to scout the main landing beach secretly beforehand, to see what the footing was, but the senior planners refused his request judging it might alert the Germans of allied interest.

A swift smash-and-grab was viable, too many smashes and too many grabs were hard work and needed too much luck. Be on the ground for an hour maximum then run, anything else was madness unless you planned to stay, in significant force and permanently.

He'd suggested several self-contained diversionary attacks to accompany the main deployment, his team would conduct one to the west of Dieppe. A radar station sat on a clifftop near St. Aubin-Sur-Mer above a small traversable sandy beach nearby. Land by dinghy after midnight, cut through the barb wire beach defences, up the slope to the station and destroy whatever was there. They'd leave several of Begley's best surprises for the Germans, timed to go off at 0400. Just enough time to perhaps make some troops go there to investigate, leaving fewer in Dieppe for the main force to deal with.

Worst case scenario, Germans dead and a radar station out of commission, there might be Enigma equipment there, he'd done that before, and he easily balanced the risks in his head. A few skilled men working quietly and efficiently, that formula presented no problems at all for Archie.

Nevertheless, he made his team practice the stages of their task repeatedly, and more than they felt necessary, but he did it anyway.

The overall Operation in Dieppe was big, far too big for Archie. At 0500, 6,000 men were to land, seize and hold the port for a short period and gather intelligence. Archie had bitten his tongue during the briefings on the objectives and initially he'd been pleased that he was capable of that. That seemed to be the collaborative behaviour that was expected of an officer. It was, and it was wrong; dead wrong.

The raid would have to be extraordinarily lucky to seize a fully defended channel port, let alone keep it for any length of time. Planning to seize one of the new 4 rotor Enigma machines while there, was a preposterous risk. He'd captured two of the previous type with a dozen men and a subtle, if personally costly, plan on the Krebs, how the hell they were going be subtle with 6,000 men he couldn't conceive.

It sounded to him as if someone had a bad idea, someone else noticed and decided to throw in a couple more that wouldn't work either. He thought the real reason was a crude experiment in preparation for a cross-channel invasion that would come sometime but was at least two years away. He also felt deeply that it was a sacrifice in men designed to illustrate to Stalin how difficult it was for Britain to take on the Germans by invading France.

So what if Stalin was engaged in a vast, deadly and costly fight with Germany, tough luck. He was a bully and a coward who'd killed more of his own people than Hitler ever would, let them fight it out. What have the Russians ever done for us? Nothing, that's what Archie thought, and Dieppe was just St. Nazaire with bells on. Deid bells.

He also knew Fleming was involved, and that irritated him intensely.

Smudger had nicknamed him.

"Labia."

"Is that because he's such a ladies man?" Archie asked.

"No, it's cos he's a bit of a cunt!"

"The word is he's writing a book about the war, spies and undercover work. What sort of wanker would write about war when they'd never even been shot at? Perhaps I should take a pot shot at him now and again just to let him know?"

Archie's team had the easiest target, though, the furthest from Dieppe. Another radar station nearer Dieppe and a six gun shore battery to the west were targets. Lovat's Commandos would undertake the raid on the shore battery, a quick manageable smash-and-grab, they'd be in and out by 0730.

Lovat was Simon Christopher Joseph Fraser, the 15th Lord Lovat, and 4th Baron Lovat. Archie had seen him once with Gubbins and knew he'd been part of the Lofoten raid. He was a Lieutenant Colonel, was going in alongside his men and intended to get them all out. That was Archie's kind of plan and his kind of Colonel. Churchill had supposedly said he was the finest gentlemen ever to slit a German throat; that was a role model Archie could aspire to.

*

Tuesday 7th July 1942 – France - The French / Swiss border

Dolf drove to Switzerland through bright July sunshine in his unmarked car, wearing civilian clothing. The car sat low on its tyres at the rear which was suspicious, but his Wehrmacht Identity Card and status ensured there were no problems while driving in France.

On reaching Switzerland he tested his new and genuinely issued, albeit bogus Swiss passport. The passport and the enclosed small envelope containing Swiss Francs ensured there were no issues at the Swiss border. If challenged about the envelope, it was some of his spending money that he'd unintentionally left with his other documents. Neither the German nor Swiss Border Control challenged him, of course, or the French passport of his girlfriend.

No one cared to examine the car or the luggage, heavy as it was, containing the spoils of war. Twenty gold bars and nearly a kilo of diamonds, mostly stolen, melted down then recast and some obtained from his unofficial fine art dealership.

Dolf could barely believe what people would pay for a piece of canvas and oil. He took his prices in gold and diamonds only, nothing traceable and all of it as good as hard currency wherever he lived or whoever he became, once Germany had lost the war.

Dolf's companion was still the same whore he'd purchased at the street café months earlier.

Unsurprisingly her name was not 'Amoreuse', her real name was Annette Abelard, a farmer's daughter.

He was certain she had Jewish blood, it was distant and not obvious from her appearance, he never asked her that question, though. He never asked questions of his whores, they would only tell lies, and he had no interest in the answers anyway.

Until Annette that was, he was surprised that she spoke German as well as French. He'd only asked her name, her real name. She'd hesitated as if trying to remember it, and he recalled the smell of a dusty brick pillbox in Calais. When she didn't answer, he asked her again, quietly and gently, then waited for the answer.

Her story was that one day she returned from her work in a shop in the town of Darois near Dijon to the family farm to find her parents and two brothers gone. A French family was moving in. They told her they bought the farm, her parents were gone then escorted her brusquely off their land.

She returned to the town where her employer, Mr Ronchamp, a Butcher, knew her family well. He took her in for two nights keeping her safe and well until he passed her on to a Policeman, who took her to Paris 'for her own safety'.

She'd worked out now that Ronchamp had sold her to the Policeman, who raped her that first night. He made it clear that she was his property. If she wanted to live, this was her life. After a week of continuing rape, he sold her to a café owner where she was to be a waitress... and more for the owner. He raped her many times, as did his son and decided to rent her out to his German clientele, who paid well. She never knew the Policeman's name, although she was sharp enough to remember his badge number and approximately where he lived in Paris.

The fact that he was her first paying customer and the previous rapes disturbed Dolf in an unfamiliar way. She told him the threats the café owner had made against her if she didn't behave as he told her to. Dolf had never thought about where whores came from or where they went when they left him. Dolf didn't wish to be last in a queue of rapists. There were enough talented natural whores in Paris, there was no need to be raping virgins, it wasn't necessary.

Annette also told him, although she looked much older,

she was only 15, which he didn't like at all. He knew he didn't have much of his soul left, but what little there was, still bound him to a few basic rules that only occurred to him from time to time. Like when he hadn't shot Archie or his friends, that act still nagged at him, and he also found comfort in it. That short meeting had been meant to happen.

He went back to Annette's café the day after he first met her, with some of Oskar's finest worst men. The father, son, wife and two daughters were arrested and taken to SS Headquarters at 84 Avenue Foch. He allowed Oskar's men to loot the café, including the wine cellar before burning it to the ground. He allowed the two neighbouring properties to burn before letting the French civilian fire brigade intervene.

Dolf followed the prisoners to Oskar's headquarters and placed them in the largest cell available. He chained the father and son to a wall, watching while a queue of guards and soldiers raped and buggered the mother and two daughters repeatedly. The females all had pretty faces, and Dolf ordered the guards not to beat them. One of the daughters was twelve, but her father should have thought of that sooner, this was his fault, his responsibility. In war, or life, you had to be prepared to take responsibility for your actions, you had to face the consequences of your actions. Had the café owner taken in the girl and treated her in a reasonable way would his daughter's arsehole be ripped to shreds? No, of course not. It was her father's fault, his alone, not Dolf's and not even the sick perverted monsters Dolf allowed to do it.

Dolf watched that Goyesce scene from Hell while sitting in a chair and although parts of the rape did arouse him somewhat, he chose not to join in. When, after an hour, he decided that enough was enough, he stopped it.

He waited for his soldiers to leave then walked casually over to the two men and told them what else was going to happen to the females. He ordered the three females to look at their men, and when they did, he shot both men in the head.

He sent the females specifically to the Buchenwald Concentration Camp where Dolf ensured that Gottlieb and Gerolf would be waiting for them. The mother and two daughters would endure an appallingly slow and tortuous death, they must have known about the rape, and if they didn't, they should have.

Dolf knew so little about mercy, Archie and nothing else in fact; but he knew a great deal about vengeance. Later, when he had time to reflect properly, he recognised that it was the vengeance that had given him the erection, not the rape. That intrigued him, he hadn't known that.

Annette sat in the passenger seat of his car, he'd treated her well and not raped her since that first night. He hadn't laid a finger on her, letting her sleep in his spare room, giving her expensive new clothes and excellent food.

He still scared Annette though, he told her, word for word, deed by deed, what he'd done to the café owner and his family. She was pleased by that and said he could do whatever he wanted to her. She was working out for herself how to survive. He'd chosen not to touch her. In a way, she'd wanted him to, she was young and naïve, unsophisticated in the darker side of life. She still knew that no one in France in 1942 could protect her better than Dolf.

Dolf told her he wouldn't touch her again until she was sixteen and it would be her birthday while they were in Switzerland. She felt a need to please him, although she didn't know how, other than letting him do whatever he wanted. She reluctantly resolved to do that, no matter how much it hurt or degraded her. She'd worked out what had happened to her parents and why, if they were lucky they were dead. Who could say what they'd do for one more minute of life, she felt she'd find out soon.

That evening, Dolf was feeling particularly pleased, he'd safely stored the gold and diamonds in a secret location. He was a wealthy man, he just had to ensure that he survived the war at exactly the right time to enjoy the fruits of his labours.

He couldn't fully explain why he hadn't touched the French whore since that first night, he wanted to. She was the perfect shape, tall, and slim, a muscled farm girl with firm breasts that didn't sag at all and the look of her face never tired him. Deep brown eyes and fairish hair, small, perfect lips, and a smile that she didn't show often enough.

Most whores lasted one night, two or three at most, one about six nights, then he grew bored of their ordinariness. The flaws in their faces or bodies soon became apparent to him, always too soon, sometimes one would arrive, and he'd just close the door and tell them to go away. Sometimes seeing a whore meant paying to fuck someone you wouldn't fuck for nothing. All whores had flaws, thin hair, a mole in the wrong place, bad skin or maybe they just smelt or tasted wrong, there was always something. Annette was different, it would probably fade after he'd had her a few times. It would be good while it lasted and he needed something different, something that wasn't, ordinary.

He took her to one of the best hotels in Zurich and stayed in the best suite, dressed her in the best clothes and didn't care who was looking. He treated her like a princess, yet still felt a great underlying need to fuck her again.

Her birthday dinner was special, a small amount of the best wine, the best food, then a small present, diamond earrings.

Annette couldn't fathom why he was treating her so well, all she could think was how roughly he'd use her later, and that she'd let him do it.

She was silently nervous on returning to their room, she felt she might throw up, and fought against the urge. If she displeased him in any way, she was dead, or worse. She forced a smile and spoke to him, telling him how good the meal was, how kind he was.

Once in the room he sat on the sofa and asked if she wanted more wine. She just took her clothes off and stood naked in front of him and told him he could do whatever he wanted to her, then lay on the bed ready for him.

She watched him undress, the urgency of his erection readily seen, scared her.

Dolf poured two glasses of white wine and placed a glass on each of the small tables on either side of the bed. He then poured two glasses of chilled bottled water and placed one on each table.

Oh just get it over with, she thought fearfully, at least he was handsome and clean.

Dolf approached the bed, climbing on next to her, she lay on her back ready for him.

"Turn over," he told her.

Annette turned over immediately and opened her legs, her face turned away from Dolf.

He carefully moved her hair from around her neck with his fingertips, stroking her gently just below the hairline and then kissing and licking her neck and ears.

At the same time, he stroked her back, first using one hand, then after finishing with her neck, using both.

He continued to stroke her body, moving gently down to her bottom, legs and feet then back up to her neck. He repeated this more times than she could count, each time moving a little closer to her anus and vagina until eventually she opened her legs wider and raised her bottom towards his hand.

He still made one more journey around her body and then stopped near her labia. Only just tickling the dry external parts before flicking his fingertips slowly up and down and around the hood of her still concealed clitoris.

Annette gasped at that touch and raised her vagina towards his hand even more. This time, Dolf put his middle finger into her, feeling the moisture he'd aroused from her. He then used that same moisture to stroke inside the hood and directly onto her clitoris. She gasped again and shivered from the pleasure he was giving her. She'd done this before, to herself, but another hand doing it was a hundred times better.

Dolf continued the stroking, each time her clitoris

became a little less moist, he recharged his finger with her juices. He kept doing that until she came and he pushed two fingers inside her, giving her orgasm something to grip onto and increasing its intensity.

Annette turned over and faced him, flushed around her face and neck with the pleasure of it, half forcing a smile; she knew what was coming next.

"You can do anything you want to me," she said.

He moved her towards the edge of the bed, placing her legs back, almost to her ears, causing her bottom to raise off the bed and giving him complete access to both her openings.

"Keep your legs back," he told her before using his tongue on her holes until she came again, shuddering. While she was still coming he entered her vagina with his penis, not huge, but hugely experienced. His thrusts were slow and gentle as he balanced on his hands above her.

She reached up and touched the back of his neck, stroking it, then grabbed it and pulled his face down towards hers, kissing him deeply, and they made love.

All night.

The following morning, he took her for breakfast on the open terrace which was already warm from the summer sunshine on the Alps around them.

"You can leave if you wish," he told her.

"I'll get you a Swiss passport and give you money to keep you while you find somewhere to live and work. In fact, I'll give you enough so you don't have to work."

Annette couldn't say anything. She didn't know if this was a test or not, she didn't know if he'd raped her again last night or not. Was he just paying her in another way? Given a choice she would turn time around and go back to her parents and farm, there was no such choice.

Dolf, wanted to set her free, he knew he'd raped her that first night and had intended to last night, he just wasn't sure if he had. He knew if she'd resisted, he would probably have done it anyway, but she hadn't and what choice did she have anyway? Would he have?

After he'd found out her history, he'd wanted to free her from her slave masters and punish them, that had been easy enough. When he realised that he also needed to free her from Dolf Von Rundstedt, it became an unfamiliar and much more complex issue.

He would set her free as the penance for his sin, he didn't want to set her free, he wanted to keep her, and that would make the penance more fitting.

"I'll stay with you," she answered breaking the silence that had lasted for a full five minutes.

Dolf returned to Paris with Annette two days later. He asked her to stay in his apartment and continued his policy of placing a pair of trusted guards to take turns on the door. He wasn't keeping her in, this time, he was keeping her safe.

Several matters demanded his attention on his return to work, but he spent the morning on some newly found priorities. A Parisian Policeman was arrested and shot for rape and corruption. Mr Ronchamp, a butcher from the town of Darois, would be arrested and shot for aiding an escaping Jewess. A French Family would be evicted from their new house and farm then deported to Buchenwald.

Only after setting those plans into motion did Dolf finally recognise what had happened and why.

By agreeing to stay beside him, Annette became only the second person who'd ever given him anything they didn't have to, or which he wasn't going to take anyway. Archie Travers had been the first.

Chapter 16

Tuesday 7th July 1942 – The Manor - Bletchley

In early July 1942, Archie had a stronger, higher, wire perimeter fence put in place around the Manor. In the summer, children took advantage of longer, warmer days to explore the countryside and the Manor became a magnet. It was clearly some secret and interesting army base, which was partly true, it was certainly no secret, just like half the world appeared to know they existed when they weren't supposed to.

There was nearly a fatal accident when two adventurous ten-year-olds and two even younger children decided to collect spent bullets lodged in a target fixed to a tree. It was Una who'd seen them, screamed and stopped Freddie from firing. Archie had only seen the follow-up and didn't get too close, he just didn't like children. He hadn't liked the child he'd been for goodness sake, and seeing the two young ones, aged about five or six, reminded him of the ones they'd rescued from Kensington.

He saw something in Freddie's face he didn't like, memories of a sister probably, and he saw something in Una's eyes that scared him a little, hope for their own children, definitely.

'Not yet please, I can barely look after myself, how am I going to look after a child?'

Seeing the children made him impatient, though. He knew he couldn't wait until the end of August to make his next move towards finding out what had happened to Freddie's sister. Archie expected to find her dead, or worse than dead, he felt that in his bones, deeply, painfully and pessimistically. Vengeance might suffice; it had done in the past, and he still had to avoid direct action against Tennent, he needed to time that precisely.

As he mulled over possible courses of action, he tried to work out in his head, how many people he'd killed and why. He tried dividing them into Germans, civilians, friends and enemies, he just lost count of numbers, never mind types and motives. The details were all in his diaries. He considered writing a list, in a ledger with dates and reasons. Then he thought of Caesar, Caesar hadn't counted, he'd written books and hadn't kept count. Did Guderian and Von Rundstedt count? Did Churchill? Would Patton?

A box opened, and he thought of how many human beings died every single day, how many, countless, stars were in the sky, how small and insignificant he was, and he became calm.

This was war, and while some of it went undeclared, he could afford no time for pity, self or otherwise.

His mind went to a name on his list, a man who favoured young girls, he had links to the Royal Holloway Children's Home and was a suitable next target. George Copeland lived in Oxford, was a Professor of Physics at Jesus College and a well-connected Freemason. Sources named him as someone who'd visited the home and specifically sought out a young girl of the same age as Alice. He was in the right place at the right time and remained the closest real connection they had to Alice.

He and Billy had watched him earlier in the year, to scout the area, his work, his home, and habits.

He had a wife and three children, he went to work and stayed at home. He travelled to and from work with a colleague every day, the colleague lived on the same street, he never stayed late, and he never arrived early. If he'd ever had any bad habits, he no longer had them. He'd lived an apparently exemplary life, but Archie had seen that false appearance many times.

He decided to speak to Rebecca about him and after careful thought asked Una to sit in.

"Well it's funny you should mention him," Rebecca said. "We've done some research. He's a dreadful flirt with the girls, only in private, though, he's careful."

"We thought he'd be an easy target for a pretty young girl who could lure him somewhere quiet," Una added.

"Una, I'm not letting you do that!"

"She's not doing it, I am," Rebecca interrupted.

"What do *you* know about luring a man?"

"Well I know more than you realise for a start, Una's been teaching me."

He opened his mouth to argue, but no words came out.

"There's no point in arguing, Archie," Una said.

"Thought not," was his resigned reply and he decided to act now, before Dieppe and before Tennent.

*

Thursday 9th July 1942 – Oxford

Rebecca had visited various Oxford Colleges, including her own St. Hilda's, several times that year. Each time looking at potential recruits for SOE or Bletchley Park when they'd completed their war-shortened two-year courses. She'd found some excellent minds for Bletchley Park, none for special ops, though. Like Archie, she didn't have the stomach to select someone to acquire a six-week life expectancy. She couldn't think now, why she'd done it herself, that was another person, another world.

Rebecca had heard of but never met Professor Copeland until she visited that year and she easily found out that he had a reputation as a pest. He persistently and unsuccessfully courted the company of young female students. He would stand uncomfortably close to a girl with tit staring, bum watching and crudely attempted humour. He was a dirty old man, the subject of ridicule, devoid of success and no girl ever went to see him alone anyway.

Until Rebecca did, discreetly in his private tutorial room. She'd fluttered an eyelash at him and made eye contact, enough to encourage him. He was inveterately sleazy and leering, he disgusted her in a way she couldn't have conceived of during her previous studies at Oxford. The slightest encouragement drew the stupid old goat into a frenzy of groping and slavering, Gottlieb possessed more subtlety. She easily put him off and moved him towards a strictly clandestine encounter that evening, to a place of Rebecca's choosing and with an outcome to match.

That night, Copeland drove on his own, without telling a single soul, to the small unoccupied cottage Rebecca described to him, ten miles from Oxford. He'd told no one where he was going, a late meeting in London he told his wife, top secret he'd said. His skewed perspective was that a sexual revolution was taking place in the forties, a revolution denied to his youth. He was therefore entitled to abuse his position to his own advantage; what use privilege if not to be abused. That he was dull, plain and without charm, played no part in his thoughts. He was a misogynist who would, in due course, believe a girl in a short skirt was asking to be propositioned or worse. He was nervous and excited, he couldn't believe his luck. The precise nature of that luck was what he wasn't expecting; bad, very bad.

He saw the car, parked outside the isolated cottage and drew his car in next to it. Rebecca opened the door and let him in. He entered the cottage and saw Archie and Una; Rebecca closed the door firmly behind him.

He sat, timidly in a chair, terrified of what he'd been drawn into, blackmail he thought.

Archie asked the questions, calmly and precisely, he was Conner again.

Copeland denied everything, denied any knowledge at all, he'd never even been to Holloway.

He was an accomplished liar, Archie thought, excellent in fact, so he gave him a hard slap to encourage him to take it all more seriously.

Copeland started crying, whimpering even. Something wasn't right, this wasn't their man, they had his name, his age, his position, his address, a description of his car.

Archie calmly put all this to Copeland and asked him to account for it.

"It must be Niven," Copeland said, "I bought the car from him last year, the bastard used my name."

"Tell me about Niven then," said Archie, Niven was the man Copeland shared his car journeys with and lived in the same street as him.

"Niven has sympathies in that way. He's written academic papers on the age of consent and the like, advocating the right of the child to consent. We all knew what his fantasies were and suspected that he must have indulged them at some point. In fact, he told me he had, some years ago, he described it to me, yes he'd been on a trip to London, which home did you say?"

"The Royal Holloway?"

"Yes, that's it, he went there to meet with others to discuss lobbying the Government, he said. Don't you see, it was him not me, it's him you want."

"And?" said Una.

"And what?"

"And what did you do about it?"

"What?"

"You were aware of a crime, the rape of a child, what did you do about it?"

"What life would these children have anyway, they get fed and clothed, they get… "

"Fucked, just like you, fucked," Rebecca finished the sentence for him and, angry, she smashed her gun into the side of his face. His bloody face slumped unconscious to his chest.

"What a cock up, that's my fault, I could have double checked that car," Archie said.

"The fault is his," Rebecca said.

"Leave the crime of the guilty unpunished rather than condemn the innocent. Marcus Tullius Cicero," he said in reply.

"What one has, one ought to use: and whatever he does he should do with all his might. Also Cicero," said Rebecca.

"All that is necessary for the forces of evil to triumph is for enough good men to remain silent. Some Irishman they told us about in school. Burke I think," Una said placing her arm around Rebecca and squeezing her shoulder supportively.

"I'm not arguing," Archie said, holding his hands up in surrender.

Rebecca fitted the silencer to her Luger and shot Professor Copeland in the heart.

"What do we do now?" she said.

"Get Niven tonight, he lives on his own," Archie answered.

*

It was late the next morning when they finally returned to their cottage. They were hungry, although it was just normal hunger.

Archie asked Una and Rebecca what they should do with the knowledge they now had.

"Do we tell Freddie?"

"No, it's false hope, telling him she might be alive and being raped on a daily basis isn't going to help the kid," Una said. Rebecca nodded her agreement, "and don't tell him I said he was a kid, I told him he was a man, he's grown up early, but he's still just a boy."

"I'll get Billy onto the name we got," said Archie, "at least we know exactly what the Animal is now."

The three killers then sat drinking tea and eating toast before they went to bed to catch up on the sleep denied them the previous night.

*

The night was successful, they had better information, they achieved a measure of vengeance, and although they'd killed another bystander, he wasn't an innocent one. Good men should not remain silent.

Niven admitted raping the girl and swore it was the only time he'd fulfilled his fantasy. He tried to explain that they'd sedated the girl to make her compliant, he genuinely believed he could make her enjoy it if he was careful with her.

A man called Michael Hunt had been his contact, he'd met him in London through his interests. Hunt provided him with erotic literature and photographs to suit his tastes, then offered to make some to order for him. Finally, after gaining his full trust, Hunt arranged a meeting to fulfil Niven's fantasy.

Niven always used Copeland's name in London for his membership of the less salubrious premises he frequented.

Niven kept the evidence in his house, trophies, photographs including one of the girl child he'd raped. Archie couldn't look at them; Rebecca told him the girl did look like she could be related to Freddie. Una said they could never show Freddie the picture, not even the face.

Hunt was in charge, brazenly boasting that the girl was his property, and took the money personally in cash.

Niven told him about another younger, skinny chap, they called the trainer or the Animal trainer, he *'broke'* the girls.

When he'd finished his pathetic sordid tale, he tried to explain away what he'd done, his audience didn't listen.

"You fucked her and left her there?" Una said.

"What else could I do, I was nice to her, I gave her money and a present, what else could I do?" he answered, pleading with her.

"This!" she said and put Rebecca's gun into his mouth as far as it would go and blew the back of his head off. She turned to Archie and Rebecca.

"We're all in this together now... until we find her, right?"

"Right," they said.

*

That's what happened, the bodies and car were gone, beyond any chance of discovery. The cottage they'd used was destroyed in a catastrophic fire. Una and Rebecca had killed helpless old men in cold blood in front of Archie and knew they'd done it for him. They did it so he wouldn't have to. So he wouldn't feel he had to do it all. So he'd know they were his, they belonged to him and him to them. They wanted to share everything with him, even his guilt.

There was already a bond of love between the three killers, now there was a bond of hatred, neither bond would ever break.

The night was over, in its box, three boxes actually and

they returned to another war.

*

Sunday 12th July 1942 – The Manor

Archie spoke to Billy privately in the garden of the Manor a couple of days later, telling him about Copeland and Niven and asked him if he could find out about Hunt.

Billy just laughed.

"You've been sold a dummy there, son, Michael Hunt's a made up name, like Isaac or Warwick."

"What?"

"Mike Hunt, my cunt, gettit?"

"Damn it, I've been down south long enough, I should have seen that, it's a bit late to ask again, we've got a description, though."

"Which is?"

"Well, he's only got one leg for a start."

"Fair hair, bald on top, hair combed over, pencil moustache, small glasses, average height, and average build, apart from the leg of course."

"You know him?"

"Knew of him, he's fucking dead now."

"Bollocks."

"It gets worse Archie, much worse."

"This was five year ago now," Billy continued, "Michael Crompton, he used to come in the Savoy and other top hotels I heard. He mixed with show business types and BBC people. He was arranging company for people who needed it, no harm in that, mostly ladies, a few gents too, professionals, always well-behaved and discreet.

"Then one trick went wrong, a client was stabbed to death in The Ritz would you believe. Sliced apart like the Ripper I heard, disembowelled by the lad he was with. Crompton was immediately persona non grata in any reputable place.

"Hushed up, of course, the lad who done it was just plain mental, off his head, just some crackpate. There was no trial, no publicity, detained at His Majesty's pleasure in some loony bin.

"Crompton worked the lower end of the market after that. He didn't last, he was on someone else's manor, didn't know the rules, so he got done in.

"I heard one of the Frasers done the job, no malice in it, no reason, no story behind it, just a plain doin' for a few quid."

"What about the nutter?" Archie asked.

"There's a different slant on that lad now, a nutter's a nutter, but if Crompton made him one, then he might have a story to tell?" Billy offered.

"He might be a lad worth saving?"

"If there's anything left to save?"

"Fuck it, we have to try, Billy, we have to try, it'll make a change from killing every cunt I see."

"An occasional taste of redemption won't do you any harm," said Billy, holding Archie's shoulder and squeezing it before concluding with a gentle pat on his back.

*

Thursday 16th July 1942 – Larbert – Scotland

Lieutenant Spencer Ward, a qualified Psychiatrist, researching Battle Fatigue in troops returning from North Africa, travelled to Scotland with two Chosen Men. He introduced himself to Professor Malcolm Etherton, the head of Clinical Care at the St. Andrews Secure Mental Health Unit, part of His Majesty's Prison in Larbert, near Falkirk in Scotland.

The transfer papers were in order, the patient/prisoner, Christopher Wrexford was to transfer to Military Custody where he would undergo experimental treatment and test new drugs. Which was partly true.

Wrexford was currently unresponsive to any stimuli and remained docile as they collected him from his single padded cell. The two men impersonating Military Police were armed and handcuffed him anyway.

"No point taking risks," they'd said unsympathetically and sternly. Professor Etherton had tranquillised Wrexford that morning, truth be told he was glad to be rid of him, he was a waste of a space.

Rebecca traced him through official prison records, he was detained for life under the Mental Deficiency (Scotland) Act of 1913. She also matched a death certificate to his birth certificate and found the real Christopher Wrexford had died as a baby. The ability to create false identities for the victims suggested a degree of criminal sophistication they hadn't expected to see.

*

Christopher woke in a new room and began to panic, a new room meant a new abuser. The bed and sheets were soft, and his pyjamas were clean and smelt fresh. He'd almost forgotten that smell. He could see the door was a strong one, it was locked, and he saw bars on the windows.

He could see trees, though. He hadn't seen a tree for a long time so he risked a walk to the window. There was a view of the countryside, but he could see a secure fence surrounding him. Still a prison he thought, stay in the cupboard.

There was food near his bedside, a sandwich, covered by a cloth, fruit, biscuits, and water, he was hungry, so he ate. Not the biscuits, he only got biscuits when he'd been a good boy, he wanted to forget about being good.

Five days later, Spencer Ward unlocked the door to one of the special POW cells at Bletchley Park. Christopher lay on the bed, unresponsive as always.

"Christopher, I'm going to let other people come and see you, to see if you'll talk to them," he said and as always there was no reply.

Spencer had repeatedly explained as gently as he possibly could, where Christopher was, he was safe and had friends now, not abusers. All to no avail, the patient remained calm, ate, used the toilet and slept, nothing else. The hidden microphones and cameras picked up nothing except him looking out of the window, apparently lost in within himself.

He tried the same technique using Rebecca, Conner, Una and Billy, Christopher remained firmly closed.

Spencer gave him no drugs, and he remained calm

without them, his medical notes stated that he needed them constantly.

After seven days of getting nowhere, Archie finally agreed to try; he didn't want to, and that weakness shamed him. Spencer had asked Una to ask Archie, she asked him once if he'd do it for her, and he agreed immediately.

Archie collected the book Una had given him as a wedding present, 'The Hobbit', and brought it with him to Christopher's room in Bletchley Park.

Outside the room, he told his mind one last time that he was Archie Travers now, took a deep breath and went inside.

"Hello mate," he said sitting on one of the two chairs.

"My name's Archie, I used to have another name, Teddy, that wasn't my real name so I didn't like it. I didn't like being Teddy either, so I decided to be Archie, and I like being Archie.

"You want to be someone else, but you don't think you can. You don't think you deserve to be someone.

"You're worried about how bad you are, what you've done. They told you, you were bad. They told you no-one would believe you. They told you, you were a liar and worthless.

"That's why you don't eat the biscuits, you only get a biscuit if they say you've been a good boy. Let me tell you what I've done," Archie said.

He told him every bad thing he'd ever done and thought of doing. Things he'd held back, even from Una. Every bad dream he'd ever had, every nightmare, it made him feel physically sick and just when he thought he might puke...

"My name's Arnold," he said.

"That's a good name."

"I have two sisters, Mary, and Martha."

"Where are they, Arnold?"

"They're dead and so am I."

"I was dead too, a few times, it's a bastard, but I came back. I'll show you how if you let me."

There was a long pause before Arnold finally said.

"Bad things happened to Arnold, in the children's home they told me my name was Christopher so I could bear Christ inside me, and it hurt. So I put Arnold away, he hid in a cupboard, Christopher stayed outside the cupboard so the bad things happened to Christopher, not Arnold, he was safe in the cupboard.

"Arnold didn't like it, so Christopher pretended he did like it so Arnold could go outside and escape. Arnold escaped once, then they caught him, hurt him real bad and kept him in. Years later, the next time they let him out he killed the man, then hid again. Arnold did the killing so he deserved to be punished."

"Where's the cupboard?" Archie asked.

"What?" said Arnold turning to look directly at Archie for the first time.

"Where is the cupboard? I can't see it."

"It's in my head."

"So it's always there?"

"Yes."

"Is it easy to get into?"

"Yes."

"Try going in it now."

"Okay."

"Come out now."

"Okay"

"See how easy that was?"

Arnold nodded.

"See how easily you can hide if you need to, a second, half a second even and you're safe."

"Yes."

"Can you read, Arnold?"

"Yes, Arnold can read, Christopher can't."

"I'd like to leave this book with you, so Arnold can read it and stay out of the cupboard."

"He'll try."

"Good, and tomorrow, I'd like Arnold to meet a special friend of mine."

Chapter 17

Thursday 23rd July 1942 - Bletchley Park

Archie and Una went together to see Arnold the next day in his room at Bletchley Park.

"I need you there with me, I can't face him alone again," he'd said to her, the statement begged a question that she couldn't ask.

"Yes, of course," she said, "I'm sorry, I shouldn't have asked you."

"You can ask anything of me, you know that."

"I know, and that's why I shouldn't have asked it of you."

"Hug please," he said.

He buried his head in her arms and started to weep.

"It's just when I'm with him, I can see it, I can feel it, as if it was happening to me, I can feel it, smell it, taste it. The pain of the victim, the malice, the evil of it, but that's not all."

He paused, she wiped his eyes, and he took a deep breath.

"Tell me you love me," he said.

"I love you."

"Tell me you'll never stop loving me."

"I'll never stop loving you."

"Whatever I say?"

"Whatever."

"I can feel the physical sensations... as if I was doing it, the pleasure taken in the evil perverted act. It makes me want to kill the whole world. One day, I think I'll be able to, and I won't stop myself."

"And I'll still love you," she said.

*

At first, Arnold wouldn't come out again, and Christopher remained silent until Una started talking about the book. The camera showed he'd read the book non-stop, not even sleeping since Archie left him. She told him her favourite part, the riddle game because it was hard to tell who was winning, who was cheating and who you wanted to win.

"It's easy," Arnold interrupted her to say, "Frodo's good and Gollum's bad. Frodo did a bad thing, but it didn't make him all bad."

Arnold paused for several minutes, apparently trying to work out in his head what he'd just said and what it meant.

"I've been Gollum, now I'll be Frodo," he said, "I've hidden from danger in the cupboard, but I hid from the sun too."

She'd cracked it, somehow Archie had known she would.

Arnold was consistently there, fragile and frightened, still knowing he could return to the cupboard instantly if he needed.

It was a long, slow, painstaking process and over a couple of weeks, they coaxed him gently from his room. They took him for walks, let him speak to other trusted people, let him eat, gave him more books, let him read newspapers, let him make some decisions of his own.

The depth and nature of the control he'd suffered struck Archie like a blade. It started with spoiling and generosity, then changed to bullying and violence akin to slavery, only worse. It was murder; murder repeated every day for the rest of your life. You were an animal, object or property, to be used, used up then discarded by stronger animals. Other than describing it as an extremely perverted form of bullying, Archie couldn't grasp the mentality of the perpetrator, how did people reach those depths? Was there a training course? A school?

Slavery was nothing new, you found something weaker than you, and you imposed your will on it, used, consumed or killed it. Was that what he was becoming? He wasn't even sure which question he should be asking? He'd always admired the Romans and Greeks; they had slaves, is this what they were? Was Caesar just a bully albeit one of history's most successful?

Maybe he just needed to be with Una, just Una, a world

with her and him, no one else.

Arnold's condition improved, although Archie and Una felt the recovery would never end. It took a toll on them personally, as individuals and their relationship. Arnold's need drained them, leeching the happiness from them, leaving them almost empty and haunted by the waking nightmare of his life. They were out of their depth, restoring Arnold to who he should be was beyond their well-meaning amateur capabilities. There was also a war to be fought and won, another bigger one.

Then Arnold asked to see them and told them to bring paper and pens.

"I'm ready to answer all your questions now," he said when they entered the room.

"I want revenge, you've saved me, now I need to save someone else."

They let him tell them his full story, he told them what had happened to Christopher in sickening, stomach-churning detail. Arnold couldn't remember his surname, date of birth or his mother and father's names, it had all been fucked out of him. He wasn't sure his sisters were dead, but that was what the people who controlled him and his thoughts had told him.

They had to get others to help, Mary Murphy helped a great deal, she had mothering instinct as a natural gift and Arnold began to trust her. In stages, they moved Arnold to a rest home for recuperating war wounded and shell-shocked men. He managed to mix with other damaged people there and began talking to them about everyday activities. They helped him to focus on what he still possessed, men there had missing limbs or were burnt beyond recognition, and there were many whose minds bore the damage.

Arnold said he'd seen Alice or Lilibeth as her captors had renamed her. He told them how popular she was with clients and thought she'd still be alive, yet so deeply broken there'd be nothing to save.

Billy drove Arnold around London, Peterborough, and

Northampton, he pointed out houses where he'd been kept and used. When they finished, they had twenty-four addresses and countless names, pseudonyms, and descriptions.

"There's just too much bloody information," Archie said exasperatedly to Una and Rebecca.

"What do we do, attack the source, attack the demand? Do we go into each address one by one? That tips them off, they'll move, they may have moved addresses already. We need to target all the addresses simultaneously, we can't manage that.

"Who do we trust? What police do we go to? What church? What government? Even the innocent ones will want to cover up the fact that they turned a blind eye, or a deaf ear, or were just too fucking stupid to notice.

"How can I go and tell any authority how I know this? If we were starting from scratch, I wouldn't start from here, I've just fucked up again, haven't I?"

"No, No," said Una, genuinely angry with him for once.

"If you've saved one person for one minute for each life you've taken, it was worth it."

"But I want... I need to stop it all, all of it. You heard him, these bastards are sick beyond any repair, they make the Nazis look benign, there's so many of them and in high places. How many Englands are there? There's one I love, it's big, and I'll fight and die for it, there's another, smaller one I'm fighting against."

"We look after Arnold, and we look for Alice, what else can we manage right now?" Una said.

"There's another war we need to fight first," Rebecca added.

"Are you still with me?" he asked.

"Yes, forever," they answered simultaneously as if it was something they'd practiced.

"I can't kill them all, can I?"

"No," they said.

*

After only a little thought, they decided they couldn't

use Arnold as a witness and force him to relive it all. They had all the evidence they needed, they just couldn't use it in any court. Whatever his real name was, the courts had already decided he was a nutter, who would listen?

Archie almost cried when Arnold asked if he could join the team or the army and help. He told him, quietly and carefully, that he'd already had enough war in his life. Quite apart from that, Archie needed to save a life occasionally to make up for those he'd taken. Arnold said he understood, but he didn't.

They kept him apart from Freddie successfully and, after intervention by Conner, found him a safe place, also in Canada where specialists would look after him properly. Perhaps in time, he could bury his past and make a life of his own, based on *his* decisions, rather than have them all taken from him. They would do their best to give him as much control over his life as he could handle. They couldn't take away the guilt he felt for what he'd done to survive. It might fade eventually for Arnold; Archie hoped it would, but he still knew he'd never let go of his own guilt, no matter how much time he had.

*

The day after Arnold left, Rebecca and Conner told Archie and Una to go away for a couple of days break. Archie took her to the Savoy, and they lived off room service and sex for their whole stay. Only when they reached the clean, fresh hotel room did they realise that they'd not touched each other since they'd first spoken to Arnold together. Speaking to him and helping him had opened a box in Archie's mind; Una helped him close that box again. When he was alone with her, the whole world was gone, the whole universe was gone, only her eyes, her scent, her touch was there. The need to look into her eyes as he gave her pleasure was all consuming. The intense pleasure she always returned always overwhelmed him. If he had one single second of time left at the end of the universe and all creation, he would give her *that* second.

He was whole, he was Archie, the most beautiful

woman in the world loved him, just him, he had everything he ever wanted, and he still wanted more.

*

On her return to Bletchley, Una went to see Billy at the Manor. She was pleasantly surprised to find him sitting in the garden relaxing and went to sit next to him.

"Enjoying the sun?" she asked.

"Exactly right Una, and the clean, fresh air, there's plenty stale bad air where I come from. You never know when the weather might change for the worse, and each ray of sun you see might be your last."

"That's deep, Billy Perry, there's a lot more to you than meets the eye, I knew that when I first saw you."

"You're pretty sharp yourself, how's the boy?"

"He seems okay now, he was just slightly different all the time Arnold was here. We spoke a lot, about, well, the most evil things you can imagine and he told me things he's never told anyone. There's more, though, like he was with me and somewhere else at the same time. I can't figure it out. Like something you see in the corner of your eye, then when you turn to look at it, it's still in the corner. Something stops me from asking about it."

"It'll come out if it needs to," Billy said.

She paused for a moment, searching for some thought in the back of her mind which just wouldn't form properly.

"Will you keep an eye on him for me?"

"Always do, Una, always will," he rose from the seat, smiling deeply at her and taking the dregs of his tea with him.

Una stayed sitting on the bench, still trying to catch that thought when Freddie approached her. He'd watched her quietly while she'd talked with Billy and waited until he was gone.

"Morning Una," he said.

"Freddie, how are you today?"

"I was thinking about that Arnold, who's gone now, what's his story?"

"He was just a badly shell-shocked soldier, Archie

helped him by talking, he's moved on to another specialist hospital."

"Oh."

"Your hair still looks good," she said trying to change the subject clumsily.

"I'll give it another trim tomorrow if you like? Let's have a closer look at that top lip."

She bent her head towards his as he sat next to her and touched his top lip, gently stroking his stubble.

"Yes that's sandpaper, not fluff, it'll grow nicely now if you let it. You'll be proper handsome then, Freddie, if I weren't married to Archie, I'd fuck you myself," she said then got up and hurried off after patting him on the head playfully.

Freddie couldn't get up, her closeness had given him an erection as soon as he sat next to her, and her touch had nearly made him come. I'm going to have to have a wank. Definitely, he thought.

'Damn, I shouldn't have said that, I'll have to fix him up with somebody, or his bollocks will explode, or he'll break a wrist wanking.'

Marion, she thought, Marion Hill, she was only 18 and had a sharp mind. She had ginger hair and freckles that blossomed more in summer. She was about the same height as Freddie. She wasn't exactly petite and had a large but shapely bottom, but the matching large breasts made for a pleasing overall picture. She'd recently joined the team, coming straight from school, forgoing her acceptance at University. Una wondered if she might like Freddie and decided to ask her to teach him how to read better, discreetly and see how that went.

*

While Freddie was out of action with his ankle in a cast, he could still help Begley, Billy, and Smudger in the stables workshop. He was a quick learner when anybody bothered to teach him anything.

He was helping Begley fit tracer bullets to Lewis Gun magazines for the Serpent when he saw a red haired girl leaning over the open stable door.

"Which one of you is Freddie?" she asked.

"It's him," said Billy when Freddie said nothing and pointed him out at the same time.

"Hello Freddie, Una asked me to help you out with… something. Are you free? She said you would be by now."

"No, I'm busy, sorry," Freddie said.

"No he's not," said Billy kneeing him in the base of his spine at the same time. "Now get out there right now, Private Knowles, this is no time for cowardice," he added from the side of his mouth, so only Freddie could hear.

Freddie walked hesitantly towards the girl, Marion Hill, who was going to teach him to read better and maybe more.

As Marion grabbed his arm, taking him and several books to the Manor Library, his three comrades stood and watched Freddie's retreating back.

"Never stood a chance," said Billy.

"No fucking chance at all," said Smudger.

"I can't read that well, you know," said Begley.

"Begs, if you couldn't read, write, count and measure as well as any man in England, we'd all be dead ten times by now," said Smudger.

"Nice try, though," Billy added, "all you need is a blonde with big tits from Building Thirteen, who also wants to know how to blow up anything ever built by mankind, and you're sorted."

"It could happen," said Begley.

*

Major Constantine Duncan of the Special Operations Executive attended his prearranged appointment with Elsbeth Brown-Wright, Member of Parliament and for many years a Government and Opposition Spokesman on Children's Welfare. She had a history of childcare and described herself as an expert. She was ready for his visit and his SOE credentials had secured her full cooperation, if not her full understanding of why he could possibly want to see her, about an issue long buried.

She was a tall, stout woman with an unflattering combination of a pig's nose and pince-nez glasses, who, despite being seated, contrived her best to make herself look down on him. He was, after all, little people.

Conner took a seat.

"How can I help you, Major Duncan?" she asked, hiding a northern accent behind her Westminster tone.

"As I explained, one of my men raised concerns with me about events that occurred during his stay in the Royal Holloway Children's Home. My understanding is that an investigation discovered misconduct, thus my duty to him requires me to raise this issue with you."

"I quite understand," she said. "What would you like to know?"

"Everything."

"You have to be more specific, Major."

"Was there any misconduct?"

"Yes, there was."

"What was the nature of that misconduct?"

"Two low-level employees were said to be not as diligent as would have been proper."

"Who were those two employees?"

"They aren't named in the report given to me, and have left that employment."

'For heaven's sake, this is like getting blood from a stone.'

"What was the nature of their lack of diligence?" he asked.

"I'm not at liberty to repeat unsubstantiated allegations against individuals, obviously."

"What made you aware of those allegations?"

"There was a detailed report."

"May I see it?"

"It's a confidential report."

"May I see it?"

"It's a confidential report."

"As you can see from my credentials, I have clearance up to Top Secret, a significantly higher level than confidential. I am formally, by law, in time of war, entitled to view any material up to that level; any denial of access would be a breach of wartime regulations."

He could see the stupid bitch becoming flustered and panic in her naïve witless confusion. Afraid to show him the report, afraid not to, afraid to breach the unwritten rules of the Establishment that she belonged to and now thought Conner might just belong to.

"The report is on your desk, I can read it in your presence if you wish, or I could take the request to the Cabinet Office if you prefer?"

He was bluffing, of course, technically he was correct, he knew he'd need to explain far too much to take it that far.

She cracked!

"Of course, you may read it, but it cannot leave this room."

"Of course," he said.

It took two hours to read the report, and he did it slowly and deliberately, there was a handwritten note at the end.

"I accept the findings of this insightful and detailed report. Es BW."

It was the biggest load of tosh he'd ever read in his life, the detail of the report clearly showed incompetence and criminal negligence at every level. It reached specious conclusions from manifestly false and illogical facts; it might well have been titled 'Whitewash'. The terms of reference for the so-called investigation were so tightly framed they precluded any meaningful result. It disgusted him that such a thing could exist when rape and murder of children were involved.

He thanked Miss Brown-Wright for her cooperation and left.

'No wonder Archie just wants to kill these people.'

The chances of any semblance of justice were so remote, he wanted to shoot her on the spot, in her office, in front of witnesses and hang the consequences. What was he fighting for? What were people dying for?

*

Half an hour later, he was in the local telephone exchange with Billy and Rebecca.

"She hasn't made a single call, as usual, nothing, not a hint, for the last two weeks since you made the appointment," said Billy. "She's not speaking to anyone, not warning anybody, nothing, beats the fuck out of me."

"She's just stupid, Billy," Conner said, "she thinks the report is a good one, she's so stupid, she thinks she's more intelligent than she is. It's a conspiracy of incompetence, no-one can admit how stupid anyone else is, or they look stupid themselves. I can't explain it any other way. She handed me a report that was the biggest load of drivel I've ever read in my life and had no clue whatsoever that it was just that."

"He's gonna kill her if you tell him that. You know he is. He'll fucking do it, he has to, it's gone too far now. There's too much, everywhere we look, every stone we turn there's another stone under it. I was born in the gutter and dragged myself out, even I can't believe how much there is. I'd rather have Sunday dinner with the Frasers than give this lot the time of day. I mean it, I'd rather be back in Wipers," Billy sighed.

"I know, I know and the truth is, I can't stop him, and I don't even want to."

"Me neither, look, we just can't let him take it all on himself, you know what he's like."

"You know him better than me now, Billy, what can we do?"

"I don't know, I thought the girls would calm him down a bit, but you just have to help him do what he has to, share it with him. You know he's right, and that's it as far as you're concerned. You know I help him as much as he'll let me, you know he's the son I never had, you know that."

"And he's the brother I never had."

"We have to do it for him then?"

"We do."

"We have to do it for him," Rebecca added, finally

saying what she was thinking. "Sometimes it just consumes him, and he can't take any more. Helping Arnold just drained the life out of him. He can look the criminal straight in the eye and do whatever he needs to, and yet he can't even look at the victims, remember the children in the cottage. There's something he's not telling me... he'll tell me if I ask him... if I ask the right question... and I just can't, I won't. I won't ask Una either. If it weren't for her he'd just explode, he'd kill the whole world if it weren't for her, I swear it," she said.

'And he's the lover I'll never have.'

"Let's do it while he's in Russia," she said.

"What's he doing in Russia?" asked Billy.

"Well, he's been told not to say and for once, he won't," said Conner, "let's do it for him."

*

Elsbeth Brown-Wright died a week later from a fatal and unexpected heart attack while working late in her office in Westminster. Her obituary praised her tireless and excellent work for the British people. It failed to mention her essential stupidity, gullibility and tireless myopic pursuit of her own advancement... and her ability to lie... especially to herself.

Only Conner knew, once Archie had dealt with Tennent, it had to stop. He didn't know how he was going to tell Archie that, or if he *could* stop him.

*

Monday 17th August 1942 – Bletchley Park

At midday on Monday, the 17th of August 1942, Archie and the Chosen Men said goodbye to Rebecca and Una at the Manor. Freddie went to London for a few days break, his ankle not yet fully healed, heavily bandaged and using a walking stick, custom-made by Billy.

He asked Conner to go to Newhaven with the men and stay there. If anything went wrong with Archie's plan for Tennent, he didn't want anyone to blame Conner, this risk belonged to him.

"Besides, if I get killed you'll kill whoever did it," he'd

said.

*

There was trepidation, the Dieppe mission, Operation Jubilee was big and dangerous. The Manor would be nearly empty for two days, they'd have some building work done, and Arthur Driver would act as caretaker.

*

Archie planned to give Briony and Asgeir plenty of time to say goodbye at Bletchley.

Asgeir Thorson was fully in command of *'The Serpent'* for the Mission. Archie, Smudger, and Billy were supposed to be on board a destroyer watching the action from a safe distance while the Chosen took all the risks.

"Just marry the girl," Archie had said, "do it, if that's what you want, just do it. Who knows how long we've got, live your life while you can. If you don't take the risk of being hurt, you don't take the risk of being loved."

Archie said the words easily enough, five minutes more with Una was worth at least two wars to him.

Asgeir said he would ask Briony to marry him if he got back from Dieppe.

"When you get back Asgeir," Archie said. "You won't die in France, I know it, I once misplaced a whole bloody army there, but I've got better since then."

Asgeir laughed, and Archie smiled.

*

The two trucks and staff car began their long journey to Newhaven to join the rest of the mission. They met Gubbins and three lorry loads of his men inside Bletchley Park itself, before going south in a larger convoy.

Once inside Bletchley Park's grounds, it was easy enough to replace Archie, Smudger and Billy with similar sized men in the staff car bound for Newhaven. Gubbins only had a little trouble finding someone as big as Smudger and as old as Billy.

"The rest is down to you Archie, remember, if a man fires at you, no court will convict you for firing back," Gubbins said.

Archie, Billy, and Smudger decided to stay for a day and a night on camp beds inside the private room in their building. Una and Rebecca remained in SOE rooms there that first night, then very obviously left Bletchley Park in their staff car after a full day's work there on the 18th of August. They'd rested and slept as best they could, they knew there was no prospect of untroubled sleep that night.

*

Asgeir was aware something big was going on with Archie, but he never questioned him. It was just another Top Secret mission, if Archie needed help, he'd only have to ask. Besides, he had Billy and Smudger with him; Rebecca and Una were hardly helpless either, he pitied anyone who took them on, although this did feel different somehow.

He decided to stop worrying about that and began to focus on his task ahead. The drive south was long and dreary, and his mind drifted to thoughts of home. A small farm near Stavanger, a port in Norway, no doubt full of German troops now. Farm life was a hard one, early starts and late finishes. He was the third of four sons; not bound to inherit the farm, he'd sought a naval career. He knew boats, so it was a natural choice, he'd still had to excel in every single aspect to ensure success and officer rank. The war changed everything, and his rank and expertise had found him a new home in England, not safe, but safer than Norway. He'd heard little of his family since leaving Norway with the retreating British. His father and younger brother still worked the farm, but there was no news of his two older brothers, he feared the worst and tried not to think about it. He thought of Briony and wondered if she'd want to live in Norway or if she'd want to leave England. He wondered if he'd want to return to Norway, whenever the war ended. Briony was far too capable to live contentedly as a farmer's wife.

Stop it, Asgeir! Concentrate on the operation, there's nothing else until it's over. Look after these men first, don't think of anything else until you're safely home.

*

Briony Samms watched the trucks pull away from Bletchley. She didn't care how the war would go, she just wanted Asgeir to come back safely. She needed to see Archie again so he could promise her that he'd come back alive, and she sought him out in their building.

Why the hell do people always expect me to know everything, was what he thought.

"He'll be fine, I just know it," was what he said.

He remembered Ben Dempsey, and how he couldn't make that one small promise to his mum and dad. Perhaps that absence of promise was what did for Ben. He'd made a huge promise to Una and Rebecca he needed to keep first, he focussed tightly on that.

Chapter 18

19th August 1942 – 0200 - The Coast of France near Dieppe

At 0200 on the 19th of August 1942, the Serpent switched off its already muffled engines and drifted gently toward the shallow sandy beach at St. Aubin. There were no large purpose-built defences, no Atlantic Wall yet and nothing like it, just barbed wire on cruciform wooden posts and firm damp sand.

Two dinghies left the Serpent, one with Asgeir, Begley, George, Henry and Hospital, the other with Bradley, Lightfoot, Gabe, and Mickey. Baldr remained in the boat with Brayden and Roebuck each manning a medium gun.

On the beach, Henry stayed guarding the dinghies, it was his turn. They silently sliced through the barbed wire with long bolt cutters. The eight Chosen Men went forward and turned left when they reached the sheer cliffs. They headed for the small rivulet that ran down at a gentle angle half a mile ahead. After almost the exact number of paces Archie had estimated, they reached the heavy concrete tank traps, designed to make a landing in force impossible, but which were no barrier to eight agile men.

Passing the traps successfully, they saw the small hut serving as a shelter for the guards. Archie guessed there would be two guards, three maximum with a telephone and a rifle each. The hut had one small window, a dim light showed inside, which was careless, it wasn't cold, and the door was still closed.

They could easily subdue the guards inside and needed to do so quietly, to avoid alerting the radar station at the cliff top. Planning ahead, they'd already decided to leave two men watching the guard post closely, who'd kill anyone who left it, as quietly as they could. Begley and Billy made a silencer for a Sten gun which worked passably well. They didn't fully trust any Sten, so George carried it as spare or for that specific silenced blast planned against the wooden hut. George took up a position opposite the door, the Sten aimed directly at it and waited, Mickey waited with him, Thompson machine gun in hand and watched his back.

Archie provided protective vests for the team and insisted they wear them on this mission. They were lighter than the Wilkinson Flak jackets but were still uncomfortable, but if someone who'd cheated death as regularly as Archie Travers ordered you to do it, there was no shame involved. They weren't in general use, they were too expensive.

"Bollocks," Archie said and paid for them when he was in America, they arrived by air a week later. He'd had them custom-made, steel and silk, and a thousand Dollars each. He'd ordered two extra large ones, for Smudger, and one did fit Gabe, who reluctantly wore it as ordered.

Time passed, and no movement or sound came from the hut so Mickey and George continued to wait.

The main party reached the cliff top, ten silent minutes after they'd left the beach. The radar station looked like an older one without the latest gear. The single guard was alert and watchful, striding purposefully and noisily around the building, his outline clear and tall against the brighter night sky over the Channel. He made an easy target for Gabe's American-made hunting rifle, and one shot through his head killed him instantly, going straight through the helmet.

That rifle shot was just heard inside the wooden hut, and three guards ran from its door. The silenced Sten fired first time, killing all three Germans crammed in the doorway with half of one clip.

Mickey made sure of the kill with a burst from his Thompson, checked inside the hut then took up a planned position to check up and down the beach for movement. George checked the path that led up to the clifftop.

Immediately after shooting the guard, the team rushed the radar station building from two angles, ensuring crossfire, but no mistakes. They smashed windows and threw grenades, Thompsons raked inside the building followed by a short wait for silence. Then a careful confirmation that all the unsuspecting occupants were dead.

The equipment was old, known and not worth stealing, nor was there any enigma equipment. The three young, lightly armed technicians on duty were unprepared for the storm unleashed on them by the Chosen Men. They looked like bank clerks to Asgeir; they should have stayed at home if they'd wanted an easy life.

He remembered Archie's words, "there must be no hesitation, no pity, just shock and unquestioned, unanswered violence."

Asgeir knew he was right, although it didn't make him feel any better then, it would help him later.

There was nothing worth stealing or destroying on the site, so Begley just added extra explosives to the decidedly unpleasant surprises he left for the next Germans who arrived. Tripwires, mines, booby traps and a larger device on a timer, hidden near the road where Archie guessed any arriving vehicles would park.

Asgeir and Bradley took stock, decided they'd completed their mission, and that waiting or further exploration was pointless. They worked their way silently down the path to the guard hut, shouting the prearranged password to George and Mickey.

"All quiet and done, let's go home," said Asgeir.

Once on board the Serpent and before starting the engines, Baldr told Asgeir that he'd seen a medium German patrol boat going east. The Serpent couldn't be seen from the seaward side against the darker shore of Northern France, but Baldr had seen the patrol boats outline clearly.

"It's heading straight for our ships en route to Dieppe," he said.

"We'll follow and take it on, now, I'll tell the men," Asgeir decided in a split-second.

The Serpent slid forward, straight and fast after the German patrol boat. Baldr was able to keep closer to the shore and cliffs, having a shallower draft, pursuing the larger vessel, the lack of light favouring their stealth.

They went full speed at the vessel and just weren't catching up fast enough, their prey would spot the Dieppe flotilla before they caught it. The small vessel itself wouldn't significantly hurt the flotilla, but it could alert German ground troops in Dieppe. Allied forces would be under heavy fire long before they got ashore. Asgeir knew how poor their chances were already, this could make it suicide. He had to gamble, Archie had taught him that.

"Prepare to fire all four torpedoes, all four," he shouted.

"But we're not in range and the target's too small," Baldr said

"Just do it. Now! Begley, man the Lewis Gun cluster, this is your big chance. Baldr, aim twenty yards to the right then twenty to the left of where he is. Then one right, one left again," He shouted above the engine noise.

"Fire one!"

"Fire two!"

"Reload!" he shouted. The men were already doing it, they could see what he saw now and worked in short order.

"Begley, open fire now and don't stop till there's no ammo left."

Begley screamed in exultation, his new toy worked like a dream, four bright yellow and orange tracer tracks of flame and countless bullets lit up the night sky. Now that's a thing of great beauty he thought, as his creation worked with an absolute perfection. It could only have been better if the German vessel was in range, which sadly it wasn't.

"Fire three! Fire four!" Asgeir bellowed above the noise of the guns and Begley's deranged shouting, they were firing anyway.

The German vessel heard nothing of this mayhem of course, but a lookout couldn't miss the hail of tracer fire behind them. He alerted the Captain, who turned his vessel immediately. He could have run, he could outrun his attacker easily, but he was a brave man with a brave crew.

Then, as they expected him to, he turned immediately starboard towards the French coast to face the danger.

The German vessels turn had the desired effect of presenting a larger side-on target for the torpedoes Asgeir had fired. Three missed, two by a distance, one by fifty feet, one hit him a glancing blow on the prow. The explosion wasn't huge and inflicted no casualties, but the vessel would sink unless they nursed it slowly to shore. They wouldn't be chasing a small British raider tonight. If anything, it might divert some more troops to the radar station.

"Come on, we've used up our luck for tonight, let's go home," Asgeir shouted. He'd heard Archie say that.

"Begley, you can stop firing now; Baldr, grab Begley please."

They'd never know, that following their action, two German vessels pursued their crossing of the channel when they might have caused more damage elsewhere and earlier at Dieppe.

They did find out later their target would have intercepted Lovat's men as they returned to England. Lovat had watched the explosion gratefully; he later told Asgeir loudly in front of a crowd that he owed the whole team a drink. That was the proudest moment of Asgeir's life.

He felt like Archie Travers, he never told a soul, and he'd ask Briony to marry him now.

Begley would never know the surprises he'd left in France would kill two more Germans later that morning when they thought they were safely inspecting the damage. One triggered the tripwire, killing him instantly with a double strength anti-personnel mine. The second was an officer, killed while his men searched the area for traps. He'd stood behind his car for safety, in the very spot where Archie had expected him to stand.

Begley wished he could plan that patiently when he needed to; he preferred chaos. The shaped charge, he'd made from Archie's design, fired a mass of ball bearings in an arc at ankle height, nearly severing both limbs, and the officer had bled to death. The German army copied and used that design against Allied Troops, as they swept across Europe. In a world war containing precious little, *that was* a genuine pity.

Shore Officers debriefed Asgeir on his return to Newhaven; he could tell Dieppe was going badly, by the faces he saw. He asked, but nobody would give him any information.

"Top Secret" was all they'd say; when something was going well, someone always gave you the news.

"FUBAR," said Bradley after speaking to United States Ranger personnel on the quayside. Asgeir knew that meant fucked up beyond all recognition.

They left their boat with Navy Personnel for routine maintenance and storage then walked thoughtfully to their waiting trucks.

Asgeir was suddenly very weary, it hit you like that. He needed to get home and see Briony, he just needed to give and receive a hug. He knew he was lucky.

As he neared the trucks, Briony leapt out and walked impatiently towards him.

"How did you get here?" he said.

"Archie ordered me to come and meet you," she said.

"Did he order you to say 'yes' when I ask you to marry me?"

"He told me you'd need a hug."

"Will you marry me then?"

"Yes, of course."

Asgeir took her in his arms and gave her the tightest, warmest hug he could manage, without ripping her clothes off. Then he gave her a peck on her lips that soon blossomed into a longer, deeper kiss.

A round of applause from around him, suddenly made him realise that all his men were standing nearby and had heard his clumsy proposal; thank goodness she'd said yes!

"Let's go home," he said.

*

19th August 1942 – 0100 – The Cottage

As the Serpent motored almost silently towards the French shore, Archie Travers waited impatiently in the English countryside. He lay flat on his stomach and cramped inside his makeshift foxhole at the end of the small track that led only to his cottage.

His MG34 barrel fed German Machine Gun, captured during Operation Claymore, was pointing straight down the track ready to fire against anyone who dared to approach his home. He'd wait until his targets were well in place, the small MG34 muzzle flash would give away his position, but that didn't worry him. He was waiting for Inspector Norman Tennent, waiting to kill him and his accomplices, hoping, against his expectations, that this might end the blood feud. He stayed awake, waiting.

His mood lowered steadily with each passing minute. He threw away the sandwich he'd kept to ward off hunger and just sipped at his water bottle. He took his tight leather gloves off, scratching the palm of his left hand until it bled. He spat on his hands, mixing it with his blood, washing his hands in that mess and pulled his gloves back on.

Although he'd pretended to, he hadn't slept for two days. What a liar he was, he lied to the people he loved, that was worse than mere deception, plain untruths, that was betrayal. Lack of sleep caused hallucinations, he should have slept.

He reached for a mantra, and none came, he felt light-headed, his eyes watered heavily until the tears ran down his face, tears without crying, the worst.

He knew he had no life, no joy, he wasn't allowed any, he deserved better and never got it. This was his life… shit, unrelenting shit from now until the day he died alone.

Despair had closed in on him with twilight then darkness; the moon was gibbous, but clouds covered it. His head contained the pounding of a headache left by hunger, hunger and more need than he could comprehend.

He had darkness in him, he knew that already and

coped with it easily. Tonight, it appeared at the edges of his waking vision. Darkness formed a circle, initially at the edges of his eyes, then slowly moved into their centre, blinding him with the absence of light. Then the darkness continued its journey from his sight into his mouth, ears, nose and lungs, suffocating him, smothering him claustrophobically. He couldn't breathe, but he wasn't choking either. The darkness moved again, this time starting in his fingertips and toes, moving up his arms and legs flooding into his groin and chest.

The darkness spoke to him.

"You're dead," it said. "You're fucking dead, just die and be done with it."

His whole body and mind were black, jet black and dead, yet the darkness still found somewhere else to go, deeper inside him.

The darkness despised the light, any light, no matter how small, tiny, atomic even and kept seeking it relentlessly, deeper and deeper into parts of him that he couldn't name or imagine.

The darkness finally found it, one tiny remaining speck of light, one atom, one neutron, one proton, something smaller, the smallest most basic fusion material, stardust, potential, life. It was the last remaining vestige of his light, but the darkness was stronger and overcame it.

His whole body collapsed in on itself crushing him, shrinking impossibly. The vast weight of darkness pressed him into an infinitesimally small space. The awesome, overwhelming weight of darkness crushed the entire Cosmos and light ceased to exist.

The light reappeared, blinding, in an impossibly huge explosion. There was nothing, no space, no light, just an absence, then there was a presence, creating and filling space simultaneously. The explosion continued forever, everywhere, omnipresent then slowed until, barely moving, it was fourteen billion years later. He returned, occupying the same familiar space, time, shape and environment.

Perhaps, just perhaps, this Universe might allow him to be at peace, and then he woke up suddenly.

At first, he was frightened this was an identical shitty Universe, fuck it, worth a try. He opened his eyes and saw a different fresh Universe, it looked identical, although that didn't fool a consummate liar of Archie's ability, it was new and... he woke up again.

He shook his head hard to focus on what he needed to do, he shouldn't have slept.

The dream left him immediately, as they sometimes did. Each thought, each picture, vivid and detailed just seconds before, vanished as he sought them out. Like points of light from flickering candles in a Church offertory rack extinguished one after the other by an altar boy with a candle snuffer. Only the feeling of despair remained, he just didn't know why.

*

As the dinghies silently touched the sandy beach at two o'clock in the morning, Archie heard, then saw a lorry drive past the cottage and stop. A car drew up blocking the gravel drive's entrance, and he listened to a second truck parking near the barn. A car and two trucks, there's more than six or seven men! Here we go again.

*

19th August 1942 – 0100 – The A1 to Bletchley

Special Branch Inspector Norman Tennent was being driven to the target cottage in the middle of the night and had laid his plans out with great care. The Animal was useful in certain limited circumstances, but his ideas were nowhere near good enough. Tennent had changed the original plan significantly; without telling the Animal, he couldn't risk a leak to his pet, Freddie.

Tennent had fought a dirty, bloody war, without truce or quarter, all his life. His parents had brainwashed him as a child, hatred, bigotry and entitlement burned into his soul alongside the songs, sashes and stupid bowler hats that his family sang and wore. He could never have been other than exactly what he was; you could only follow the example you were given. If born German he'd be in the SS enthusiastically killing Jews, or other sundry Untermensch. He was a vicious murdering bastard in any nation and any language; his God gave him that right.

His mission was to kill the Catholic whore and her friend, the clever bitch. The whore needed to die specifically because she'd killed a British soldier and generally was a Catholic whore, born to the wrong family. The clever bitch needed to die as revenge for Packard. That would hurt Travers, hurt him hard, so hard he'd break cover and open himself up to ruin.

Tennent was an expert at ruin, a lie here, a false complaint there, evidence planted, unreliable witnesses, a false confession obtained through torture if he found the scope. False exposure as a tout was his favourite, one carefully crafted lie reaching the right ears and someone else did the killing for him, then he could stitch the killer up too.

Tonight, Tennent had kept the plan simple, only the level of violence was in question. He didn't trust the Animal and the Animal didn't trust this Freddie. True, he only had six trusted men in London including the Sergeant from Holloway Police Station. He knew what was good for him and his family, he'd already faked the arrest records for the whore and was in over his head. Another favourite of his, long-term blackmail. Sergeant Finch would be his driver and his involvement that night would secure his unquestioning services for a lifetime.

The Animal and Freddie knew about six men, one car, and truck, they didn't know about the ten men fresh across the Irish Sea for a secret mission. Ten men who asked no questions, Tennent owned them; body, soul and mind.

They'd kill them, and not one shred of evidence would link any killing to Tennent. Unless someone admitted killing Packard, of course, and that wasn't going to happen. Travers' people played a hard game, and they'd lose to a better player. *We* are the people, not them, he knew beyond the slightest doubt.

Freddie, the witless tout had no future, the Animal would ensure that detail was attended to. The Animal might need to be put down too, depending on his performance tonight. Sure, he'd given this Freddie cash up front, but he'd see no more, and he wouldn't get a girl either, the cheeky little rat. He thinks he's somebody does he, I'll do him myself. He might even fit neatly into a frame if necessary, a perpetrator found at the scene or perhaps he'd hang himself later, consumed by guilt, 30 pieces of silver at his feet, he laughed inwardly.

The two girls were dangerous, they'd be well armed and well trained, he'd heard; they knew how to kill and had done so before tonight. He'd enjoy a measure of pain or torture, if an opportunity arose to use them, he'd take it. He insisted on no chances being taken, though, his plan was to kill them quickly, nothing less.

That's why there was a twin barrelled Bofors anti-aircraft gun in the first truck.

They'd blow that house to bits at close range, 50 yards from the tarmacked road. The extra men were merely additional insurance against unexpected resistance by the pair. The Animal liked odds of six to two, did he? Sixteen to two was better!

The first truck would park by the wasteland immediately after the hard gravel side road. Five riflemen would take up firing positions in the tree thicket behind the cottage. The second truck would park in the barnyard, two men in the hayloft overlooking the cottage and garden. Three men to cross the stream and through the hedge covering the front door. Two men operating the ack-ack gun would blast the house from the wasteland, then the men would advance from two sides, the river behind the cottage would bar any retreat that way.

Freddie would be secure with the Animal and Finch, Tennent would barely have to leave his car.

The truck and mobile anti-aircraft gun were stolen to order in the East End of Glasgow a month earlier. His three best men in London were in the front.

The second truck, stolen the night before would join the convoy when they reached the A5 junction of Watling Street and Sheep Lane. A right turn there would take them to the old woodland called Circuitt's Covert. The second truck was his own little secret, his own covert action, ten of his own volunteers, fresh from Belfast. Not all policemen, just kindred evil spirits who adhered to his version of God's law.

Best of all, he'd already identified two Sinn Fein men who'd make convenient scapegoats. Revenge for a deserter was near enough the truth, and they'd already disappeared the previous morning, their prints already on two rifles securely in his car boot. The English would find their bodies in a burnt-out truck later.

*

Freddie Knowles sat fidgeting in Inspector Norman Tennent's car as it went up the A1, driven by the ginger-haired Sergeant he recognised from Holloway. He didn't know him by his real name and didn't ask, his nickname was Ginge, obviously. Tennent was bolt upright in the front passenger seat, the Animal in the back seat with him. He was nervous, something just wasn't right. He'd boarded the car at 2200 in an empty back street in Holloway, a canvas-topped truck with three men in the front had followed the car. He asked why they needed a whole truck if only three men were sitting in it.

"Surely another car would be better for a getaway?" he said.

"Shut it," said the Animal.

The Animal was puzzled too, this wasn't the plan he'd agreed with Tennent earlier. He still had his handcuffs ready, and when he was told to, he slapped one on Freddie's right wrist before securing the other cuff to his own left hand.

"That's to make sure you don't run, you little wanker, you've got previous."

"Stop just here," said Tennent pointing out a layby on his left. As the car pulled up, so did the truck and a second truck joined the small convoy. Tennent left his car to approach the second lorry then the first.

"What's goin' on?" Freddie asked.

"No idea, son, looks like reinforcements," Ginge said just before the Animal punched Freddie full in the face.

"I told you to shut it," the Animal spat at him.

Freddie felt for the walking stick at his left hand, it was no use in a car.

Chapter 19

19th August 1942 – 0100 - The Cottage near Bletchley

Rebecca and Una sat crouched closely together in the cottage. Archie hadn't wanted them to, but they'd swallowed a couple of wake ups earlier so they were more than wide awake. They were slightly bored, calmly ready for the fighting to start, not reckless, not stupidly keen, just possessing the certain knowledge of a need to act and to get it done.

Making something happen suited them better, at least they had weapons next to them, pistols and two Thompsons and each had worn body armour as Archie insisted.

*

Smudger crouched close to the rear of the cottage, concealed by fully grown trees nearer the river, with a couple of Thompsons, six magazines and a dozen grenades available. His back covered by the water, he knew he was unseen in those tall trees and could easily handle anything approaching on that flat waste ground.

He had that taste of excitement in his chest, a dangerous feeling, massive butterflies, enticing, like the moments just before sex. He knew it could mean his death, and he embraced it nonetheless. He'd enjoyed escaping Calais and he'd enjoyed the killing too. The simplicity appealed to him, we were right, they were wrong, you killed them without fear of conscience. He was helping his best friends, for these few short minutes they mattered more than his wife and kids. Anyone intending to hurt those two brave, beautiful girls was going to die tonight.

*

Billy waited in the old barn's loft, overlooking the cottage and Archie's foxhole. He couldn't see Smudger's position, only the tops of the trees above his hiding place.

He checked his weapons one last time. The Thompson was sound, the Webley service pistol was perfect for his grip, Archie had lent him his Mauser for any distance work and grenades in a kit bag if needed.

He was strangely content for a man poised, ready to kill and risk his life; as content as he'd been for decades.

He was alive, well-armed and with friends; he was with his boy and his two girls. He had a daughter he still loved and a wife he'd loved until she'd died in childbirth. When his wife died, she'd taken a chunk of him with her that he'd never replaced… until he'd met Archie and seen what he was. He'd seen his eyes, their darkness, the smell of bloody gunpowder, the need to kill, and still with a spark of light. Archie was Billy, thirty years ago, like looking in a mirror, but with a better chance at life, a chance Billy was going to make damn sure he took.

His daughter was safe and always would be, he'd kept her safe like a Guardian Angel until she'd met Archie. Then Archie, in turn, had kept her safe by setting her free from him. Grace wasn't meant for Archie; Una was born for him and Rebecca too. Billy couldn't figure how Archie would work that, but… a creaking timber, just the wind, made him stop thinking and focus on the job.

*

Smudger only saw the first truck park next to the flat wasteland, not the car or second truck. He did see the tarpaulin being pulled back immediately revealing a twin-barrelled Bofors anti-aircraft gun.

"Fucking hell," he said, picking up two grenades, pulling the pins and relishing his chance to be back in action.

*

Billy watched all three vehicles arrive from his position in the hayloft, he'd planned to cover the driveway and more, from his elevated level. The third vehicle, the second truck pulled up right next to the barn. About ten men left it, in complete silence. He saw some go north towards the cottage, and he could clearly see five coming towards the barn. They entered the barn by the front entrance, he heard some leave the rear entrance heading towards the stream and cottage. Some came up the creaking wooden stairs to the hayloft, only two he thought, reaching for his knife.

*

Through the cellar's small side window facing the rear of the cottage, Rebecca and Una heard the noise of heavy vehicles pull up and stop.

They rose to their feet, eagerly checking their weapons in complete darkness, as Billy had taught them.

*

Billy crouched deep in the shadows of the hay loft waiting patiently for the two men to take up positions overlooking the cottage. Quietly waiting for his best chance to kill them as silently and quickly as he could. He couldn't give the game away just yet.

He couldn't afford to make a noise or a mistake, they were big lads, and he wasn't a young man. He could take one easily with his blade, but two were bound to make a noise he wasn't ready for. He wished he'd opted for a silenced Luger now.

He decided he couldn't just sit waiting for the shooting to start, those two might start it, and they had a Lewis Gun.

He moved forward as carefully as he possibly could, Thompson in his left hand, blade in his stronger right hand.

He took one small step forward then two then... one small badly balanced step from his half crouched stance creaked a timber, just loud enough for them to hear. They turned round and moved towards him, fast.

*

As soon as the tarpaulin was off the Bofors, the trained gunner opened fire, and the other man next to him stood ready to reload. The heavy calibre shells ripped two sides of the cottage to shreds. Old brick and plaster shattering at the short range, windows and frames splintering and scattering immediately, parts of the old roof fell to its rear.

*

Archie's foxhole was shallow, and he lay there aiming his MG34 machine gun down the gravel track.

He heard the explosive rattling of the ack-ack gun

smashing the cottage and that didn't concern him, he knew his two girls were safely in the basement and well-armed. He just needed someone to leave that car so he could kill them.

No-one left the car, then two armed men surprisingly emerged from the hedge five yards in front of him. He fired directly at them, tearing legs and groins apart from his low angle and short range, they fell dead to the gravel.

He saw a figure leave the front passenger seat of the car, holding a machine gun and moving towards the cottage. The figure began firing short blasts towards Archie and the flash of his weapon. Not Freddie then, he thought and fired off the rest of his magazine at the man, replaced the magazine and rattled the car again to make sure. Keep your head down, Freddie, he pleaded.

His pleading was interrupted by five quick bullets from behind him. The third man who'd left the barn found a clearer path and came through the hedge behind Archie. Archie's position given away, the third man had fired through the thin top covering of the foxhole, directly into Archie.

*

The Bofors gun began firing before the tarpaulin was fully off, and Smudger ran headlong from his cover with his grenades, getting a better throwing arc for the longer distance involved. He instinctively guessed the distance to the gun and lobbed two grenades as far as he could manage. One exploded near his target, the other missed wildly, so he ran forward, twenty yards closer and lobbed another two. This time, they resulted in a fiery explosion that illuminated the night sky, the fuel and ammunition in the truck had exploded alongside the two cowardly killers manning the Bofors.

Lennard Smith never learned cricket at school, he'd learned how to throw stones at windows, though.

The huge flames allowed him to see five other men leaving the trees to his left. Before he could take one of his two Thompsons off his shoulder and aim, a fusillade of single shots from five rifles hit him, his huge outline clearly visible to his attackers. Most of the incoming bullets rattled his armour, staggering him, although enough bullets hit arms and legs to cripple him and take him to his knees, unable to stand or use his arms. He knew he was dead, he'd bleed to death, but he clung to consciousness, and hatred.

The Bofors had stopped firing, he was sure he'd taken a couple with him, but a couple wasn't enough.

*

Tennent watched his ack-ack gun blasting the cottage and saw two of his men pushing through the hedge and wondered where the third was. He saw a muzzle flash at the end of the track an instant before he heard the crack of heavy machine gun fire and saw those two men fall.

That wasn't in the plan he thought as he opened his car door gripping his own Sten gun and started firing at the machine gun's flash. The rate and direction of the MG34 fire were heavily loaded against him, his Sten fired perhaps a dozen shots while fifty from the MG34 ripped into him and his car. He fell to the ground, without realising how soon Sergeant Finch and the Animal left the right side of the car and took cover. The Animal dragged Freddie alongside him as he fled into a ditch on the roadside. Tennent was severely wounded, but with proper hospital care, he'd recover and make someone pay for this. He saw and heard the firing onto Archie's machine gun position, and it stopped firing. That's one down then.

*

In the hayloft, Tennent's men leapt instantly towards Billy, barely leaving him time to press the trigger on his Thompson. Its fire just hit the legs of the man to his left. Part of his mind heard the sound of the ack-ack gun. The man on his right moved sharply towards him, punching him in the chest painfully and pushing him breathlessly onto his back. Instinctively, Billy kept his finger pressed hard on the Thompson trigger, and a spray of shots took the left-hand man in the chest, heart and arms. He dropped, dead and lifeless, his torso ruined beyond recognition by the short-range bullets.

Billy knew nothing of that, as the bigger stronger man battered the Thompson violently from his left hand onto the floor, the earth floor, twenty feet below.

The bigger man was on top of Billy, his knees pinning down both sides of his chest, his two huge hands on the wrist holding the knife, he was heavy and well trained. He positioned his hands tightly around Billy's wrist, getting the best position from which to break it. One steady twisting bend snapped it, the knife dropping to the floor.

Billy reached up with his left hand to pinch the pressure point on the big man's neck. That hand wasn't strong enough, and the man's neck was thickly muscled; Billy hurt him, but only enough to earn him a vicious smack in the face, dazing him.

Billy's left hand floundered around, searching blindly for another weapon. He was close to his stash, but could feel nothing, he knew there was panic in his face, and the big man saw it.

"Is this what you're looking for, you old bastard?" he smiled at Billy, waving his revolver above the reach of his searching left hand, before letting it drop near the hand. Billy's heart sank as he heard the gun plop to the floor twenty feet below, his hand had been searching thin air for a weapon. Billy was a dead man, he knew it.

*

Three bullets hit the back of Archie's armour, two doing no damage, one piercing the weaker side armour and cracking a rib. The two others, poorly aimed in panic went through his left shoulder and into his right thigh.

Archie decided to play dead, then heard the sound of a rifle clip ejecting and acted instantly.

Pushing upwards through the light camouflage above him, he jumped at the man and his rifle, with Dolf's knife in his right hand.

With no bullets left in his weapon and without time to reload, the man smashed the rifle butt into Archie's head, enough to concuss any man, but not a man protecting two women he loved.

The rifle's impact knocked Dolf's knife from his grip, but it was still tied to his wrist by a thin leather strip. He flipped his wrist upwards, swinging and pulling the knife with it, he caught the handle of the knife first time, restoring it to the secure grip of his right hand. Lightfoot had taught him that, an old Apache trick he'd said.

Archie's blade struck upwards, under the ribs, towards the heart then twisted until his hand and blade were inside the man.

The weapon fell from the man's hand, but he wasn't quite dead yet. He pushed forward towards Archie, whose legs gave way under the weight, as the man collapsed dead on top of him. Archie felt his right arm snap as they hit the ground and still continued to twist his knife to make sure.

The man's blood flowed onto Archie's stomach and chest. He pushed him off with his one good hand, grateful there were no brains in his mouth, and he didn't smell as bad as Mike.

He turned immediately to the foxhole, recovered his Thompson, cocked and held it in his left hand. Then he just stumbled tortuously towards the sounds in the rear cottage garden.

*

The big man on top of Billy looked him in the eyes from only a few inches and started talking. Taunting him and spitting abuse into his face.

Billy relaxed, smiled and breathed deeply and slowly for two seconds then head-butted him, classic forehead to bridge of the nose. Not satisfied with that, Billy bit him on the lips, squeezing his teeth like a death grip, drawing blood, spit and snot from his face.

Then, as quick as a cat with one life left, he used his hands and knees to twist and roll the man once to his left. The movement took them into thin air where they plummeted twenty feet to the hard ground.

He'd never be sure how he did it. Sheer luck or maybe animal instinct, but when the bigger man hit the ground, he fell on his back with the added weight of Billy and his vest on top of him. He was still only dazed, then Billy saw his Webley revolver lying nearby, snatched it in an instant and blew the brains out of the big man's head. Then screamed with excruciating pain from having used his broken wrist for the fatal shot.

Billy moved immediately towards the cottage garden and the mayhem he could still hear outside. He had to move fast now, and he was wading the stream before he spat out a chunk of lip and blood from his mouth.

That's better, Billy thought, the big lad was well trained, but hadn't done this for real before. Billy had fought hand to hand in France many years before, for real. The rules were – no hesitation, no quarter, no pity and no gloating.

He heard a frenzy of Thompson fire and moved quicker into the silence that followed. He had his Webley with five bullets left, and he'd take a few others, even if it killed him.

*

The shock of the first shells hitting the cottage knocked Rebecca and Una off their feet. The shells had burst through the kitchen window and smashed apart the cellar door above them, wood, stone, plaster and brick tumbled down the stairs next to them. They smelled gas then burning and saw the flicker of flames licking the wooden cupboards in the kitchen. Rebecca tried the trapdoor that led to the rear, she'd heard heavy wreckage falling on top of it, and it was jammed tight shut.

The kitchen was no longer open to them, and smoke was drifting into their limited fresh air supply. They had to remove their armour and leave through the single small window, no grown man could have escaped that way, but two elves could.

*

In the ditch, Freddie knew he was finished unless he escaped from the Animal and Ginge. He seized his chance to unscrew the stiletto knife that Billy had concealed inside his walking stick. It took one second too long, and the Animal was on him. His stronger right hand overpowering

Freddie's left, grasping the knife in his fist as he pummelled him in the face before Freddie could use the blade on him.

"You little shit cunt," the Animal said as he held the blade within an inch of Freddie's eye ready to stab it into his brain.

"I should have fucking killed you long before I left home, you always were the runt of the litter."

*

Una placed her Thompson out of the narrow window, then, pushed by Rebecca, escaped but only after a struggle with her blouse and trousers, ripped by the ragged catch on the window frame. Rebecca took her own blouse and thick heavy trousers off as well as her shoes to avoid that delay and climbed out as quickly as she could, pulled by Una.

Both emerged bedraggled and scantily clad into the chilly night air, expecting to join the fray. They turned to recover their weapons, only to see them being kicked aside by two of five armed men. All with rifles aimed straight at them.

Rebecca bent over, coughing badly from smoke she hadn't yet inhaled, knowing that her breasts would be seen.

Una fell to her knees, retching loudly.

All five men stared at them, even in the darkness and prepared to gloat.

*

Archie moved toward his girls, his progress was slow, less than walking pace. He held the handle of the Thompson in his left hand and balanced the barrel in the crook of his broken right arm. His right leg in excruciating pain, his body almost useless, but he'd never felt more awake, never hungrier and never more ready to kill.

*

Was it seconds or minutes later? Smudger couldn't tell. His eyes showed him some slow motion film in black and white. He saw five armed men with rifles pointing at Una and Rebecca, unarmoured and on their knees. The flames from the cottage kitchen showed the figures clearly, the girls were bent over, coughing and choking. The firing must have hit the gas cylinders the cooker used.

Then, to the right of his dying vision, he saw Archie approaching from the direction of his foxhole. He had a Thompson in his left hand, his right arm bent unnaturally, and he was limping badly. Smudger knew he'd stumble into the riflemen's field of vision as soon as he rounded the corner.

*

"Right get Tennent, tell him we've got them, and they're ready to be used," he heard one of them say in a strong brogue.

Lennard Smith wasn't having that, not one chance in Hell.

"Hoy, you cunts!" he shouted in that impossibly deep foghorn bellow that only he could manage. All five men couldn't help but look in his direction, and they swung their weapons automatically towards him searching for a target against the dark earth.

*

Una and Rebecca each spent only a single second working out which men to take first.

The sound of a shout from the field in front of them distracted all five men for an instant, and they made their move towards them, then... "Down!" shouted Rebecca to Una as she felt Archie's presence in the hairs standing up on the back of her neck.

*

Sergeant Finch's police service revolver smashed into the side of the Animal's face, knocking him bloody and sideways onto the ground, unconscious. Finch undid the cuffs from Freddie's wrist.

"Come on son, there's more work to be done, with me."

Freddie was stunned at first, then managed to retrieve his blade from the ground, stabbing the Animal once in his leg.

"Just enough to stop him running, I need to have a word with him later," Freddie said to Ginge, before smashing his fist into the Animal's nose, breaking it.

"That's for Alice too," he said then dragged him back to the car and cuffed him to one of the door handles.

*

Archie moved to turn the corner to his right behind the cottage and heard Smudger shout, "Hoy, you cunts!"

That shout made Archie stagger forward more quickly and fully around the corner. More rifle shots finished off Smudger, but his dying distraction had presented Archie with targets he could see clearly silhouetted in the flames from the truck and the cottage. All in a neat row waiting to be mown down with a full Thompson barrel magazine. He pulled the trigger with his left hand and continued firing until all the ammunition had gone, long after they'd all fallen, dead to the ground. Dolf's knife still hanging uselessly from his right wrist.

Archie just had time to register that Smudger must be dead and that Rebecca and Una were alive before his legs gave way and he dropped to his knees.

They were stars, not candles, they were stars dying, and I can't stop that. This fight must be over if I've dropped again, I don't drop till it's over, do I? Smudger saved me again just like last time.'

Then he collapsed face first into the soft earth of the cottage garden and lost consciousness.

*

Billy reached his girls in time to see them cradling Archie in their arms and pulled some field bandages from his pockets. Rebecca had already checked Smudger, he'd taken more bullets than she could count.

*

The mayhem of firing had stopped. Ginge went behind the Bofors truck, finishing off the remains of two bad coppers who'd been thrown out of the truck by the blast of the grenades.

Freddie found Tennent next to the car at the front, the

headlights still dimly giving some light to the scene.

Tennent was still conscious, and gulping blood from internal bleeding and his legs looked shredded.

"How are you today, Inspector Cunt?" he asked, crouching down beside him and looking him in the eye.

"We don't surrender to nobody," he spat out the words at Freddie.

"We're not asking for surrender, there's no quarter today, not for the likes of you, and I ain't nobody, I'm somebody," he said and stabbed his blade through Tennent's eye and into his brain. When the last death gasp escaped from his lips, Freddie took the blade from the eye socket wiped it on Tennent's suit and spat in his face.

"Nobody fucks with my mates. Not anymore, those days are long gone."

*

Freddie and Ginge approached the scene behind the cottage cautiously.

"Everythin' all right Billy?" Sergeant Ginger Finch asked.

"Well it's over at least, we've lost Smudger and my boy's fucked up, needs an ambulance, but we've stopped the bleeding okay."

Billy saw Freddie looking at Finch.

"Ginge is an old mate of mine, Freddie, he said he'd keep an eye on you for a pint. I might have to make it two, a small scrap usually turns into a full-scale battle where Archie's involved. We should know that by now."

Just as he said that, they heard sirens and saw two ambulances pulling up beside Tennent's car and then the sounds of other trucks behind the old barn.

"Don't worry, that's looks like the help, Archie must have sorted that. Fuck knows how?" said Billy Perry, who suddenly felt his real age.

He flinched as Rebecca tightened a bandage around his right hand. He tried to explain it wasn't his blood, and his wrist was broken. She wasn't listening, and he was too tired to explain.

Una would have done that, but she simply wouldn't let go of Archie's hand.

*

The fire in the cottage kitchen wasn't spreading anymore, unable to find more fuel to feed it.

"D'you think that's proper, Miss?" Billy said to Rebecca.

"What are you talking about it's a perfectly good dressing?" was her reply.

"No, not the bandage, you Miss, you need to put some clothes on."

"I've got a clean hankie if you need a blindfold, Billy Perry."

"Not me, it sounds like there's about fifty men comin' our way and there's enough stories about you already!"

"Oh... right, they're in the cellar, though."

"Let's get in there then," he said and started moving the debris that was preventing the cellar door from opening, using his one good hand, and they climbed down.

*

Lieutenant Jimmy McKay, approached the scene of utter chaos.

A ruined cottage, one wrecked truck and car, corpses everywhere, a ginger police sergeant in full uniform with his hands in his pockets, one man being bandaged by a girl whose blouse was hanging off. What looked like a fourteen-year-old boy, taking a bandage off his ankle, explaining there had never been anything wrong with it anyway.

"Medic!" he shouted, and two men with a stretcher ran towards Archie.

From his left, he saw Billy Perry come out of the cellar, one arm bandaged poorly and dangling uselessly. He was using the other arm to pull up Rebecca Rochford, who was doing up her blouse, wrongly, using the wrong buttons in the wrong holes.

"We was just checkin' if the fire was out proper, sir," said Billy. He was stifling a laugh that was interrupted by an exploding gas canister rising from the kitchen like a rocket and landing who knew where.

"It is now," Rebecca added.

"Sorry about this Jimmy, I never seem to be properly dressed when we meet," Una interrupted, "I wouldn't want you to get the wrong impression."

"I get the distinct impression you're all stark raving mad," Jimmy McKay replied.

"Do you mind, I'm just as sane as the next man," said Freddie from his spot on the ground.

"Yeah, but you do stand next to Begley a lot," said Billy.

Chapter 20

August 1942 – Bletchley Park – Hospital Room

Archie woke up gradually in a hospital bed, drugs clouded his mind, bright sunlight shone on his closed eyes, and he couldn't mistake the fresh smell of the sheets.

He didn't know where he was, his body told him it was past midday, three or four o'clock, not the same day he'd lost consciousness. He concentrated on his limbs and moved his toes carefully, two legs, that's good. He moved his fingers, two arms, that's good too. Damn, the wound on his left palm had cracked open, and he could feel the sharpness of stitches holding the flesh together, he'd thought that was part of a dream.

He tried to breathe deeply through his mouth and couldn't, the pain in his right side was blade sharp, at least one rib gone then. He took shallow breaths through his nose to remain calm.

His right leg had a wound in the upper thigh, he singled out that pain and concluded it was just flesh, not bone, about twenty stitches there.

A needle was fixed into his left arm at the wrist, fluid, blood or plasma.

There was a wound at the top of his right shoulder, no more than a nick.

He tried to open his eyes and could only open the right one. He tried to lift his right hand to his other eye then realised his right arm was broken and in a cast. He screamed with the pain of the motion and for the loss of the eye. His lip split as he screamed.

"I can't see!"

He heard a door being thrown open and caught the scent of Una rushing towards him, pressing him down onto the bed.

"It's okay, you're all okay, the eye's just swollen, and there's a cut above it. There'll be a scar, you'll be fine."

She searched around for some safe part of him to hold

and kiss, and found only his left upper arm and left cheek, so she gently kissed that again and again.

"Dieppe, the men?" he asked, croaking.

"They're all back safe. All of them, not a scratch. Asgeir proposed to Briony, and she said yes."

"And the op?"

"Fucked, I asked Jimmy McKay, and he won't say a word, so that means fucked."

"McKay?"

"Yes, I'll let him tell you."

"Is Dad okay?"

"Yes Billy's fine, Smudger's gone I'm afraid. He's gone where you wanted, though."

"Okay, and Freddie?"

"He'll talk to you later too."

"I love you... so much. I should have said that first."

"I love you even more... I should have said that first as well."

"And... I love Rebecca too... you know that?"

"Yes, we both know that."

"I love you more."

"I know that too, the bad news is you won't be able to fuck me for weeks. The good news is I'll come back later to suck your cock just so you remember it's me you love most."

After one final gentle kiss she left and let McKay in to see him.

Archie looked at the palm of his left hand again, puzzled.

*

Jimmy McKay came into the room.

"Hello Archie, you look bally awful, old chap. I'm afraid your small private matter turned into something bigger than any of us expected. Still, my remit was to remove all evidence of some accidental fatalities that occurred during a live fire exercise. There were more bodies than we or you expected. A small ferry will sink tonight on its way back to Belfast I suspect, very sad, men returning from a secret mission, a tragedy. Anyway, it's done now, nothing for you to worry about."

"I don't understand."

"Churchill told Gubbins to make sure you got away with it, he said not to help, you wouldn't want help, just clear up afterwards."

"Why would he do that, how would he even know?"

"I don't know the full story, Churchill knew you could have stayed in America that last time, wanted to even, and you gave it up to come back here to help him. The Americans have hidden microphones in strategic places, a bit like the ones we have in the Senior Officer POW's quarters. Does anyone ever tell you about all that?"

"No, they don't. Apparently, I don't need to know."

"Anyway, he wanted to know what the other danger you'd talked about was, so he asked Gubbins. There are things Gubbins tells him and things he doesn't. There are things Churchill doesn't want to know about, but if he asks a direct question, then Gubbins always gives him an answer."

"Right, I think I can follow that now. Thank you, Jimmy, that's another one I owe you."

"Perfectly all right old chap."

"And Dieppe?"

"A complete and utter cock up, losses over 50%, about a hundred aircraft and a destroyer lost. Your job and Lovat's were the only ones that worked to plan."

"How will they explain that?"

"It'll be a complete success."

"What?"

"In war, truth is the first casualty, and we know that the truth isn't always a useful commodity, don't we?"

"You've got me there, Jimmy. We'll have to make sure we learn from it, that's all we can do. Make the best of the poor hand we're dealt. This is going to be a long war, and I'm so tired, get them to wake me in two years or so," he sighed.

"You'll be lucky. You've got more visitors."

*

Freddie came in next...

"All right boss?"

"Well I've been better, mate, you don't look great yourself," said Archie, seeing his bruises and black eye for the first time.

"This is fuck all, he did worse to me when I was a kid."

"Who? The Animal? You knew him as a kid?"

"Yeah, well he is my big brother... Nicholas, he was called 'Old Nick' aged six, that's how bad he was!"

"You never said a word."

"Well you ain't gonna be proud of that kinda thing are ya."

"Spit it out Freddie, we've known each other long enough, mate."

"Sorry, he got away, he was unconscious, knocked out and with a nice stab wound in his leg and handcuffs on, we weren't gone five minutes, and he'd disappeared when we got back. We searched, and there was SOE everywhere, but not a fucking sign of him. Billy's put out the word on him, and he's got no friends left. He's a dead man if he goes near Holloway after what he done to the Dempseys.

"He had a load of cash with him when I saw him, a lot was supposed to be for me and the rest was his bonus. I did make him give me two hundred quid up front, though, still got it, well most of it. You don't mind if I keep it?"

"It's yours, you worked for it, mate."

"But, I don't think he'll be back soon and nowhere near London, or here, that's for sure. An animal has a fight with another animal, he knows when he's lost and won't try again; that's the law of the jungle, he knows that. Without backup he's nothing, and he's lost his owners. He'll be just another mad dog now, and he'll only fight if he's cornered like a rat, I know it. Trouble is I have to find him now, I have to corner him."

"We can track him down and have him taken care of, the Frasers'll take that job for nothing if he's in with bent coppers and we can pay plenty if we need to."

258

"No there's more to it. My sister, Alice, she's alive, and he knows where she is. I could see it in his eyes when I asked him for money and her, for helping with this job. He said, *'I'll show you where she is, you can see her and then decide if you still want her'* and he laughed."

"When I said a girl, he thought I meant Una at first, that's how sick he is, I can't tell you what they were gonna do to those two girls if they'd got them alive. It's like a business for them, I can't explain it, it's like slavery with whites instead of blacks, they buy and sell, swap, it's worse than murder. We've seen some bad stuff, and we've done some bad stuff, Boss, we done stuff we had to do. These do it cos they enjoy it, cos they think they've got the right."

Freddie paused, and Archie continued for him.

"Because they're entitled to do it, because they deserve to do it, and it deserves to be done to the victim. Like a dog attacks a cat, like a cat eats a mouse, like a mouse can eat a snail, and a snail can eat a fish. Everything eats something else, and it's usually alive when they start eating. Sorry, mate, I've read one too many books, and it's the way I justify what I do, they deserve what I do to them, they deserve death, and I deserve to give it to them. I can't explain it any better."

"Will you help me, Boss?"

"When I've got two working arms, legs, and eyes, he's next on my list, and you'll be helping me; he hurt Una remember. Ask Billy to keep his mates on the lookout."

"Thanks, Boss."

"Will you stop calling me Boss?"

"No."

*

Rebecca was next...

"For God's sake is there a queue out there, have you got coupons or a ticket with a number on it?" he said.

"You shut up right now, or I'll tell Una not to suck your cock!"

"Do you girls tell each other everything about me?"

"Yes, I thought that was self-evident."

"I'm doomed aren't I?"

"Yes."

"I told her I love you."

"I know you did."

"But I love her more."

"I know you do."

"Can you come closer so I can give you a kiss?"

She leaned in towards his face and gave him a chaste peck on the lips, but it did linger.

"Thank you, I really am tired now, if I can sleep now, I should be able to come home tomorrow."

"You are joking!"

"No, I'll be fine honestly."

"We haven't got a home now, remember."

"Find somewhere else then, wherever you and Una are, will always be home."

"Okay, that sounds like a plan, I'll send in Una, you won't be able to sleep unless you know she's safe, will you."

"How do you do that?"

Una came back into the room carrying the book she'd given him when they'd married, the one he hadn't read and had lent to Arnold.

"Now, you've got plenty of time to read this, no excuses now."

"Okay."

"Right, drink this water carefully and go back to sleep, don't worry I'll be here when you wake up. I'll always be here when you wake up."

*

Archie slept for a few hours and woke to find Una with a cup of lentil soup for him, a little lukewarm, so he gulped it down, and she fetched him a warmer one.

Even that little snack filled his shrunken stomach, and he returned to sleep until the next morning and more soup, this time with bread and butter.

Una kissed him and left his room, she sent Billy in next, but not before giving him a huge, welcome and painful hug.

"You all right, son?" said Billy.

"Yeah."

"Cos you still look like shit."

"You old bastard, don't make me laugh," he said, laughing, "are you okay?"

"A bruised rib and a broken wrist, while you were asleep a specialist drove from London to see me and set it proper. Told me you'd sent him, you know how to plan ahead, son. I won't even ask how you did that."

"I'm not sure I know, tell me what happened exactly, please Billy. I need to know."

"Let me get a couple of mugs of tea first, this is going to take a while."

Una opened the room door with her knee and brought them two mugs of extra strong tea.

"How do they do that?" Billy asked, looking at Archie and wincing from the clout on the head he expected and duly received from Una. Billy talked him through the ambush at the cottage as best he could.

"So Tennent was smarter than we thought?"

"Yeah, but not as smart as you, playground bully nothing more, just another piece of dog shit we stood in. Stinks at the time then washes off easy enough. You put about 20 rounds in him, I counted the holes so I could tell you."

"Is he gone forever?"

"Oh yes, he's gone and forgotten already, Ginge says. He's got no friends left in England, there's a mess in Belfast, there always is, we can't worry about that."

"Freddie?"

"You know he still needs to find the Animal and his sister, at least we know she's definitely there to look for now."

"Fuck knows what we'll find?"

"Can't worry about that, it needs doin', that's all."

"How do we do it then?"

"Can't worry about that either, son. This Alice, she's trouble, and trouble finds you, you could sit in this bed for your whole life, and she'd walk through that door sooner or later. I'm surprised you've been here two days, and nobody's tried to kill you yet. I've been sat next to that door, just in case."

"You haven't?"

"Have I bollocks... " he laughed, "the girls took turns as well. I couldn't keep them away, and there's no arguin' with them."

"I do know that, Billy."

There was a long pause.

"Billy, there's so many cunts out there, how can I kill them all? How dare I even think of it? Who the hell am I anyway? I have to do it, I just have to, there's a need inside me, a need I can't deny, I'm good at it. Absolute shit at giving life, but fucking good at taking it, and now that I've started I can't stop, I can't ever stop. How can I possibly do it all, there's so many, one goes down and two more stand up? How can I do it, Billy?"

"One cunt at a time, that's all I can say, son. I can't stop you, don't want to, won't stop you... and I'll help."

"But what's going on, Billy? I've asked Conner, and he hasn't got an answer. What's happening, why am I at the centre of a thousand things, a thousand bad things and another thousand good things. I do my best, but I still kill people I love. I've killed Smudger now, we tried our best, we broke that ankle, we faked the Doc's report, and I still killed him."

"I don't know, I can't work it out, so I don't think about it too much. I was retired, I was safe, I had a nice hobby at the Savoy, I was comfortable. Then you turned up, and I was drawn to that flame again.

"And if you'd told Smudger he was goin' to die, savin' those two girls, he'd still have done what he did.

"I am where I'm supposed to be and so are you, there's fuck all we can do about it.

"I think it's like you said to the team, one percent, one percent can make a difference between life and death, between good and evil. Maybe that's what we are, that one percent?"

"Or one percent of one percent of another percent?"

"You see, there you go again, thinking about it too much. Just relax and go with the flow. That's what I do."

"Am I the flow then?"

"Yes, you are, son and I'll be with you all the way... Listen, you'll be knackered now, I'll get Una to bring you another cuppa then you rest again. You need it, and you need her too."

"Okay."

"One last thing before I go, it'll make you laugh, I'm warning you, but you'll want to know. When that lot were all dead, your Rebecca went around them and kicked each one of 'em as hard as she could in the balls, and more than once I can tell you. She scared the living daylights out of those SOE boys. There was even one they'd put in a bag before she'd kicked him. She made them take the body off the truck and out of the bag so she could get a proper swing at him. I don't know how the hell you'll do it, but you need to look after her as much as your Una."

Archie smiled, he knew he couldn't laugh and knew he'd have to do just that.

"Thanks, Dad," he said and watched Una come back in the room exactly when she was needed and with a fresh mug of tea.

"I need a few minutes with Rebecca please," he said.

"I know, I'll get her for you."

Rebecca was there ten minutes later.

"Have a seat, Rebecca, please," Archie said.

"Is this the Headmasters study now then?"

"No, it's a friend's room."

"You're being serious, though."

"Yes, I need you to do something for me."

"Anything. I think?"

"I need you to stop the groin kicking, it's not what you are, it's not healthy anymore."

"Okay."

"Thank you."

"Just remember how easy I made it for you," she said, giving him a light kiss on the forehead and rushing out of the room, presumably to avoid any questions about what she meant.

*

The funeral of Lennard Smith, Smudger was held within seven days, officially he died of wounds received in the Dieppe raid.

The doctors forbade Archie from going, the leg wound was still fragile, and they'd pulled the broken rib from his badly bruised right lung and refused to risk moving him. He paid no attention at all to them and made plans to go anyway until Una forbade him from going, and he truthfully agreed not to go.

Even then, McKay put two guards on his locked door until it was over.

*

Rebecca and Una broke the news to Smudge's wife in person, just the two of them, as they'd insisted. Archie would make sure the family never wanted for money, ever, but they'd never replace a man like Lennard. His body was frozen though and with a slim chance in the future.

The entire team including Conner, who'd stayed away for several days after Dieppe, turned out for the funeral, a huge South London affair for a huge South London man. Archie would never face the widow Mrs Smith in person. He'd tried to save Smudger from France and the rest of Europe, and he'd killed him in a rural English field instead. His ability to kill his friends knew no bounds.

The whole team paid their respects to Smudger because he'd earned it; they also did it so it would spare Archie the need to do it.

*

Dolf Von Rundstedt sat in his large plush office in Paris, a week after the Allied raid on Dieppe. He had the newspapers and the official report, first draft. The German controlled media made great play of the Allied defeat, and they were right to do so. He couldn't see what they were trying to achieve unless it was an experiment.

He knew more than that; the Allied Prisoners of War from Dieppe had been talkative with little persuasion, and they didn't know why they were there either.

An experiment costing that many lives showed the Allied determination to win, he needed them to win from the west, not the Russians from the east.

Yes, it was a dry run to see if they could capture a full-sized port, they couldn't, and they'd learned a harsh lesson. They'd have to land on beaches as they had in North Africa using flanking movements.

No words were spoken about it, but Dolf saw the concentration of troops in Dieppe just before the raid, as unusually high, suspiciously high. There was a spy or excellent intelligence, and he needed to find out which. He was in a better position to do that now, following the raid on French soil, his posting was upgraded to Oberst, full Colonel. Notwithstanding his criminal activities, Dolf was excellent at his job.

He decided to think about that tomorrow, and went home for the weekend.

Annette was waiting for him in his apartment, she gave him a warm hug and was making dinner for him. She was an accomplished cook. He let her leave his apartment occasionally to do some shopping. He always sent two guards with her, discreetly, at a short distance, no one would notice. Just knowing Dolf might be enough to get her killed.

*

After two full weeks of bed rest, Una and Rebecca came into Archie's room with a wheelchair. The same huge contraption they'd used for Smudger after Archie told Billy to break his ankle on the boat in Norway.

"I've finished The Hobbit!" he said.

They were up to something, but he was getting out of his room so he chose to go with that flow. Not that he had any choice when they ganged up on him like that.

Una wheeled him out towards Building Thirteen, he

265

could see a crowd near the rose bushes and knew what was coming.

Freddie stood next to a hole, dug some distance from their building, preparing to plant a small sapling

"An oak," he said, "for an oak of a man, I swear when we first saw action in France, Jerry thought he was a tree, and three of us hid behind him an'all. My mate, Lennard Smudger Smith, a man who never swore in his whole life."

There was some laughter then applause too, then Billy and Freddie sang their own relatively clean version of the 'Unfortunate Rake,' a young trooper cut down in his prime.

No one stared at him, although everyone noticed that Archie Travers looked in a terrible state for a man who hadn't left England recently. They saw his wife, Una at his right hand holding onto his fingers and cast tightly, and Rebecca Rochford standing separately and to one side. They also saw Una wave Rebecca over towards them and motioning for her to hold his other hand, which she did with a smile.

They saw the tears flow down Archie's unemotional face, tears without crying. No wailing, no ululation, no spreading of arms and shouting for God or vengeance. Just an Englishman trying to preserve his composure and dignity out of respect for his fallen friend and failing to do so.

No one saw Conner Duncan or Alan Turing, standing behind and apart, without a hand to hold.

*

Later, after Archie finally talked to Conner, Rebecca, and Una about Dieppe, he was calm and measured, still angry, but in a controlled way. It was a monumental cock up, no objectives achieved, with so many high ranking people to blame it was beyond counting them all. Even Archie felt guilt, perhaps if his mind had been clearer that summer he might have said something and someone might have listened.

No, the lunatics had taken over the asylum. Operation Jubilee was a brilliant, worthy plan and if you told a lie often enough, it became the truth.

For a military operation of that size and complexity, you needed a logistics expert in overall charge, to plan every detail. Divide that detail into a series of smaller, manageable tasks, each given to a separate team who knew exactly what to do and why. Tell them why for goodness sake! Decades later those poor souls who'd been forced to surrender on that shingle beach still wouldn't know why they'd been there.

You needed to build in several levels of contingency planning, multiple redundancy, Alan had explained. It was an engineering principle and would have to be a crucial component in his thinking machine theory. Archie said it was the difference between a chain and chainmail.

If something needed to be done properly, plan to do it twice or even three times, Plan A, B, and C, have a man, a spare man then another one. Julius Caesar knew that, a thousand years ago, why did we have to relearn the lessons of history? Archie had been bold enough to tell Eisenhower just that, when he met him at Hyde Park, he wished he'd taped that conversation now, maybe it had been.

This was going to be a long war, but he was just that little bit more ready for it, just that one percent of one percent of...

*

It wasn't until the 10th of September 1942 when Archie left his hospital bedroom and walked unaided to Building Thirteen in Bletchley Park. Archie wondered why Una and Rebecca weren't there to see him, no Freddie and no Billy either. Just Conner and Alan, who were waiting for him, sitting on the bench by the rose bushes and Smudge's sapling.

Archie knew something was up, he always knew it now.

He sat down between Conner and Alan, who'd left a man-sized space there for him.

"Spit it out then," he said.

"You have to stop it," Conner said.

He knew what he meant.

"Who says?"

"Gubbins, Churchill and… Alex too."

"Are you telling me, are you ordering me to stop?"

"No."

"What are you doing then?"

"I'm asking you, as a friend."

"And you, Alan?"

"I'm asking you too, as a friend, I hope?"

"Of course, you're a friend."

Archie paused for a while.

"Let me think," he said, counting the rose bushes and the tree, counting the list of dead enemies and friends in his head, it was a big list and, as always, he lost count.

"What does Alex say?" Archie eventually said.

"There are other things you need to do first."

"What things?"

"He won't say."

Archie paused again, gritting his teeth. If he stopped it was going to cost him so much, what did he have left? He knew he was right, and the whole world was wrong, but he knew he couldn't fight the whole world. The harm he did was all that kept him safe, the madness was all that kept him sane, and they'd ganged up on him, Conner and Alan outnumbered him. Una, Rebecca and Billy had stayed away because they couldn't ask what was being asked, but wouldn't interfere. His two friends were asking him, not telling him.

Archie sought a mantra, and one appeared, one where his loss would be balanced by a gain, a chance he might never have again.

"I'll stop," he said, "if you stop lying to each other about what you feel."

Neither Alan nor Conner did anything other than look straight ahead.

"Yes," said Conner.

"Yes," repeated Alan.

"I'll stop," Archie said with a deep sigh, and his tears

held back.

"I'll tell Freddie myself. Una, Rebecca and Billy will know what I've decided. I can still look for Alice without killing anyone?"

"No, you have to stop that too, Conner said, "you need to focus entirely on one war."

That cut into him like a knife again, through his heart and the soul he no longer had. He took all the hatred, harm, vengeance and violence that filled every fibre of his being and squeezed it, crushed it in his fists. He reduced it to the smallest size he could manage with all the strength he could muster and pushed it into a box in his mind, shut it and locked it tight.

"Okay then," he said, "can you get Una for me please, I need her really badly."

The End

The story continues in Book Three – Love to Justice.

Other titles by Richard A. McDonald are available on Amazon in paperback and Kindle formats.

If you have enjoyed this novel, please feel free to put a review on Amazon. If you haven't, please give it to someone else who might.

For more information see the author's website.

http://www.richardamcdonaldauthor.com/

17734639R00163

Printed in Poland
by Amazon Fulfillment
Poland Sp. z o.o., Wrocław